L...

It v... gifted with the blond-haired, blue-eyed
'ooks of a careless beach boy, the crooked
...in of a man who didn't sweat the
...all stuff. He'd also wound up with the
...reternatural athletic talent to be one of
he top skiers in the world, a millionaire, a
nedia darling.

And with, of course, the preternatural ego
o go with it.

'What are you doing here? Aren't you
...upposed to be somewhere in New
Zealand, embarrassing yourself on
...amera?" She could cheerfully have bitten
...er tongue the minute the words were out.

As for JJ, he just grinned. "And here I
didn't think you cared. You keep track of
me. I'm flattered."

"I keep track of hurricanes, too. Mostly
because I'm hoping they'll go somewhere
else…"

Available in October 2008
from Mills & Boon®
Special Edition

The Rancher's Family Thanksgiving
by Cathy Gillen Thacker

Capturing the Millionaire
by Marie Ferrarella

I Do! I Do!
by Pamela Toth

A Mother in the Making
by Lilian Darcy

The Tycoon Meets His Match
by Barbara Benedict

Under His Spell
by Kristin Hardy

Under His Spell
KRISTIN HARDY

MILLS & BOON®
Pure reading pleasure™

*First published in Great Britain 2008
by Harlequin Mills & Boon Limited,
Eton House, 18-24 Paradise Road, Richmond, Surrey TW9 1SR*

© Chez Hardy LLC 2006

ISBN: 978 0 263 86079 5

23-1008

*Printed and bound in Spain
by Litografia Rosés S.A., Barcelona*

To Stephen,
River deep, mountain high

KRISTIN HARDY

has always wanted to write, starting her first novel while still at school. Although she became a laser engineer by training, she never gave up her dream of being an author.

Kristin lives in New Hampshire with her husband and collaborator. Check out her website at www.kristinhardy.com. *Under the Mistletoe*, the second book in Kristin's HOLIDAY HEARTS mini-series, was nominated for a RITA® Award for Best Long Contemporary.

Dear Reader,

Sometimes books go together as you expect, and sometimes you wind up with characters that are so feisty, they do what they like, whether you want them to or not. So it was with Lainie Trask and downhill ski racer JJ Cooper. I had plans for Lainie when I first tucked her into *Where There's Smoke*, the first book of the HOLIDAY HEARTS books. She was supposed to meet the South Shore lawyer of a series that I'm cooking up that takes place in Cape Cod, Martha's Vineyard and Nantucket. I figured Lainie would be the tie from HOLIDAY HEARTS to the new books so that we could keep visiting with the Trask family for another year.

Then JJ walked on stage in *Under the Mistletoe* and that was that. The chemistry between Lainie and him formed spontaneously in the air, like steam – all I did was write it down. Of course, they pretty much demanded that I give them their own book, and they weren't about to take no for an answer. I guess the Cape Cod lawyer will have to find a woman of his own, because Lainie is…well, read on and find out.

And when you get done, drop me a line at kristinhardy.com. I'd love to hear what you think.

Happy reading.

Kristin Hardy

Prologue

July, Crawford Notch, NH

There was nothing, J. J. Cooper thought as he pushed off, quite like the feeling of being at the top of a mountain. Granted, he was on a mountain bike instead of skis, and hurtling down a steep slope of grass, not ice and snow, but the adrenaline fizzed in his veins just the same. It was the speed, the motion, the challenge.

The risk.

Going fast in a car had never done much for him; he wanted—no, needed—to be out there making it happen himself, just his body, the environment and as little equipment as possible.

The wind of his passage ruffled his dark-blond hair, sun-streaked by weeks of activity in the northern New Hampshire summer. He swerved off onto a newly built ski run that he'd watched the graders build to his specifications earlier in the summer. Director of ski at the Hotel Mount Jefferson Ski Resort—not a bad off-season gig for a World Cup ski racer. Now he just needed to test his work.

Going off the knoll he'd had built into one side of the run, he caught a few feet of air and came down with a bone-rattling thud that the bike's graphite composite forks couldn't entirely absorb. For a moment he swerved dangerously on the steep slope but he wrestled the bike back into control. This was what it was about, the buzz of letting it all hang out there and dragging it back in.

This was when he felt most alive.

And for once he wasn't orchestrating every moment of his day around winning races. For once he was doing something for the sheer kick of it. Early summer, his time to play. Not that he didn't also spend time training—he *always* spent time training—but in this summer idyll it was less about the focused repetitions of the weight room than about moving outdoors, about running and hiking the hillsides, mountain biking, doing his jumps.

No, there was never really time to slack off entirely, not if he wanted to keep the steel hawsers of muscles and tendons in his quads strong enough to hold his line while he was flying through a turn at ninety miles an hour, pulling three Gs of force. But it didn't all have to be boring reps. He could work himself to exhaustion and still have fun doing it, because ultimately, fun was really what it was all about, right? A challenge? Sure. An adrenaline rush? No doubt. But the day his life as an athlete stopped being about the pure joy of the moment and the competition would be the day he'd retire.

Good thing it hadn't happened yet, because the idea of life

without racing was nearly unfathomable. Sure, he'd hit thirty a couple of years back, but he was still going strong. All those people who talked about him retiring were nuts. He'd come in second in the World Cup overall the previous season, won it all the year before that. Oh, and a gold medal in Torino. That wasn't the performance of a tired old guy who needed to go out to pasture, was it?

To wipe away the question, he attacked the slope headlong, wrenching the bike into a turn, feeling the pull in his shoulders and arms. The speed, the motion, the risk. Today he was in New Hampshire in the late-July sun. In a couple of weeks he'd be blasting through training runs on an icy slope in New Zealand, then heading to speed camp in Chile, all while people back home were still grilling on the back deck. A World Cup ski racer lived for winter, and if the winter wasn't where he was, then he'd go find it.

Ahead, a water bar designed to provide drainage during rainy months and snow melt cut across the trail. A grin spread across J.J.'s face and a moment later he'd turned straight toward it.

And a minute after that, he'd parted ways with the bike and gone flying. At least, he thought, he'd been going less than ninety….

Gabe Trask stared down at the clipboard in his hand, ignoring the throbbing roar of earthmovers as they worked to smooth the final hundred yards of the new ski run, where it came down to the lift house. Between running the hundred-year-old Hotel Mount Jefferson and overseeing the upgrades to the newly acquired ski resort across the highway, he was beginning to have a lot more sympathy for those circus clowns with all the plates on sticks. It had taken some mad spinning, but so far he was keeping it all on schedule and under budget. If the new run passed muster with J.J., they'd be all set. The Hotel Mount Jefferson Resort and Ski Area would be the hospitality powerhouse of New Hampshire.

"So I've got good news and bad news," said a voice behind him.

Gabe glanced over to see J.J., who sported an odd grin on his sunny beach boy face. "What have you screwed up now?" he asked, glancing back down at his clipboard.

"The good news is that the top of the run checks out fine," J.J. continued, ignoring him.

"And the bad news?" Gabe glanced back up. J.J. stood there with his right hand curled around the gooseneck of his mountain bike and his left arm hanging down loose. Weirdly loose. Almost as if—

"The bad news is I'm calling in my marker on all those rides I gave you when we were in high school," J.J. continued, a little note of strain tightening his voice.

"You need a ride home?"

"I need a ride to the clinic." He gave Gabe a wry grin. "I think I dislocated my shoulder."

Chapter One

August, Salem, Massachusetts

"Nice pair a melons you got there, lady."

Lainie Trask glanced from the cantaloupes she held to the fruit vendor standing behind his table. Her brown eyes glimmered with fun as she hefted them higher. "They are, aren't they?"

"Buck for the two of 'em. Can't do any better than that."

Lainie handed over a dollar and tucked the fruit into her canvas carrier bag. "And here I thought I already had a nice pair of melons," she said out of the corner of her mouth to her girlfriend Liz.

Liz glanced at her judiciously as they turned away from the fruit stand. "More like guavas, I'd say."

Lainie laughed and swept her glossy dark hair back from

her face as they walked deeper into the confusion of color, noise and scent that was the Salem farmers' market. Tables and pushcarts groaned under the weight of baskets filled with crimson tomatoes, sunburst-yellow lemons, green zucchini, the strange, otherworldly fuzz of kiwi.

"Get yer bay scallops here. Bay scallops, fresh off the boat. Hiya, Lainie."

"Hey, Pete." Lainie stopped at the stall and studied the seafood on ice, then the man who stood behind it. "Fresh, huh?"

The weathered, sixty-something fishmonger gave her a roguish wink. "Any more fresh and it'd be hittin' on you."

She grinned and looked at Liz. "Scallops for dinner?" she suggested.

"Nah, I'd rather go out, assuming there's anyplace around here you want to go to."

"There's a McDonald's on the highway. We could splurge on Chicken McNuggets. Sorry, Pete." She gave him a quick smile. "Next time around. Come on, Liz, let's go get coffee."

The two women began walking again. "Chicken McNuggets," grumbled Liz. "You know the owner of Tremolo just opened up a new bar and restaurant two blocks away from me? Small plates to die for and a six-page cocktail menu. You should have come down and visited me in Boston for the weekend."

"It was your turn to drive up here," Lainie argued. "I'm sick of driving down."

"Then *move* down. I mean, why are you still living up here in Siberia, anyway?"

"Salem," Lainie corrected, leading the way out of the farmers' market and onto the main drag.

"Salem, Siberia…it's north and it's cold. Same difference."

"It's not that far north."

"Far enough. You don't belong up here. You belong down

in the city. I thought that was the plan. I mean, you don't have a life up here."

"I have a life," Lainie objected. She did, and one she increasingly loved.

"Oh, yeah? When's the last time you had a date?"

She glowered at Liz. "Don't start sounding like my parents. It's not my fault. Most of the people I know are married."

"Of course they're all married. You're living in the burbs. You've gotten it out of order. You get hooked up first, *then* you move to Siberia."

Lainie rolled her eyes. "Sorry, I guess I missed that part in the manual. Anyway, I don't even know if I want to date," she said grumpily.

"You don't want to date?"

"I mean, come on, be honest, it sucks. You sit around, trying to make conversation, trying to figure out what you've got in common, trying to remember why you ever even bothered to say yes. I'd rather be at home watching a movie."

"But it would be better with some guy's arm around your shoulders."

"Well, is it my fault they never ask me out?"

"Maybe you intimidate them."

"Is that because of my six Nobel Prizes or my seven-figure income?" Lainie asked.

"Ha, ha. No, it's because you're…you. I mean, you're never exactly shy of an opinion."

"You're shy of an opinion in my family and you'll never get a word in edgewise. So I say what I think, is that a crime?"

"No, but maybe it's a little much for the average Joe right off. Maybe you could tone it down a little."

Lainie stared at her. "Whatever happened to the 'be yourself' advice? Isn't a guy supposed to love me for who I am?"

"He can't if you chase him away before he figures you out."

"Forget it. I'll stick with my idea about taking time off." If it took pretending to be a fragile flower for her to lure a guy, she wasn't interested. It was too much work, anyway. She was happy to give the opposite sex a rest for a while.

Liz wasn't, though. "I know a couple of nice guys I could introduce you to but you're G.U."

"G.U."

"Geographically undesirable."

"For God's sakes," Lainie grumbled. "It's only forty-five minutes to your house."

"The way you drive, maybe. It takes me an hour. Guys don't want that. They want someone who's right there. When are you moving?"

Lainie shrugged a shoulder. "When the time's right."

"When the time's right? That's what you've been saying for almost four years."

"When I find a job down there."

"Have you been looking?"

"Museum jobs don't exactly fall off trees. I've been keeping my eyes open." Lainie stopped in front of a store-front with the legend Cool Beans painted above a rendering of a steaming cup of coffee.

"There she is."

Lainie turned to give a brilliant smile to the grinning, grizzle-haired man behind the counter. "Hey, George."

"You've got some kind of sixth sense, don't you? I just pulled a pan of blueberry coffee cake out of the oven. I shoulda known you'd be here. What is it, some witch thing?"

"That's me, using my powers for baked goods."

"Hey, if you've got powers for baked goods, come over and do something about my oven," he invited. "It's been running hot for the last two months. I'll pay you in coffee cake." He waved the pan before her.

Lainie sniffed blissfully. "My powers work best in the presence of an appliance repairman. Get one over here and I'll come chant a success spell. For advance payment." She reached for the pan but George pulled it back.

"Nope, I'm not buying it. Maybe I'll just stick with the repair guy."

"Probably best," Lainie agreed. "Does that mean I don't get any coffee cake?"

"I don't know. We start the new project next weekend. You gonna show?"

"Have I ever let you down?"

"Not so far," he agreed, and reached for a plate. "So who's your friend?"

She grinned. "George, this is Liz from Boston. She was my college roommate."

"Any friend of Lainie's," he said, nodding at Liz. "What can I get you, young lady?"

"Some of that coffee cake and a mocha, if you've got it."

"If it's got coffee in it, we've got it," he told her, putting together her drink with quick, economical motions.

"Aren't you going to ask what I want?" Lainie pouted.

He set an already filled mug on the counter and put a slice of coffee cake beside it. "I already know what you want."

"Marry me, George," she said seriously.

"I couldn't afford to keep you in coffee."

"Wow, that coffee cake was pretty amazing." Liz patted her belly as they wandered along the Salem waterfront, past docks lined with fishing boats and white sailboats.

"See? There are some good things about Salem."

"'Some' being the operative word. You really are just a small-town girl at heart."

"I'm not a small-town girl," Lainie replied, stung. "At

least not anymore." She wasn't. She'd left the tiny burg of Eastmont, Vermont, where she'd grown up, and she'd never once looked back. She was a cosmopolitan girl who knew her way around a Cosmopolitan, and she fully intended to live in the city one day.

When it made financial sense.

And if lately her visits to Boston had seemed mostly noisy and rushed, that was probably just coincidence. "I'm going to look harder," she said, as much to herself as to Liz.

"It's about time." Liz stared out at a nearby boat where a shirt-less deck hand was raising the main sheet. "Yum. You suppose Popeye over there would give us a ride if we asked pretty?"

Lainie grinned. "Down, girl. You're cradle robbing. He happens to be in high school."

"How do you know?"

"I know his parents."

Liz rolled her eyes. "Do you know everyone in this town?"

"I know enough, and unless you want to get arrested, you might want to keep away from Jared. At least until he turns eighteen."

Liz squinted. "He looks older from here."

Lainie patted her shoulder. "It's your eyesight, dear. Anyway, we've got a job to do before we can relax." She steered them toward the shop-lined pedestrian street that circled near the wharf. "I've got to buy wedding and shower presents for my cousin Gabe's wedding."

"I seem to remember you asking me up to have fun, not do your errands."

"But this will be fun, and you'll find it even more satis-fying knowing you're helping me get a little item or two out of the way."

"Somehow I doubt it."

"Not at all. So, what should I get?"

"Dish towels," Liz grumbled.

"Too boring."

"Candlesticks?" Liz moved to step inside the crafts store they were passing.

"Wow, and you're calling me small town," she said firmly, closing the door Liz had opened. With a wave of her hand, Lainie headed toward an art gallery down the way.

"Hey, he's your cousin, you figure it out," Liz protested. "It's not like I was—'The Salem Witch'?" She stopped in front of a gift boutique and stared at the gothic letters painted on the window. "Is that like being the town mascot?"

Lainie turned around and came back to her. "She certainly manages to show up here and there."

"You have an official town witch. Are you people nuts?"

"Hey, you play to your strengths."

Liz opened the door.

"What are you doing?"

"Playing to your strengths. Maybe you can conjure up a present for your cousin. Among other things."

"It's a gimmick, Liz," Lainie protested, following her in. "You know this stuff doesn't work."

"What? The woman who runs the witch museum says witchcraft doesn't work? Aren't you an honorary Wiccan by default or something?"

"Oh, yeah, that's me, the family witch."

"So you should feel right at home. Besides, every marriage needs a little magic." Liz wandered along the wall, studying the candles and herbs, the spell packets and charms. "So, let's see, how about a potency charm?"

Lainie rolled her eyes. "I'm thinking Gabe can do without that."

"Oh, really." Liz's eyes brightened. "Does he have any brothers?"

"You're about a year too late. They're all spoken for."

"Just my luck."

"We could always get you a love spell," Lainie said, picking one off the wall and scanning the back. "Here. You just make tea with these herbs, light the candle and dance buck naked in the moonlight for three nights running."

Liz eyed her. "Buck naked?"

"I'm just reading you the directions," Lainie said blandly.

"I live in the middle of Boston."

"I'm sure if your dance is quick, you can get it over before you get arrested for indecent exposure. Better yet, do it on Friday night and the spell will probably be effective immediately."

"I've got a better idea."

"What's that?"

Liz's eyes gleamed. "A love spell for you."

Lainie cast a glance at the ceiling. "Trust me," she said. "The last thing I need is a love spell."

It was the fondest wish of Al and Carol Trask to see their children all married off eventually, with families of their own. Lainie didn't have any problem with the idea in concept; she just had a few differences of opinion with her parents on the particulars. Like, for example, their definition of the word eventually. To Lainie, that meant before she turned, say, forty. Or fifty, if it suited her.

To her parents, twenty-six was high time to start thinking about settling down.

Which was why she was happy, quite happy to be going to her cousin Gabe's Jack and Jill party as part of the run-up to his wedding to Hadley Stone. After all, Gabe's wedding would buy her at least six months of peace from the reminders and questions. Given that, springing for a shower gift and driving a couple of hours to the party was a pleasure. She'd cheerfully have driven twice as far, if that were the sacrifice required.

Although, to be honest, it wasn't much of a sacrifice. She and Hadley had become good friends over the past year. Lainie was looking forward to a nice, long gossip after the party. Besides, it was a perfect day for a drive and she was itching to see the renovated ski lodge where the party was to be held.

Gabe and Hadley had bought the eyesore as a fixer-upper the year before. And fix it up they had, Lainie realized as she pulled in. The grubby, underprivileged-looking buildings she remembered had disappeared, replaced by a soaring complex of two- and three-story cedar-and-glass structures that were the architectural equivalent of a breath of fresh air. The Crawford Arms, the once-faded Victorian grande dame at the edge of the property, had been pulled back from the brink of seediness to boast a subtly gorgeous multicolor paint job and windows that sparkled with newness.

Even the brilliant white stripes on the freshly paved parking lot gleamed. The positively enormous freshly paved parking lot, she amended as she whipped into a spot and turned off her car. In fact, if a natural disaster ever hit the New Hampshire International Speedway, they could probably just move the race to Gabe's lot. Clearly, her cousin and his bride-to-be knew how to do things right.

Lainie stepped out into the summer afternoon and reached into her back seat to pull out a gaily wrapped package. None of that tired, old white-rose bridal paper for her. A person should make a statement, she figured; all the better if it was red and silver stripes.

A light, warm breeze whisked under her pale aqua skirt, lifting up the short flared silk, making her laugh. Summer might have come late to the north country but it was well worth appreciating when it finally arrived. And appreciating it, she was, with her stretchy, bare midriff top and strappy high heels. After all, in two or three months they'd be back in the frigid temperatures of late fall.

And three-inch heels didn't go so well with snow and ice.

Nope, she was a summer girl at heart, happy to toss aside her tan-in-a-bottle for the real thing. Fall was for prickly people; winter was for the melancholy; spring was for the ambitious.

Summer was for people who knew how to enjoy life.

Ahead of her, the path curved toward the broad double doors that led into the main lodge. Ski racks flanked the wide cedar porch; come winter, they'd be filled with colorful snowboards and wide downhill skis with their bindings. Come winter, the whole area would be frosted with snow and ice, and crowded with people. She was looking forward to seeing it.

But not before she'd gotten everything she could out of the warm weather.

The breeze whisked at her skirt again, flipping it up as she stepped up onto the porch. Hastily she reached behind her with one hand to push it down. And, distracted for a crucial instant, caught her toe on the underside of the wooden step.

The next thing she knew, she was pitching forward, trying desperately to hold on to the gift package and trying equally hard to avoid doing a face plant on the deck. When the door opened before her, she gave up, dropping the box and groping for the door handle as though it were salvation. The shower gift would survive; her nose might not. Somehow she missed the door anyway, though, and instead found herself doing a four-point landing on the cedar.

"Falling at my feet again, Lainie?" The voice was lazy and mocking, and she recognized it instantly, even before she looked up to see the hand before her eyes.

J. J. Cooper, golden-boy ski racer, finding her sprawled before him just as he had fourteen years before, on the mountain where she'd tumbled into the snow with a broken binding. Then he'd been her knight in shining armor, helping her up, dusting her off and, to her infinite astonishment, piggybacking her down the mountain on skis, his shoulders strong under her fingers.

Was it any wonder that her twelve-year-old self had fallen madly in love with him? She'd pined, positively pined over him for the four long weeks that stretched from that Thanksgiving weekend encounter to Christmas vacation. Writing his name in her notebooks, she'd dreamily imagined how he'd look at her with those denim-blue eyes and hold her hand when he came back from his ski academy for the holidays, her grown-up high school boy.

Of course, when he had, he'd demonstrated quite clearly that he had no interest in a skinny little kid like her. He hadn't insulted her, he hadn't been mean. He'd just been…oblivious. Ski god J.J. was exclusively interested in the very curvy and very grown-up blondes who buzzed around him like a bunch of flies, Lainie had thought ungraciously. He hadn't even bothered to snub Lainie when she'd hung around, desperate for his attention. He'd barely recognized her at all, until she'd crashed before him, trying to daredevil ski in a desperate attempt to attract his attention from the inept ski bunny he was escorting around. "A little kid like you shouldn't be up here," he'd scolded, hauling her up like a sack of potatoes. "You could get hurt."

"You're so sweet to help that poor little girl," the ski bunny had cooed as they'd schussed off, leaving a redfaced, furious Lainie to watch them go. Clearly, J. J. Cooper had no use for Lainie.

And from that moment forward, Lainie had had zero use for J. J. Cooper.

She scowled and rose, ignoring the hand and smoothing down her skirt. "Well, well, well. Speed Racer. How lucky can a girl get? Here I figured you'd be in training by now."

He raised a brow. "Why, Lainie, I didn't realize you kept such track of me."

"I prefer to keep an eye on minor annoyances. It helps me avoid them." She dusted off her hands. "Let me guess. You've broken training to show up here."

"Considering that, as best man, I'm the host, it seemed like the right thing to do." He leaned over to pick up her box, tucking it under his arm. "Want an escort in?"

Lainie folded her arms and stared at him. It wasn't fair that he'd been genetically gifted with the blond-haired, blue-eyed looks of a careless beach boy, the crooked grin of a man who didn't sweat the small stuff, a chin and jaw only sharpened by his Vandyke. He'd also wound up with the preternatural athletic talent to be one of the top skiers in the world, a millionaire, a media darling.

And with, of course, the preternatural ego to go with it.

"I'm fine. Why don't you go inside and find your posse?"

His eyes crinkled irritatingly. "You should know I'd never bother with a posse when I have you."

Scorn radiated off her. "Aren't you supposed to be somewhere in New Zealand embarrassing yourself on camera?" She could cheerfully have bitten her tongue the minute the words were out.

As for J.J., he just grinned. "And here I didn't think you cared."

"News bulletin," she told him, reaching for the package he held just out of reach. "I don't."

He lifted the box just a few inches higher. "But you do keep track of me. I'm flattered."

"I keep track of nor'easters, too, mostly because I'm

hoping they'll go somewhere else. And if you'd give me back that box, I'd go somewhere else myself."

He burst out laughing. "Oh, Lainie, life just isn't the same when you're not around."

"That's funny, life's always the same when you're around," she said sweetly. "You're nothing if not predictable."

That wiped away the smile. "Maybe when it comes to going fast."

She shook her head pityingly. "Oh, Speed, everything you do is predictable. Where do I start? Let's see… I'm betting that your last six girlfriends—the ones for this season, I mean—bought their lipstick using euros."

"Give me a break. I live in Europe seven months out of the year. Who else am I supposed to date? After all, you never come to visit me," he said with a leer.

Lainie folded her arms. "Okay, how about the CD changer in your car?"

"Yeah?"

"It's got at least one oldie disc by Lynyrd Skynrd."

"Lucky guess."

"Not a guess. Like I said, Speed, predictable."

It was his turn to scowl. "None of that counts."

"Speaking of your car, twenty bucks says you bought a new one a week after you hit the ground in Montpelier last spring."

"Yeah, so?"

"You did buy a new car, didn't you?"

He shrugged. "Maybe. The question is what?"

Given his image, the ultrasexy sports car would be the obvious pick. But she knew better. "The biggest mean-ass four-by-four hemi on top truck in midnight-blue metal flake." She smiled in enjoyment. "And if they didn't carry it in midnight-blue metal flake, you had them do a custom job for you."

To her infinite pleasure, his mouth fell slightly ajar.

"Well, am I right?"

He recovered. "You could have looked right out in the parking lot and seen it."

"Maybe, except that if I know you, you tucked it away in the back row." When he was silent, she merely crossed her arms and looked satisfied. "Oh, yeah, Speed, I know you. I know you through and through."

And she plucked the package from his hands and walked inside.

Chapter Two

One thing she had to give him: he threw a hell of a party. At a glance, Lainie would have sworn the spacious lodge held the entire population of Crawford Notch, where Gabe lived now, as well as Eastmont. People crowded together in the main room, laughing, joking, sipping drinks. Off to one side, in the lounge, a band played U2. As far as opening events, it was a humdinger.

Then again, so was the lodge. Gabe and Hadley hadn't bothered to renovate. Instead they'd just knocked down the old structure and put up something inspired, something open and airy and inviting. The cathedral ceiling of the main room soared overhead; skylights brought the day inside. The two walls of the lodge that faced the mountain were sheets of glass, looking out on the vivid-green turf of the final slope of the ski runs. In five months the grass would be covered in snow, dotted with the bright flashes of speeding skiers. Then this room would belong to the après ski crowd.

But for now it was theirs.

Lainie watched the bartender in the lounge pour a martini. Discreet waiters circulated with canapés. She took a blissful sniff as a tray of scallops wrapped in bacon passed by. Later, she promised herself. For now she needed to find the guests of honor and figure out someplace to drop her gift.

"Look who's here, it's Witch Girl," she heard a loud voice say.

"Gabe!" She found herself swept up in a bear hug by her dark-haired cousin. "How have you been? It's been forever since I've seen you."

His teeth gleamed in a smile, and she thought, as usual, that he could have made a fortune in Hollywood. "Not that long. Nick's wedding was, what, three months ago?"

"Two," corrected the slender blonde who stepped up beside him. "Still too long, though. Thanks for coming."

"Hadley, sweetie, no way would I have missed this." Lainie hugged her in turn. "I am so happy for you guys."

Hadley pushed back a sheaf of pale hair and gave her a skeptical look. "Don't give me that. You're happy because we're keeping your parents off your back. You don't fool me."

Lainie grinned. "You love me and want me to be happy, don't you? Besides, I really am thrilled for you. You're perfect together."

Gabe gathered Hadley against him, his dark hair mixing with her light. "That's what I keep telling her. We're made for each other. I was made to look good and she was made to wash my socks. Oof." He released her, rubbing his side where she'd elbowed him.

Hadley smiled prettily. "We've already agreed, he'll wash his own socks."

Lainie laughed out loud. "I think you'll both do fabulously." And an arm looped around her from behind.

"What do you think, Lainie," J.J. asked, "will you wash my socks? *Ow!*"

She removed her elbow from his side and turned to see him bent over. "I'll wash my hands of you, if that'll do."

"You're roughing up my best man, there," Gabe said mildly.

"Consider it for the good of mankind."

"That's not very friendly," J.J. complained. "What did I ever do to mankind?"

"For the good of womankind, then," she amended. "On general principles."

"Underneath that mask of hostility lies complete devotion," J.J. told Hadley.

She stuck her tongue in her cheek. "I can see that."

"If I wanted to be devoted to you, Speed, I'd have to line up behind the entire female population of Scandinavia," Lainie said. "I mean, granted, with your attention span, you'll go through them quickly, but I don't have that kind of time." She winked at Gabe and Hadley. "So where do I put this?" She raised the gift box.

"I'll show you," Hadley said, leading the way across the room.

"So are we going to be able to get off somewhere this weekend and catch up?" Lainie asked as they threaded their way through the crush. "We are so due."

"I think it sounds like a great idea." Hadley set the box on the gift table and flicked her a conspiratorial look. "How about now?"

It didn't take them long to find a table in the corner and order wine. "So what's going on? How's the wedding?"

Hadley sighed. "A headache, mostly."

"Why? It sounded like you guys had it all worked out."

"We did. Or at least we thought we did. Then my mother got involved."

Lainie frowned. "But you guys are paying for the wedding yourselves, right? I thought the whole point was to have it the way you wanted."

"You haven't met my mother."

"Come on, sweetie, you're standing up to them now, remember? You're not letting them run your life anymore."

"And I'm smart enough to pick my battles," Hadley said as their wine arrived.

Lainie raised her glass. "To Gabe and Hadley and happily ever after."

"Assuming we get that far," Hadley muttered, and clinked her glass.

"So what's going on?"

"With my mother? Everything. I've managed to keep her out of it all so far, but now she and my sisters are having fits about the wedding party."

"What are they having fits about? Your sisters are in it, aren't they? They ought to be happy." They ought, in Lainie's opinion, to consider themselves lucky to have a sister like Hadley.

"There are two of them, and Gabe's got three groomsmen."

"So? Small weddings are the new black."

"They're worried about the exit processional. My mother insists that the numbers should be even."

"But you guys are going low-key. Give one of them two guys to lead out, it's no big deal."

"It is to them," Hadley said grimly. "No one throws better fits over nothing than they do."

"But it's *your* wedding." Hadley's complicated relationship with her family was a source of constant amazement to Lainie. No wonder the woman had moved three states away.

"Like I said, I pick my battles. I've kept her out of everything else. I figure this one's not worth it." She let out a breath. "So I have a favor to ask you. I really hope you won't be offended at the late invite but, pretty please with sugar on top, will you be in our wedding?"

Lainie blinked. "Be in your wedding? But don't you have a childhood friend or someone that you'd like to ask?"

"This is me, remember? The compulsive overachiever who didn't have time for friends? Anyway, people have a tendency to get offended at being asked five weeks before the wedding."

"People can be idiots," Lainie pronounced, slinging an arm over Hadley's shoulders.

Hadley grinned. "That's part of why we get along so well. Anyway, I'm sorry about the short notice. Just please say you'll do this for me. It'll save me a world of grief."

"Hadley, sweetie, whatever I can do to make your life easier, let me know."

"You just did. My mother will be thrilled. It'll be so symmetrical, my sisters with Gabe's brothers. You'll be maid of honor. That'll put you with J.J."

That'll put you with J.J.

Lainie glanced across the bar to where he stood with his arms around two women who looked about eighteen. He whispered something to one of them, and she burst out giggling and pressed a kiss on him.

Lainie scowled. "Great. J.J. and me. Just what I've always wanted."

J.J. leaned against the lodge wall, beer in hand, listening as Tom Phillips, a guy he and Gabe had known in junior high school, hit the punch line in a joke. So it wasn't an après ski party in Gstaad. It was still good to be entertained, especially now, when he was sitting around at loose ends. It made him feel itchy in his own skin. He was accustomed to having a focus. He was accustomed to having a goal. He should be finishing up with speed camp in Chile right now, ready to head to Innsbruck in a couple of weeks to prep for the first World Cup race of the year at Sölden. Instead he was here, trying with admittedly little grace to be patient with physical therapy and the healing process of his shoulder while he waited for clearance to start training in earnest. He wasn't used to being forced to sit back and let other people get a head start on him.

He wasn't used to feeling like he was falling behind.

Of course he wasn't, he reminded himself. Maybe he'd be starting the season at a slight disadvantage, but he'd catch up quickly. Dry-land training would help, and once he got on the slopes, it would all come back.

And he wasn't going to think about what the future held, the all-too-near prospect of the day he'd miss speed camp not because he was rehabbing, but because he was retired.

J.J. made an impatient noise. Only a putz worried about things he couldn't change, and the future wasn't now. Right now he was just biding his time until he got going again. So if he was stuck waiting, he'd make the most of it. There were beautiful women in New England. He could hang out with friends, see his family.

And maybe harass Lainie some more.

Lainie.

Something about her today seemed uncommonly delectable.

He looked across to see her standing and talking to a guy whose eyebrows seemed to blend in with his hairline. As he watched, she threw her head back and laughed, not a giggle but the full-fledged belly laugh of a woman who wasn't afraid to have a good time.

J.J. took a drink of his beer, letting the conversation flow over him. He wasn't sure if he enjoyed needling her so much because it was so easy to get a rise out of her or because she generally managed to give as good as she got. Or maybe he just liked watching those brown eyes dance with devilry when she hit him with a really good zinger. If Lainie Trask were an animal, she'd be one of those seals that balanced balls on its nose, with her sleek dark hair and her quicksilver sense of fun. There was something irresistible about her, something happy and feckless and free.

Even when she was glowering at him.

Their sparring was so long-standing, he hardly remembered when it had started. One minute she'd been the skinny little drink of water who'd hung around him and Gabe when the two of them were in junior high. The next, he'd come back from his first modest experience in the Winter Olympics to find her all grown up into a leggy high-schooler with the eyes of a woman— a woman who seemed completely immune to his charm.

At first the acerbic retorts had annoyed and then they had begun to amuse. Sure she was hot but she was also the next best thing to Gabe's kid sister. Dating her was out of the question—even if she had had more than two civil words to say to him.

It was better this way, he thought, studying the long legs and smooth, golden skin left exposed by her stretchy white top and little blue skirt. If they'd dated, it wouldn't have lasted, and it all fell too close to home. When things went south, he'd not only lose a girlfriend, he'd maybe lose two people who were the next best thing to family. This way it just kept being fun.

Except when he had to watch her being monopolized by some guy. Not that it was jealousy or anything.

"…let's ask J.J.," a loud voice said beside him.

J.J. tuned back into the conversation. "Ask me what?"

"Whether Eastern European women are more beautiful than Swedish women." The speaker was another old school friend named Dennis, currently glowering at Tom.

"Everybody knows that Swedish women are the babes of Europe," Tom argued. "Except Dennis, here."

"Didn't you look at your last swimsuit issue? It's the ones coming from Russia and Eastern Europe who are the beauties. Anyway, J.J., what do you think? You're probably hooked up with one of each right now, right?"

J.J. grinned. "Ah, gentlemen, I'm flattered by your faith in me but I've given up my evil, worthless ways. No more gorgeous blondes with mile-long legs and big, uh," he glanced at a nearby mother with kids, "personalities. I'm dating only schoolteachers and librarians, now."

The remark earned him snorts and jeers.

"Give us a break, Cooper. Who's the babe of the month? C'mon, fill us in," Tom demanded.

J.J. grinned and finished his beer. "Not on your life. I'm going after another drink," he announced, and ambled across the room toward the bar—and Lainie.

She never glanced in his direction as he walked over. "The bar's to your left," she said pleasantly as he came to a stop beside her.

The guy with her looked at J.J., goggle-eyed. "Hey, J. J. Cooper, wow, I saw you in the Olympics. Remember me, Bart Ziffer? You dated my sister."

"Now there's a surprise," Lainie said under her breath.

"I'll have to tell her I saw you. She lives in Worcester, now. Got three kids. Hey, I bet they'd like an autograph. Can I get one?"

Lainie gave J.J. a derisive look. "Sure, Speed, give him an autograph. It might be worth a buck or two on eBay if you ever do anything impressive."

J.J. picked up a cocktail napkin. "Got a pen?"

Bart gave a blank look and patted his pockets. "I don't think so. Lainie?"

She held up her empty hands. There was something to be said for a woman who didn't bother with a purse, J.J. thought. It showed a certain independence of spirit. He grinned at Ziffer. "Catch up with me when you've got a pen and I'm all over it," he said, "but right now I need to talk to Lainie for a minute." He caught her arm, ignoring her suitor's crestfallen look, and began leading her away.

"That happened to be someone I've known since junior high." She pulled loose from him.

"You've known me since way before junior high."

"I know, and I never have figured out what I did to deserve it. So what, exactly, did you need to talk with me about?"

"Something important," he told her, trying to figure out just why he'd been compelled to get her to himself.

She crossed her arms. "Oh, really?"

"They did a nice job with the lodge, huh?"

She raised an eyebrow. "I'm waiting."

"So, uh, what are you doing with yourself these days? Still working at the witch museum?"

"Yeah. So?" She tapped her fingers, but he noticed she was in no hurry to go back.

"Just wondering. Still living in Salem?"

"It's as good as anywhere else."

"What ever happened to New York and Europe and all that? Or do you just like small towns?"

Her chin came up at that. "Salem's not a small town," she retorted, ignoring his snort. "And I'll move on when I'm ready."

"I guess that means you never did take that trip to Vienna and Prague you were talking about."

"I will at some point. Not that it's any of your business."

"Look, Gabe and Hadley are starting to open their gifts," J.J. said hastily, stepping back to lean against a nearby wall.

With a glower, Lainie subsided to lean next to him.

J.J. watched Hadley exclaim over a set of dish towels. "Now there's an exciting gift."

"It is if you've got dishes to dry," she said.

"I suppose orange and yellow stripes will be easy to find in the dark."

Lainie shook her head as Hadley tore open another package. "Okay, a magenta and gold lava lamp. Now that one's worse."

"Not necessarily. I think it's got style."

She looked at him as though he'd sprouted another head. "Style? You want look at those two people out there and tell me that's their definition of style?"

J.J. glanced over at Gabe and Hadley and pursed his lips. "Maybe."

"Oh, wait, don't tell me. That was *your* gift."

"Nope, but it's not a bad choice."

She just snorted.

"Well, what did you get them, anyway? Since you've got such great taste," he added.

She opened her mouth and stopped. "None of your business."

"It's not a state secret. Yours is in the on-deck circle anyway, unless I miss my guess. Come on, Lainie, spill it." When she only stared at him mutinously, he tilted his head. "Okay, then I'll guess. I'm thinking you didn't get them anything they registered for. 'That's for people with no imagination,'" he mimicked, doing his best imitation of her.

Lainie looked at him, startled.

"Nope, I'm thinking you didn't even go to a store for house stuff. I'm guessing you either went for the Trump factor and got them a statue of Venus or something at an art gallery or got something off-the-wall like a set of wrenches or an extension cord. Am I right?"

She set her mouth and glared.

"Let's make a little bet. If I'm wrong—"

"You leave me alone the rest of the night."

"I leave you alone the rest of the night." His eyes gleamed in enjoyment. "If I'm right, you dance with me later."

"Does the phrase 'a cold day in hell' mean anything to you?"

He just crossed his arms and leaned against the wall with an easy smile. "This is the north country. Gets cold early around here. Look." He pointed. "You're up."

Gabe set the red-and-silver-striped box on the table in front of Hadley. She peered at the tag. "Oh, this one's from Lainie."

Lainie gave her a halfhearted wave from across the room as Hadley began tearing off the paper eagerly. She opened the box inside…

And pulled out an extension cord.

"Yes!" J.J. crowed and pumped his fist. "Now who's got who down?"

"It's not an extension cord," Lainie protested.

"What's that orange snaky thing she's holding there, witch lady? That would be an extension cord. Score one to the gentleman in blue."

"The present isn't an extension cord," Lainie repeated as Hadley dug into the box. "It's a—"

"Mosquito zapper?" J.J. fell against the wall laughing. "Oh, Lainie, Lainie, Lainie, you are priceless."

Her cheeks tinted. "What? They have a lot of mosqui toes here."

"I'm sure they do," he said, wiping his eyes.

"It's practical," she muttered. "Stop laughing." She thumped him in the stomach. "Anyway, what did you get them? Something goofy that you picked up on your travels, I'm betting."

He looked down his nose at her. "Something refined and stylish. Something that didn't come from a hardware store, and don't tell me yours didn't because I recognize that orange sticker on the side."

In the center of the room, Hadley read a tag. "The next present comes from J.J., our host."

"Let's go get a drink," J.J. said quickly.

Lainie gave him a look. "Not a chance, Speed. I want to see this."

Hadley tore away the paper to reveal a large carton.

"A cardboard box," Lainie said. "How clever. Just what everyone needs."

Gabe tore open the flaps of the box and dug into the pool of packing peanuts inside to pull out—

"A cuckoo clock?" Lainie snorted. "Refined and stylish, my ass."

"Hey, it's practical," he defended as Gabe turned the ornately carved dark walnut clock to and fro. "Besides, it's handmade. I got it in Bavaria. Anyway, don't change the subject. You owe me a dance."

"I do not."

"Did she, or did she not pull out an extension cord?"

"Well, yes but—"

"No buts."

"It's a technicality," Lainie protested. "It was an accessory, not the gift."

He shook his head. "Did she or did she not pull out an extension cord?"

"You can be truly annoying sometimes," she muttered.

J.J. grinned broadly. "And I'm not even trying."

"Do you live to harass me?"

"No, I live to ski. But harassing you makes the time off the mountain go faster."

* * *

The pile of gifts had long since been opened and the toasts were over. Champagne fizzed pleasantly in Lainie's bloodstream as she nodded to the sound of the band. Good thing she was staying with Gabe and Hadley, who lived directly behind the Hotel Mount Jefferson, across the highway. She could hitch a ride with the happy couple, or walk, if need be. The night air would probably do her good.

She finished dancing with Ziffer, shaking her moneymaker to a Dave Matthews cover. It was impossible to be heard over the music or to move much on the crowded dance floor, but she did her best to come up with sign language for "thanks," and "I'm going to take a break."

A glass of water, maybe, and a few minutes of sitting would be just fine with her. She stood at the bar nodding to the beat, swaying a little, and then a hand stole around her shoulders. "You owe me a dance, remember?" she heard J.J. say, his breath warm on her ear. Something fluttered inside her.

Fluttering?

It was the champagne, that was all, Lainie told herself. Everybody felt a little giddy when they had champagne. It didn't have a thing to do with J.J.

Almost certainly not. Still, it made her want to do nothing so much as get away from him, pronto. She knew that look on his face, though, the look that said he was enjoying himself hugely. She could dig in her heels and refuse, and only wind up amusing him even more, or she could just get it over with. After all, it was a dance, three minutes. How bad could it be?

Then the band swung into the Romantics' "What I Like about You" and she was immediately energized. "I love this song," she crowed and dove into the crowd on the dance floor without even bothering to see if J.J. followed.

It seemed everybody else had had the same reaction. In seconds, the area before the bandstand had transformed into a mass of surging bodies, driven by the beat. Lainie stopped in a small patch of open floor and the irresistible chorus of the song took her over. With giddy joy, she raised her arms, head whipping back and forth, and stepped and spun in time to the music.

She wasn't dancing with J.J. really, just in his vicinity. She might just as well be dancing with every person on the floor, just a part of the motion and flow and sound of the crowd surrounding them. Then the music shifted to another dance staple with an irresistible bass hook, and it just became about the beat, nothing else. Jostled by the crowd, they bounced and shook, hot and sweaty and laughing, drawn on by the song, and the song after that. The band played the crowd, knowing that when you have the floor filled you never relent, just keep pushing them with one more irresistible song, and one more.

Finally, when people began filtering off the dance floor in self-defense, the band gave in. "Okay, we're going to slow it down a little," the lead singer said.

Breathing hard, Lainie looked at J.J. as the band swung into a slow ballad. "Okay, you got your dance."

"And then some." He grinned. "You're more talented than I realized."

"I'm so glad you approve," she said dryly.

"I always approve. In fact, I—"

And just in that moment, a slightly worse-for-wear Bart Ziffer barreled drunkenly back into Lainie, sending her off balance. Sending her into J.J., pressing her up against him for a blinding second, so that his arms went around her reflexively.

Something happened then, something that she didn't even want to know about. Champagne, Lainie thought, but she was very afraid it wasn't, because it was the same treacherous thing that always happened every time they got a little too close. Normally she kept her distance. Normally she could laugh him off and get away until her system settled. But this night, with the champagne fizzing in her system, the dancers holding them together, it was too late.

She looked, she couldn't stop looking, and it was as if some part of her vision widened so that he was all she could see, looking more alive, more real, more there than anything or anyone else in the room. Everything else faded away, and there was just J.J., looking at her first with surprise, then confusion, then some special attention that sent a shiver through her. His hands tightened, pulling her closer rather than releasing her.

She should look away, she knew, but she couldn't stop staring. And, dammit, she couldn't stop feeling—the hard lines of his athlete's body, his arms tightening around her even as they stood, the warmth of him as he leaned just a bit closer…

And utter panic vaulted through her.

Lainie wrenched herself away, turning without another word to flee blindly through the couples dotting the dance floor.

"Wait a minute." A hand landed on her shoulder, and J.J. spun her around to face him, staring at her with a hint of the same confusion she felt herself. J. J. Cooper, the man with the ego the size of Mount Washington, the man who couldn't even commit to a facial-hair style for more than a few weeks.

Not to mention a woman.

And it was that that had her turning toward the door.

"Where are you going?"

She barely threw him a dismissive glance. "Sorry, Speed, but my fairy godmother told me to be home at midnight. I'm out of here."

"Out of here? The party's just getting started."

"Clock ticking, got to go." She definitely had to go, before she got caught up again. Before she threw common sense aside and planted one on him just to find out what it was like. Before it was too late.

Chapter Three

It made her cranky, pure and simple, Lainie thought as she shepherded a school tour into the main room of the museum. Fourteen years after her brief obsession with J.J., and here she was, once again thinking about him every time she turned around. Only, this time she was twenty-six, not twelve.

It was ridiculous.

So what if they'd had that weird little moment of chemistry at Gabe's party? He was a lightweight, a good-time guy who was only out for himself and his own fun. Skiing, parties, women. She didn't know many things conclusively, but one thing she did know was that she'd be better off volunteering as a crash test dummy than starting something with J. J. Cooper. In fact, if she got involved with J.J., she'd *be* a dummy, of high proportions. He didn't bear thinking about, not even for a minute.

Realizing that she *was,* in fact, thinking about him just put her in a bad temper. Better to concentrate on work.

Lainie looked around the throng of avid-faced fourth graders before her, and her mood brightened. "Okay, who knows what a witch looks like?"

The whole crowd of them raised their hands.

"Ugly," offered one.

"Warts."

"Flies on a broomstick."

"Plays Quidditch," someone shouted. "When does the match start?"

Lainie smiled. "If you want Quidditch, you'll have to come back Halloween week for the Hogwarts Festival. But let's talk about witches, okay?"

"Yeah!"

One thing she loved about working at the Witchcraft Museum was that the kids showed up eager and bright eyed with curiosity. They were lured by the promise of witchcraft, the sensationalism of the trials. Instead of a lot of dry display cases to stare into, they saw the story told by the characters. The learning almost sneaked up on them while they were concentrating on other things.

"Who knows where the word *witch* comes from?" Lainie asked.

A little girl with dark corkscrew hair and red shorts raised her hand. "Wicca," she announced.

"That's right—the word *witch* comes from *Wicca,* a religion of the earth."

"Religion happens in churches," the little girl countered.

"Not always," Lainie corrected. "Religion happens wherever a person wants it to. There were and are people who worship the earth outdoors. Some of them call themselves Wiccans. Long ago, that word turned into *witches.* A lot of times they learned how to use herbs to help people feel better. Sometimes people appreciated them for the good they did. And sometimes people persecuted them as being in league with the devil. Sometimes even non-Wiccans were persecuted as witches. Do you know what persecuted means?"

The little girl raised her hand again. "People were mean to them?"

It was the most apt definition she'd heard. "Yes, people were mean. If you got accused of being a witch, there was no real way to prove you weren't. Lots of times, people accused of being witches were killed."

"By mean people."

"No, by ordinary people who just didn't know any better. That's what happened here in Salem. But instead of me telling you the story, I'm going to let the people of Salem tell you the story. Look above your heads."

Lainie pressed the wireless control in her palm. Even as the lights went down, the Wiccan wheel of the year set into the floor began to glow a pulsing red. A little murmur of excitement and alarm passed through the crowd of children. They all backed away from the medallion a little as a basso voice greeted them.

"Witchcraft…possession…trials and hangings. The story you are about to hear really happened here in Salem. The year was 1692. It began with a group of girls…"

On the perimeter of the room, on a level above their heads, a roomlike section grew bright to reveal the figures of three young girls crouched by a fireplace and staring up at the figure of a housekeeper wearing a colorful headkerchief. In the next moment the figures began to move and speak, drawing "aahhs" from the audience, taking them back to the seventeenth century and a time of madness.

One after another the dioramas lit, and bit by bit the tragic dance played out. And Lainie felt the familiar sadness. Fear, ignorance and boredom, a toxic brew under any circumstances. Add a little fanaticism and power lust and you had a destructive force that had spelled the ruin of dozens. It might have happened long before, but the story still touched her every time.

As it touched the people who visited the museum. They came from near and far, young and old, all drawn by the story. And the numbers were rising by the week. Halloween was the high season for a town whose name was synonymous with witchcraft. Ghost walks, festivals and galas, costume parades and reenactments, the events began at the start of October and ran all month long. Of course, the planning started well before that, which was why only a day or two into September, Lainie found herself with barely time to think.

Even as the show went on, she was busy reviewing her to-do list. Her alarmingly long to-do list. Phone calls, e-mails, requisitions, contracts, and no thoughts of J.J.

Specifically no thoughts of J.J.

Finally, the show ended. Lainie pressed her remote to bring the lights back up and bring them all back to reality.

The kids stood around, blinking in the sudden light, looking interested, even sober. It was a lot to absorb, and they were just getting to the age to do so.

"So, what did you think?" Lainie asked.

One of the boys nudged another. "Tituba looks just like Emma."

The little girl in red scowled. "Does not."

"Does too!"

"Does not."

"Emma! Boys!" the teacher said reprovingly.

Lainie stuggled not to smile. "Well, I think Emma looks just like herself, and I don't think—"

The words died in her throat. Because there, leaning against the wall at the back of the room was J. J. Cooper, a grin on his beach-boy face.

In the first instant of surprise, all she could do was stare, heart thudding in her chest. He didn't belong there amid the confusion of kids. It was the last place he should have been, and yet somehow, curiously, he looked at home.

Then again, J.J. managed to always look at home, no matter where he was.

There was a cough from the teacher. "Miss?"

Lainie tore her gaze loose from J.J. and cleared her throat. "Sorry. I was going to say, I don't think Emma's the type to accuse anyone of giving her fits."

"Only Cassie, maybe," Emma grumbled.

"Who's Cassie?"

"My little sister."

J.J., Lainie noted, looked amused.

"But witches don't give people fits, remember?" J.J., on the other hand, was pretty good at it.

"How do you know witches don't give fits?" one of the little boys demanded. "Are you a witch?"

"Joshua," the teacher said warningly.

Lainie laughed, relaxing a bit. "It's all right. No, Joshua, I'm not a witch. I'm not even Wiccan. I'm just a plain old ordinary person, just like Bridget Bishop and the rest."

"How come you work in the witch museum?"

"Because it's fun and because I think their story deserves to be told. People need to remember what can happen when they get scared and stop thinking." She pointed to a case on the back wall that held the figure of a storybook witch, complete with warts, pointed hat and broom. "This isn't real. *The Wizard of Oz* is just a movie. Real Wiccans are people just like the rest of us. They don't do spells, at least not that I know of."

"There are spells in Harry Potter," Emma piped up.

"Well, Harry Potter's something different."

"I love Harry Potter," Emma announced.

"So do I," Lainie said. "The Harry Potter books are great. How many of you have read them?"

Hands shot up all over the room.

"The author of the Harry Potter books has a great imagination," she continued. "That's why we read, to get carried away by our imaginations. I like getting carried away. How about you?"

Across the room, J.J. raised an eyebrow. Lainie could feel the flush stain her cheeks. "Getting carried away by your imagination is a good kind of carried away, but you want to watch other kinds of carried away, the kinds of carried away that can hurt people. Like the way the Salem witchcraft trials got carried away." She paused. "Anyway, if there are no more questions, that's our tour."

"What do you say?" the teacher asked.

"Thank you, Ms. Trask," they chorused obediently.

Lainie smiled. "Thank you for spending the morning with me. The exit's right through here."

There was nothing like being the head of a procession of fourth graders to give a person dignity, she thought wryly as she shepherded the tour into the gift shop.

"Lainie, do you have a minute?" a voice called. Lainie turned to see her boss, Caro Lewis. Small, dark, positive, Caro had taught Lainie a tremendous amount in the three and a half years they'd worked together. Somehow in that time, they'd also become fast friends. Because they were both scrupulously careful to do their jobs to the nth degree, it worked.

"What's up, chief?"

Nearby a pair of little boys menaced each other with goblin

heads. Caro watched them, the corners of her mouth curving up. "They look like they found the museum intellectually stimulating. Who do you have today?"

One of the boys crossed his eyes and stuck out his tongue. Lainie's lips twitched. "The fourth-grade class of Daniel Dunn Elementary School."

Caro glanced beyond the boys to where J.J. stood, leafing through books. "Fourth grade, huh?" she said, eyeing him. "My, my, they just get bigger every year. He must take a lot of vitamins."

Lainie snorted. "He's just a delinquent."

Caro laughed so loud that J.J. glanced over. "But a tasty-looking one. Listen, Jim over at the Seven Gables Inn had to reschedule our planning meeting. He wants to know if we can do eleven."

"Eleven o'clock?" Lainie glanced at her watch and frowned. "That's only fifteen minutes from now."

"I know, but the next window he's got isn't for another week, and Halloween's coming for us."

"I have to print out the schedule and get my laptop."

"I know. I'll head over now and get started. You come on as soon as you're done. Have fun with your fourth-graders." Caro winked and sashayed away.

Lainie stood at the doorway to the store and eyed J.J. As though he'd felt her look, he glanced up. Definitely too gorgeous for his own good, she thought. The Vandyke had changed to a Fu Manchu, she saw, sharpening his chin, making that mouth of his look far too interesting.

A crash made her jump. She looked around to see a display of wands and spells scattered on the floor, courtesy of the boys with goblin heads.

"Richie, Matt, that's enough," the teacher scolded. "Now you go over and help clean that up."

"Don't worry about it," Lainie said. "I'll take care of it." The last thing she wanted was for them to walk away with bad memories of the museum. She knelt down next to the colorful pile of plastic and glitter, righting the magenta canister that had held the wands.

Out of the corner of her eye saw J.J. head over. She glanced up at him.

And it took her breath.

She'd known he was there, she'd watched him walk over. Even so, there was something about the jolt of that blue gaze that sent adrenaline flooding through her system. She frowned at herself. It was one thing to have the heart-thudding thing happen when he'd popped up out of the blue. It shouldn't be happening now.

He bent down next to her to help, picking up the packets and examining them. "Love potions?" he asked, holding one up.

She took it from him. "What's the matter, Speed, losing your edge?"

"Not me."

"What a relief. It would be the end of civilization as we know it. Although I use that term loosely where you're concerned," she added, picking up the rest of the wands and rising. "To what do we owe the honor of your presence?"

He grinned. "I've got an appointment."

"In Salem?"

"In Boston."

She snorted. "I hope you're better at staying on the *piste* when you're racing than you are at following directions. This isn't Boston."

"I thought something looked funny," he replied.

"South. A long way south. The highway's right out there," she added helpfully.

He didn't move. "Trying to get rid of me, Lainie?"

"Why, Speed, whatever would give you that idea?" She reached out to toy with a leaflet that promised step-by-step directions to putting a hex on someone.

"Should I be nervous that you're holding on to that?"

"No, the time to get nervous is when I go after the voodoo doll."

He gave her a quick glance. "You wouldn't, by any chance, have broken one of those out already?" He rubbed his shoulder. "It would explain a lot."

"No, it's an inspiration I've never had until now. Worth keeping in mind, though," she added thoughtfully. "Why, are you having problems?" Not that she should care, of course.

J.J. shrugged, a little stiffly, now that she noticed it. "Ah, I screwed up my shoulder back in July."

"Screwed it up?"

"Dislocated the son of a bitch."

"What, did you trip over your ego?"

He grinned. "Mountain biking."

"I am so not surprised."

Suddenly his eyes seemed darker and he was much closer than he had been. Suddenly she was neatly boxed in between him and the corner shelves. "You know, Lainie, one of these days I will surprise you."

For an instant she didn't move; she couldn't. Then she forced herself to swallow with a throat gone bone dry. "Yeah, well, I'll be right here holding my breath for when that happens." She pushed past him, out into the center of the shop.

But he'd gotten to her in that moment, and he knew it. She could tell from the enjoyment flickering in his eyes.

"Gee, it's been fun, J.J. I've got to get to a meeting," she said briskly.

"Over at the Seven Gables Inn?" At her startled glance, he shrugged. "I heard you talking with your friend."

"My boss, but yes at the Seven Gables Inn. Anyway, I'm late, I've got to go."

"Nice day for a walk," he added.

J.J. stood in the museum courtyard, waiting for Lainie. He wasn't entirely sure what ridiculous impulse had led him to stop in Salem, only that when he had an impulse, he usually found it worthwhile to ride with it. Traffic had cooperated on the drive down from New Hampshire. When he'd glanced at the dash clock and seen that he had a few hours to kill, he hadn't thought but just gone with the first thing that came to mind.

And in the two days that had passed since the party, Lainie had come to mind a lot.

It wasn't an entirely unfamiliar situation. She'd always had a way of flickering through his thoughts at the most unexpected of times—when he was thousands of miles away, flying down an icy mountain, standing at a party in a room filled with the music of a dozen languages.

And sometimes, unsettlingly, in his dreams. Best not to think of that, he reminded himself. Better to banish those pulse-pounding images to the dark corners of his mind where they belonged. The problem was, this time out of the gate he wasn't being so successful at the banishing stuff, maybe because he was at loose ends, maybe because he wasn't involved with anyone.

Or maybe because of that moment at Gabe's party, that strange little snap of connection that had whipped through his system before he'd been prepared for it.

"You still here?"

It was Lainie, frowning at him, laptop slung over her shoulder. She wasn't wearing the little skirt and crop top this time but a long summer dress made of some intriguingly fragile-looking fabric that shimmered over the slip beneath and flowed around her calves like water.

It should have looked demure, with its faintly old-fashioned looking pattern of pale blossoms, but all it did was make him itch to unfasten the row of buttons that ran down the front, beginning with the hem and rising to where the fabric dipped down around the slender column of her throat. She wore a necklace with a single bead like a flat pearl, pierced from side to side with a string-thin leather thong so that it sat atop the hollow where her collarbones came together.

"Earth to J.J."

He'd been staring, he realized.

"I have to go. You shouldn't have waited."

And she clearly hadn't wanted him to, though that didn't bother him. Not when he saw the faint pulse begin to beat in her throat. "Salem could be a tough town. I owe it to your parents not to let you walk around alone. Although—" he eyed the black bulk of her laptop case "—that thing probably counts as a lethal weapon."

"Try to remember that," she advised him.

He reached out and curved his fingers around the black webbing of the strap. Her eyes widened. "Maybe you'd better just give it to me to carry," he said.

She tugged it back from him. "I thought you had a bad shoulder."

"It's the other one, and it's getting better all the time," he told her. She finally gave up, and he slung the bag over his shoulder, trying not to look smug. "So, where to?"

She didn't bother answering, just headed toward the iron gates that led to the street, and the trapezoidal town common beyond.

She could needle him, she could pretend all she liked that she didn't want him around. He knew better.

He was used to women with quick hungers, women who

knew what they wanted. And what they wanted was him. He'd had more memorable times than he could count and none of them were anything as hot as that moment in the gift shop when he'd stood just a little too close to Lainie and seen the flare of desire in her eyes.

He wasn't sure what to think about it, what to do about it except that he knew there was no way he was just going to walk away.

Not until he figured it out.

She didn't know what he thought he was up to, but the last thing she needed before an important meeting was a distraction. Especially a distraction like J. J. Cooper. Out of habit, Lainie walked between the stone pillars that led into the common itself. Even if it was only a few dozen yards, she liked wending her way along the graceful oaks and the grass-edged paths instead of the narrow concrete sidewalk that threaded along the street. On drowsy, Indian summer mornings like this one, it was quiet and tranquil.

Usually.

She blew out a breath.

"Careful," J.J. said. "Hyperventilating isn't good for you."

Lainie glanced to the heavens for patience and headed toward the side of the common by the hotel.

The warm breeze slipped over her skin as they walked a few steps in silence. "Nice common," J.J. said. "Do you spend a lot of time here?"

"Sometimes."

"I can see why you would. It must be something in the fall. There are some beautiful places in the world, but there's nothing quite like New England."

Lainie stopped to stare at him. "I thought you had an appointment."

"I've got time." He just smiled and began ambling again with that loose, careless stride. He didn't move with the controlled grace of an athlete, and yet something in the way he held himself suggested that he could do just about anything he wanted to with that body of his.

Like she needed to think of that.

Lainie made an impatient noise and caught up with him. "What's the appointment?"

"Dry-land training. Rehab."

She snorted. "I don't think you can be rehabilitated. I think you're stuck with yourself just as you are. And so are we, sadly."

It didn't do a thing to wipe away that confident grin. "You know, you talk tough, but deep down inside, I think you've got a soft spot for me." For an instant, there was something almost velvety in his voice.

"So young to have terminal delusions," she said.

"In fact, I think deep down inside, you can't resist me."

"It'll be an enormous effort, but I think I can just about see my way to it. In fact, I think I'll manage pretty well." She threaded her way between the stone pillars on the side of the common and started across the street to the Seven Gables Inn.

"I don't know if I buy that."

There it was again, that velvet note. He flicked a glance at her and their gazes tangled for a moment. Awareness of him dragged at her like some kind of a gravitational field. His smile this time was slow, almost dangerous.

A horn tapped and Lainie realized that she'd come to a stop in the middle of the street. "Well, you stand right here until you're sure." She shook her head and strode across the pavement as he followed. "Anyway, you told me why you're going to Boston. That doesn't explain why you're here harassing me."

"Because it's so much fun?"

"There's something deeply twisted about you," she muttered.

He laughed in genuine amusement. "So I've been told."

"Why are you here? A town like Salem can't hold anything for a guy like you."

"Maybe I came here to sightsee."

Lainie snorted. "Next thing you'll be telling me is that you came here to get your fortune told by the Salem witch."

"No. I came here because I wanted to see you," he said simply.

It stopped her in her tracks. In the middle of the sidewalk that ran in front of the plate glass windows of the hotel, cars whizzing past in the street, she turned to stare into those blue-gray eyes. And for the first time since she'd been twelve, found herself at a loss for words with him. She moistened her lips. "Why?"

He reached out for her hand. Heat vaulted up her arm, making her dizzy. "I don't know," he said, staring at her palm as though the answer might be there. "I thought maybe I'd figure it out when I got here."

And suddenly she was very afraid of hearing what that answer was. "I have to go," she said faintly, telling herself to pull her hand away. But instead she just stood there, staring stupidly at him.

"I know." He placed something in her fingers and closed them over it, then raised her hand to his lips.

Heat bloomed through her, making her dizzy. She wouldn't let him throw her off balance, wouldn't give him the satisfaction of playing Casanova and making her look the fool.

"Is that one of those moves you've learned in Europe?" Lainie asked unsteadily.

"We haven't even scratched the surface of what I've learned in Europe yet," J.J. said. "I'll see you around, Lainie."

And he turned and walked away.

She opened her hand and found one of the serenity stones they sold in the gift shop.

Carved into its surface was the word *beginnings*.

Chapter Four

"I can't believe I let you talk me into this," Lainie said, puffing as she struggled to raise her toes, already pointing at the ceiling, even higher in rhythmic bursts. "Nobody should work this hard at six in the morning."

"Just think of all the good it's doing you." Caro lay on the mat next to her, doing the exercises as though they cost no effort at all.

"I'd rather be running any day. Tell me why I'm doing this again?"

"To strengthen your core."

"I think my core's as strong as it needs to be."

"If it were, you wouldn't be puffing," Caro said serenely.

"I'll tell you what my core needs," Lainie said, rolling to her side to do the plank. "Coffee and scones at George's."

Caro turned to stare at her before getting into position.

"Work out and then go pack the calories right back on? Isn't that contrary to the whole point?"

"What do you mean? Coffee and scones *are* the whole point. This is just what we do to earn our right to them."

"I feel sure there's something really off about that statement, but I can't quite figure out what," Caro said.

"Come on, guys, no talking," the instructor reprimanded them gently from the front of the class. "Concentrate on your core."

"See?" Lainie whispered. "Scones."

"Isn't this the guy who was kissing your hand outside the hotel yesterday?" Caro looked up from her newspaper.

Lainie froze, a bite of scone halfway to her mouth. "Kissing my hand?" she repeated faintly.

They sat at the window counter in Cool Beans. Caro held up the sports page. On the bottom, in living color, J.J. stared out at her with his crooked grin. Local Champ Down as Season Looms, read the headline.

Lainie cleared her throat. "You, um, saw that?"

"It was kind of hard to miss."

"You didn't say anything."

Caro gave a Mona Lisa smile. "I was biding my time. It was the fourth grader from the gift shop, right? Funny, we don't often get Olympic medalists dropping by."

"Oh, he's just…" Lainie flapped her hands.

Caro raised an eyebrow. "Yes?"

"Someone I grew up with."

"That didn't look like the move of a childhood friend."

"I never used the word *friend*," Lainie said darkly.

Caro's mouth curved. "Now, this is getting interesting."

"It's not interesting. There's nothing going on."

"It sure didn't look like nothing."

"I ran into him at a family event over the weekend. Lucky me, he decided to stop by and bug me." Lainie took a drink of her latte and set the cup squarely down on the picture of J.J.'s face.

"Looks like he did a pretty effective job," Caro observed.

"Oh, that's the one talent he's got."

"Judging by the hand-kiss thing, I'd say he's got a few more."

Lainie sucked in a breath of annoyance. "Yeah, well, he's not going to use them on me."

"You so sure of that?"

"Positive."

Caro stirred her cappuccino. "What's the problem, is he a jerk?"

Both less and more. "J. J. Cooper cares about three things—skiing, parties and women, and not necessarily in that order. He has the biggest ego on three continents and the attention span of a gnat."

"Big breeders, those gnats."

Lainie finished her coffee and thumped down the cup a little too loudly. "He's just yanking my chain. He's stuck here for a while instead of being Mr. Continental and he's bored. Showing up here gives him something to do."

"So are you going out?"

"Not in this or any other universe." Lainie finished the last bite of scone with a decisive munch and screwed up the napkin.

Caro took a meditative sip of her coffee. "Why not?"

"The same reason I don't hit myself on the head with a hammer. It's dumb, it's unhealthy and I know for a fact it's going to be painful before I ever start."

"So you've got a thing for him." Caro nodded wisely.

"I do not have a thing for him," Lainie retorted, stung. "And

Speed Racer is dreaming if he thinks for one minute that I'm going to be the one to take him off the hook while he's stuck here."

Caro nodded. "Understandable."

"Because I am so not."

"You've got me convinced," she said mildly.

"He's not my type. He never has been."

"Don't forget to invite me to the wedding."

Lainie gave her a narrow-eyed stare. "Does the phrase 'when hell freezes over' mean anything to you?"

"Winter's coming," Caro said genially.

It looked, J.J. thought, like a medieval torture rack, an open-sided, metal-framed cube built of steel bars as tall as a man. Levers and steel weight plates and leather belts dangled on the inside. "You're weren't part of the Spanish Inquisition in a previous life, were you?" He turned to the short, muscle-bound man in sweats who stood outside the cage.

Manny Turturro grinned at J.J. from a face misshapen from a decade in the boxing ring. "Me? I'm the milk of human kindness."

"The milk of human kindness," J.J. repeated. Actually, to his eye, Manny looked more like a human fireplug with a smile. "So how does this work?"

"I use the lever to raise the weights, then lower them so that all the pressure is on you. Your job is to use your legs and abs to stay in place for a count of ten, then I pull the weights off. The idea is not motion but maintaining peak muscle contraction."

"And it's not going to be a problem with my shoulder?"

Turturro shook his head. "The weight's going onto your trapezius. I checked it all out with your sports med doc and he was fine with it. How's the shoulder feel, anyway?"

J.J. moved his arm around a bit. "Good. A little twinge if I try to move too fast, but otherwise it's fine." Not fine enough to let him get on the slopes, though, which was why he was at Turturro's. Manny Turturro's methods may have been unorthodox, at best, but the iconoclastic trainer had brought countless elite athletes to the peaks of their professions with a few months of work at his training compound north of Boston.

"I can pretty much guarantee it won't be pleasant, but you want to be ready for the slopes, we'll get you ready for the slopes."

J.J. grinned and stepped into the metal cage. "Okay, let's do it."

Unpleasant, he quickly discovered, was a mild word for it. *Agonizing,* maybe, or *excruciating.* And Manny just kept grinning at him like a demented gnome and calling for another set.

"Come on, Cooper, show me what you got." He levered up the weights without breaking a sweat.

"Anybody ever tell you you're a sadist, Manny?" J.J. said through gritted teeth as his quads trembled with effort.

"Hey, all you have to do is convince yourself you're having fun. Just ignore all this. Think about something pleasant. Take your mind off it."

Something pleasant? And that quickly, Lainie popped to mind. *Stop it.* He'd been tempted, oh, so tempted, to stop in Salem again the previous day, and even that morning. Unfortunately he'd been running late—figuring out he hadn't needed to leave at the crack of dawn to make his appointment had made sleeping in far too tempting. As it was, he'd still gotten up earlier than he'd have liked, and if he had to spend more days in the car than he was out of it anymore, he was going to start clawing his face off.

Time to think about Plan B.

"Come on, Cooper, another set."

He glowered at Manny. "I'll give you another set."

"If distracting yourself doesn't work, then visualize. Isn't that what you fancy athletes do? Close your eyes, feel the weight and imagine it's the g-forces from going around a gate."

Fine idea in the abstract, except that when he closed his eyes, the image in his head was Lainie, staring at him, stunned, as he kissed her hand. J.J. sank down into another rep, pushing aside the pain of fatigue. He liked seeing Lainie stunned, her control and assurance gone. He liked knowing that for a moment all she thought of was him.

So maybe he should get in her way a little more, see where it all went. He had the time; she wasn't attached the last time he'd heard. Maybe they ought to run it around the block, see how it did. Of course, she might take some convincing.

He smiled broadly. Then again, the convincing might be the fun part. After all, he'd never set out to charm a woman yet without succeeding.

"There you go, imagine yourself winning," Manny said. "It works—you know as well as I do. You get a goal, then concentrate on it and make it happen. It's as simple as that. Give me one more."

J.J. swiped away the sweat that was starting to drip into his eyes and tried to ignore the trembling of his legs. *Think about something pleasant.* Like the feel of Lainie folded against his chest at the Jack and Jill party. Like the way she'd feel, warm and naked against him in bed.

"There we go, that's what I'm talking about," Manny said. "Focus, concentrate on what you want."

And J.J., in the midst of another rep, concentrated.

The mountains were where he felt best, he thought as he stood on the terminal slope of the Mount Jefferson ski run with

Gabe. Something about being there always felt right. Not that he didn't love the beach and the city, or that he couldn't find a sort of quiet beauty in the desert. They weren't the same, though.

Up among the peaks, he somehow felt more alive, as though he could breathe more deeply, stand taller, become more than what he was. Whether it was because skiing was in his blood or whether he'd become a skier because of his love for the mountains, it was the place that was right for him.

They stared down at the sweep of turf that spread out below them. To their left, the sculpted curve of the new half pipe was already lightly grassed over. Across the valley, the Hotel Mount Jefferson gleamed white in the morning sun.

Gabe turned to stare thoughtfully at the point where the new downhill run tapered into the main slope. "You did a hell of a job."

J.J. shrugged. "All I did was draw a couple of things and wave my hands around. You and Hadley were the ones who made it happen, you guys and your construction crews."

"Team effort. Besides, if Hadley and I can pull off planning a wedding in three months, we can sure as hell pull together a ski resort remodel."

They began walking over down the slope toward the new lift.

"So, you ready for this?" J.J. looked across the valley at the peak that was Mount Washington, rising into the clouds.

Gabe held his ever-present walkie-talkie phone in one hand, his clipboard in the other. "The resort opening?"

"Your wedding, dummkopf."

Gabe grinned. "Oh, that."

"Yeah, that. It's a big step." An enormous step, one that J.J. thought might happen for him some distant time in the future, but certainly not soon.

"Nah. I'm looking forward to getting it over with, actually."

J.J. looked over to him with interest. "Why's that?"

"I don't know, I guess I want real life to start. Right now it keeps feeling like we're in a holding pattern. I'm ready to go."

Always before, they'd kept pace in their lives professionally and personally. Maybe J.J. had been a slight trailblazer when it came to girls: the first to knock teeth in a clumsy kiss, the first to dive into the dating dance, to discover the mystery of just what was underneath those sweaters and skirts. They'd been cohorts exploring the country of woman side by side.

Suddenly, it felt as though Gabe had found a map through some new territory that J.J. didn't know.

"You know, it's funny, I remember some guy who looked just like you telling me all the reasons he needed to keep away from Hadley," J.J. observed. "What changed?"

"I don't know that anything did outside," Gabe said slowly. "I just took a look one day and all the reasons why not didn't mean a hell of a lot stacked up to how I thought it would be with her."

"So you just said what the hell."

Gabe shrugged. "Aren't you the guy who always says rules are there for breaking?"

"You've got a point."

"Anyway, why are you giving me a hard time over this? I figured you'd approve on her babedom alone."

"Just doing my job as best man." J.J.'s voice was serene.

"Grilling me?"

"Sure, grilling you. It's on the list, right below hitting on the maid of honor."

Gabe coughed. "Yeah, well, you know the maid of honor is now Lainie?"

J.J. gave him a sharp look, then his face relaxed into a smile. "Really? Well, how about that?"

Chapter Five

Lainie walked out onto her front porch, feet thudding hollowly on the wood. The sunny morning held a breath of chill, a reminder that winter lurked on the horizon. She rubbed her quads a little. Running shorts weren't exactly the best thing for this kind of morning, but she'd warm up soon enough once she got moving.

She raised her hands over her head and stretched first to one side, then the other. Okay, admittedly she didn't live in Salem's best neighborhood. Or even the third or fourth best, for that matter. Working as an assistant curator at a local museum wasn't exactly a high-buck job. Still, the flat in the century-old triple-decker house worked for her. Given that she didn't own much of anything valuable, adding an extra deadbolt to the doors when she'd moved in had seemed sufficient.

Lainie rested one of her feet on the porch railing and bent over it to stretch her hamstrings. Most of the people who lived in this section of town were as hardworking and honest as she was; they just hadn't gotten the breaks. In a way she was living in relative luxury, with a whole flat to herself, as opposed to being crammed in with a dozen other people in order to be able to afford a roof over her head.

"Hiya, Lainie."

Lainie jumped. She whipped her head back and forth, staring along the empty porch. Then she let out a breath of relief as she spied the toffee-haired little girl behind the screen of the front door, over to the left side of the broad porch. "Kisha. Wow, I didn't see you there." She took a breath and waited for the adrenaline in her bloodstream to dissipate. "What are you doing hiding in the hall? Why aren't you outside?"

"Gran doesn't want me to play on the grass. She's worried I'll get dirty for today." As though the lure of the outdoors was irresistible, though, the little girl slipped out from behind the screen and onto the porch.

Lainie looked out at the weedy, coffee-table-size square of dirt that Kisha called grass. It made her heart twist. No kid should grow up with only a little square of bare ground to play on. But she was trying to do something about that, Lainie reminded herself. She just needed to be patient.

"If your gran told you to stay inside, you'd better listen," Lainie advised, and dipped low into another stretch. "You don't want her to come after you with her wooden spoon."

Kisha giggled. "She won't come after me with the spoon."

"I wouldn't be too sure." Even with two jobs and three young grandchildren on her hands, Elsie Banks never seemed to miss a thing. "I'd play it safe."

"I'll stay on the porch," Kisha said, grabbing the railings as if they were part of a jungle gym. The wood creaked and shifted.

"Over here," Lainie suggested. "We need to get that part fixed."

"Okay." Kisha moved closer to her.

Meanwhile, Lainie stretched, catching hold of her ankle to fold her calf up against her hamstring, feeling the good pull in her quads. "So how is first grade?"

Kisha's eyes lit up. "It's really fun. They've got swings and a slide and my teacher, Mrs. Cornelli, has a bunny rabbit in a cage by her desk. Mr. Nibbles," she elaborated. "He's really soft."

"I bet he is." Lainie stretched the other leg.

"I brought a carrot for show-and-tell, so I could feed it to him. I like carrots."

"So do I. In fact, I've been eating so many lately, my nose is starting to wiggle like Mr. Nibbles'." She demonstrated until Kisha giggled.

"You can't turn into a bunny."

"How do you know?" Lainie asked, and hopped once, holding her hands up like little paws.

"Stop it, fool." Kisha laughed, sounding just like her grandmother.

"I can't help it, Kisha." Lainie hopped over to the stairs. "It's too late. I'm a bunny fool." And she hopped down to the sidewalk and started to run, Kisha's laughter ringing in her ears.

He should add parallel parking to his training regimen, J.J. thought to himself as he finished backing into the tiny spot he'd managed to find on Lainie's street, then whipped his head around and reversed his tires to straighten out. Good for flexibility, good for the arms. And with a truck the size of his, God knew he got his reps in.

He turned off the ignition and got out, squinting again at the slip of paper in his hand. It definitely wasn't the kind of neighborhood he'd been anticipating when he'd driven in to find her. He knew Lainie well enough not to expect to find her in some condo complex. A house, maybe, or a duplex in one of the picturesque older neighborhoods of Salem. He'd been right about the older part, at least.

Of course, there was old and there was just plain decrepit.

He walked down the block and stopped in front of a run-down-looking house that had been painted white in some happier time. Now it was more a dirty gray, roughened and peeling in some places, mildew spotted in others. But flower-boxes sat on the railings of the broad front porch, spilling over with fat purple and magenta blossoms. Lainie? he wondered.

On the porch, a little tawny-skinned girl about seven or eight played with a smaller boy. Down the street a clot of teenagers hanging out aimed sullen looks at him.

J.J. studied the building as he walked up the cracked front walkway. The address he had was for apartment D, which, given that the building had three stories, three mailboxes and three doorbells, was kind of a puzzle. He stopped at the base of the stairs and glanced at the little girl. "Hi. Does Lainie Trask live here?"

She swung on the porch rails like they were monkey bars. "My Gran says I'm not s'posta talk to strangers." The look she aimed at him made him feel like he should be producing a résumé, or at the very least a photo ID and references. "Are you a stranger?"

"He's about as strange as they come," a voice said behind him and he turned to see Lainie. She wore a T-shirt advertising the Macon Whoopie hockey team and eye-popping, hot-pink running shorts. Of course, the shorts weren't nearly as eye popping as those long, gleaming legs of hers. Her face still held the flush of exertion—or maybe a flush of something else, given the wary look she aimed at him. "Showing up out of the blue again, Speed? That's a habit you need to break." She walked past him and mounted the stairs.

He grinned broadly and followed. "It's a free country."

"That's right. Maybe you should go see some more of it," she suggested. "That's your specialty, isn't it? Moving on? How's your new condo?"

"How'd you know I had a new—" He stopped and tipped his head to her. "Fine."

Her smile held a certain smugness that he itched to wipe away—and he knew exactly how.

"Because you get a new condo every year," she said in answer to his question. "Why don't you just buy someplace and stick with it? You've got more money than God."

"If I bought, I'd have to worry about keeping it up. Besides, I like variety."

"So go find some variety now," she invited.

"I already am." He reached out and brushed at some flaking paint on one of the porch pillars. "Who knew that Salem had this kind of—" At the clearing of her throat, he broke off. "Variety," he substituted, flicking a quick glance at the two kids, who were watching him avidly. "Do your parents know you live here?"

"My mommy and daddy are passed away," the little girl told him, mistaking the question as aimed at her. She'd apparently decided that if Lainie thought he was trustworthy enough to talk to, she should, too. "My gran's raising us all, 'less we drive her to an early grave," she added.

He crouched down before her. "I'm sorry to hear that."

She nodded gravely. "I was sad when it happened, but I was a pretty little kid. Tyjah still cries over it," she said with a sidelong glance to the little boy. "I'm grown-up now, and Gran says Latrice and me have to help watch after him. Latrice is my sister," she elaborated. "Do you have any brothers and sisters?"

J.J. nodded. "One. A little sister."

"You have to stick together," she said seriously.

"Yes, you do." He rose and grinned at Lainie, who stood a few feet from the door. "You want to stick together with me?"

Before she could respond, a voice came from behind the screen door with the snap of a drill sergeant's. "Kisha Tonisha Banks, you and your brother better not be playing in that dirt." The door opened and a tall, gray-haired woman with cocoa-colored skin stepped out. "Hi, Lainie." She looked back at Kisha and her brother. "Are you bothering Miz Trask and her friend?"

"Lainie said I could talk to him."

"Don't you go calling her Lainie. She's a grown-up. She's Miz Trask to you."

Kisha dragged her toe over the wood of the floor. "Yes, ma'am."

"It's okay," Lainie said.

The woman shook her head. "They need to respect their elders." She lowered her voice. "I'm outnumbered. I don't drill respect into them, I'm sunk." She winked.

Lainie laughed. "Self-preservation's important."

"Especially when you're living with these hooligans," she replied, but the affection was ripe in her voice.

"Elsie, this is J. J. Cooper, from my hometown," said Lainie. "J.J., this is my neighbor Elsie."

Elsie reached out to shake his hand, without a flicker of recognition. "It's a pleasure. Are you here for the kickoff?"

J.J. frowned. "The kickoff?"

"Don't worry about it, it's a Salem thing," Lainie interrupted, "and no, Elsie. He just stopped by to say hi."

Elsie started to say something and then looked beyond Lainie to where the two children were on hands and knees beside a bug crawling across the porch. "Kisha, Tyjah, you get up from there. Go on inside, you two, and get cleaned up.

We have to leave in an hour." She threw Lainie a good-humored look. "It never ends. Nice to meet you, J.J. Hope to see you around again."

As the door closed, J.J. turned to Lainie. "See? Elsie's happy to see me."

"Elsie doesn't know you like I do."

He walked up to examine the row of bells by the front door and turned. "So how come you live in apartment D if it's a three-story house?"

"That's easy. We've got the basement. Roscoe. His door's on the side."

"You've got a basement named Roscoe?"

"We've got a welterweight UPS driver named Roscoe. He just lives in the basement."

"So he's in A and the ground floor is B?"

She nodded briskly. "Now that you've got that worked out, I guess you can go." She reached past him for the doorknob but he just stood, studying her mouth.

"Any chance I could get something to drink? I'm thirsty."

"You're breaking my heart, Speed."

He stepped a little closer to her and was amused when she stepped back toward the railings. "You could invite me up for coffee."

"Aren't you the optimist?"

"Orange juice?"

"Keep dreaming."

"Tap water?"

"The spigot's right around the corner," she said sweetly.

He liked the fact that she took keeping up with. It made life interesting. Not nearly as interesting as the way that T-shirt fit her, though. "How about if we go somewhere and I buy *you* a cup of coffee? And breakfast, even. What about that?"

"I don't have time for coffee. I need to take a shower."

He shrugged. "Hey, a shower, coffee, I'm easy."

"Alone," she emphasized. "And then I've got plans with Elsie and her family. You've got to learn to stop just showing up. The world's not all about you."

"I never thought it was," he said.

Lainie just eyed him. "What, are you bored and looking for entertainment?"

"It's a nice morning for a drive," J.J. allowed.

"Says the man who's never out of bed before noon."

"Funny you should say that. All last week I heard the alarm ring for me to get up and come down here for my workouts, and I kept thinking there had to be a way I could sleep later and still make my appointments."

Lainie gave him a narrow-eyed look. "Don't even think about it."

"Salem's the perfect place."

"Salem would bore you to tears in five minutes."

"I've been here at least fifteen and I'm not crying yet. Anyway, the location's right. It puts me maybe ten, twenty minutes from the training center."

She frowned. "I thought you said it was in Boston."

"I drive fast." He grinned and reached out to toy with a purple blossom in a nearby flowerbox. Soft and velvety smooth. He wondered if Lainie's skin felt the same way. "So, what's a good neighborhood?"

"Anyplace far from me. This is way too low rent for you."

"It's too low rent for you. Want to move in somewhere together?"

"Only if I can change the locks." He was standing too close again, but she was damned if she was going to give him the satisfaction of stepping back. The hair on her arms prickled.

"I was serious," he complained.

She smiled pleasantly. "So was I."

"Hey, you could stand to upgrade. I can rent a house and we can share it."

"For the week and a half you were here. No thanks. This place suits me just fine. I've got good neighbors."

"Okay." J.J. looked at the street meditatively. "Maybe it's a good place for me, too. Maybe I should find a place around here." He tipped his head. "Like that."

Lainie turned to look where he pointed, craning around the corner pillar behind her, and saw the For Rent sign in front of a building kitty-corner from them. She frowned. "That's new."

"It's a sign. Don't you witches believe in signs?"

"I'm not a witch," she said automatically. When she turned back, he was pulling out his cell phone. Suddenly it had ceased to be funny. The last thing she needed was J. J. Cooper, Party Boy, underfoot. He wasn't a part of her life. He didn't live a lifestyle she wanted. Her eyes narrowed. "Don't even think about it."

"What? I don't have a whole lot of time to spend looking." He squinted at the sign and dialed. "Yeah, this is John Cooper. I'm calling about the house for rent on Maple Street. Is it still open? Yeah? When can you show it to me? I'm here right now. Great. See you then." He cut off the call and folded his phone shut with a satisfied smile. "Fifteen minutes. He says it even has off-street parking. I can hardly wait."

"You are not moving into my neighborhood," Lainie told him indignantly.

"You were the one who said good neighbors watch out for one another."

"I don't need watching out for."

"Maybe I like doing the watching."

She took two steps so that she was standing toe-to-toe with him. "You are not moving here." She punctuated each word with a stab to his chest, her face inches from his. "You can buy anywhere you want, live any place you want. Go somewhere else."

"No way. I can't do that."

"Why?" she burst out.

"Because of this." Before she could react, he'd pulled her to him and brought his mouth down on hers.

A pure, hot, blinding surge of sensation whipped through her. Her hands flew up to clutch his shoulders, because if she didn't grab on to something she'd be lost. Over all the years she'd watched and, yes, wondered, she'd never thought it would be like this, his mouth, his hands, the feel of his body, all of it rolling over her like an avalanche, pulling her in, taking her over, reducing everything to elemental desire. There was no thought, no focus. There was nothing but him, all around her. Overwhelming.

J. J. didn't invite, he took, and in taking dragged her deep down into wanting. One of his hands speared up into her hair, the fingers of the other spread squarely over her ass. Hard, familiar and entirely too proprietary.

He shifted to press his mouth to her throat, and she couldn't prevent the soft, shuddering exhalation of breath.

And she heard his low chuckle as he released her. "I think that's definitely worth moving to the neighborhood for. Now go get your shower."

Chapter Six

"So now I've got Speed Racer as my neighbor. Of all places he could go, he's got to move here." Lainie scowled at her salad, not even bothering to pick up her fork. "And not just here, but *here,* here."

"The hand kisser?" Caro looked at her across the table at the cheerful café they'd chosen for lunch.

Lainie scowled and stabbed at a bit of lettuce. "A truly kind friend would have forgotten about that."

Caro fought a grin. "I'm sorry. It must be frustrating."

It was mortifying, was what it was. He'd kissed her on her front porch in broad daylight and she'd just stood there and let him do it. Not even let him, she'd practically climbed all over him. After all the years of thinking she was impervious to his charm, all it took was him crooking a finger at her and that was that. It was infuriating.

And it scared the hell out of her.

"This is my town. I've got a place here. It's not fair for him to just breeze in."

"It is a free country."

"I know, and I should be free of J.J. It's so annoying. And he *knows* it's annoying. He's doing it deliberately." And if she could stay annoyed, maybe she could stop thinking of the way his mouth had felt on hers.

"Maybe he just wants to be closer to Boston."

"And of the twenty or so towns he could have chosen, he just happened to pick here?"

"Okay, unlikely," Caro acknowledged. "All right, so he wants to be closer to you."

"Well, he'd better get over it," Lainie said briskly. "There is no way J. J. Cooper's getting anywhere with me." *But he already has,* a voice in her head taunted.

"You know—" Caro picked up her iced tea "—for someone who's not interested, you seem awfully focused on him. Why not just have a quick bonk to get him out of your head and call it good?"

If she thought it would be that simple, she'd do it in a heartbeat. "A quick bonk?"

"You do remember how it's done, right?" Caro took a sip of tea.

"I remember." Lainie met Caro's eyes. "He kissed me."

Caro choked. "He kissed you?" she spluttered. "*Now* you tell me he kissed you? After we've been sitting here for twenty minutes?"

"We were talking about other things," Lainie said with dignity.

"We were talking about *him*," Caro corrected. "So what happened? Did he kiss you or did you kiss him or did you kiss each other?"

"I think we kissed each other," Lainie admitted grudgingly. "But he started it. On my porch," she added in response to Caro's unspoken question. And she blushed; she could feel it.

Caro's brow rose. "I guess the man knows what he's doing."

"Of course he does," Lainie said bad temperedly. "With the amount of practice he's had, he pretty much has to, doesn't he?"

"Which begs my earlier question—why not bonk his brains out and get it done with? I mean, it sounds like it would be memorable."

"Because it's not that easy, Caro."

"Why not? The women?"

Lainie let out a breath of frustration. "Look, the women are only part of it. They're the symptoms, not the reason."

"I'm not following you."

"It's the disposable lifestyle. Everything. He doesn't keep anything, he doesn't stick with anything. His whole life is about whatever's new today. Salem's just something to do in passing, and as soon as he gets used to it, he'll be off to something else. I don't want to be his disposable woman," she said.

Because she was very afraid she could get in way too deep.

"You could wait until he retires."

"And he'll be the same person, just with a different job. No, thanks."

"And you don't think a quick, superficial affair—"

"No way am I getting naked with J. J. Cooper," she said firmly, remembering the kiss, the flash, the fire. "I don't even want to go there." She sighed. "I just need to get him out of my head and I'll be fine."

"Maybe it's time for a change of scenery," Caro suggested.

"Who's got time for a vacation right now?"

"I don't mean a vacation. I mean moving on, really moving on. Different city, different job. Maybe what you need is a complete change of pace. I know I do."

"You're moving?" Lainie stared. Caro was one of the best things about Salem. If Caro was gone, life would be a whole lot less fun.

"If I get lucky. I'm applying for a museum in New York. It's a long shot, but you never know. I'm sure as hell never going to go anywhere if I don't try. Jobs don't just fall from the sky."

"Headhunters," Lainie offered.

"Headhunters don't recruit at regional museums like this one. They hunt the A-list places. Nope, if I want to get out of here, I've got to do the work."

"What's the museum?"

"The Museum of Antiquities. A friend of mine from college, Julia Covington, works there. She tipped me off about the spot."

"Manhattan," Lainie said, tamping down a little curl of envy. "Wow, would you live in the city?"

"Depends on what they pay me. Maybe not at first, but once I know my way around I might."

Living in Manhattan. It was what she'd planned, back when she'd been in college. She'd taken it as a given that it would happen, but somehow, she'd never quite managed it. Somehow, she'd wound up back in a small town. "I've always wanted to live in a city like New York."

"So do something about it. Start looking. Forget J. J. Cooper, it all starts with you."

Forget J. J. Cooper.

That was the trick.

One thing to be said for not having a home, there was less to move when it was time to go, J.J. thought as he set down the box of books and CDs in his new living room. A couple of suitcases, his iPod and laptop and he was pretty well good to go. Weights, of course, but he'd installed those in the garage the day before. Everything else, the furniture rental store had delivered that morning.

The place could have used the attentions of a couple of determined handymen, but it was fine for the month he'd be living in it. The rooms were big and the light was good. The garage and yard out back gave him a place to stash his truck and a place to work out. It was wired for cable, so he pretty much had everything he needed.

He flopped down on the couch and picked up the remote. The chance of any skiing being on was practically nil, but maybe he could catch the Sox game. When he tuned it in, he leaned back with a sigh, feeling the good exhaustion in his muscles from his workout. It didn't get much better than this.

His stomach growled. Okay, he could think of one or two ways to make it better, like oh, say, pizza. Better yet, pizza with Lainie.

Lainie.

He'd kissed a lot of women in his time. He'd never been rocked back on his heels quite like the way he had been with that little interlude on her front porch. So what if the better part of a week had passed? He still kept flashing on it and feeling the want, as fresh as it had been in the moment. Feeling the urge for more. It had been an impulse, as things so often were with him. He'd been curious, expecting something pleasurable, but not necessarily something to take seriously.

Not something that would leave him awake and wanting.

He'd always been a big fan of chemistry. How else to explain all the lost days at various European hotels? Dive in, burn it out, go on. As long as both parties involved were on the same page, it wasn't a problem. And he'd found chemistry, over and over. But this chemistry wasn't the kind that stayed in a little test tube.

This chemistry was the kind that blew the roof off the lab.

If he'd ever guessed how it would be, he could never have kept his hands off her all those years. And it had been there for her, too. He'd felt it in her body, in her mouth, heated against his. Something was brewing between them. After all these years, it was time.

Thoughtfully, he reached for the phone. It didn't do him any good to be in the neighborhood if he didn't take advantage of the opportunity. He had a pretty good idea that he could grow old and die waiting for Lainie to roll out the welcome mat, but there was no reason he couldn't do it in reverse.

With a smile on his face, he dialed her number.

Lainie sat at her desk, scratching out a hasty grocery list. Her lunch break was just long enough for her to scoot out and pick up a few things, to ensure she didn't starve over the weekend. Opening her desk drawer, she rummaged for her purse just as her phone rang.

"Lainie Trask."

"I guess so."

He didn't even bother to identify himself, just assumed she'd recognize his voice.

And the most annoying part was that she did.

"Why are you bugging me?" And why was it that her first thought was of the feel of his mouth on hers? She almost didn't recognize the person she'd been on that porch, the person dragged down into hot and greedy wanting by the taste of him.

"It's done. I moved my stuff in today. I'm now officially your neighbor."

Nerves stirred in her stomach. "Gosh, how thrilling."

"I think so."

"So what are you up to tonight?" J.J. continued. "I thought we could go out. You know, welcome to the neighborhood?"

"Tonight? As in a date?"

"Seems that way, doesn't it? Dinner, movie, whatever. I can guarantee you won't be bored."

"Boring is the last word that comes to mind when I think of you, Speed."

"Brilliant? Charismatic?" he offered.

"Unreliable. Erratic."

"Are you still mad that I kissed you?"

"Did you kiss me? I didn't notice."

"Then I guess I need to do a better job of it next time."

Something in his voice made her shiver. "I'll pass, thanks. I've got things to do tonight."

"Hot date?"

"None of your business."

"I'm not so sure about that."

"I am." Making a face, she slammed down the phone.

It rang again, almost immediately. *"What?"* she demanded.

"Jeez, Lainie," said the voice of her cashier, "we just need some change in the gift shop."

Squeezing her eyes closed, she counted to three. "I'm sorry, Marla, I thought it was someone else."

"Not for work, I hope. What's going on? You've been in a bad mood all week."

Lainie scowled. "Bugs. I'm having problems with bugs."

The day was headed into dusk by the time Lainie walked in her front door. The summer weather in New England was fleeting enough as it was; it was absurd to spend so much of it at work that she missed it. She'd been going flat-out from the time she'd hit her desk that morning, but she was damned if she could point to a single thing she'd knocked off her to-do list.

Which only made her crankier.

Of course, she knew exactly why she was cranky in the first place, she thought as she wriggled out of her work clothes and into shorts and a T-shirt.

So what if J.J. was living in her back pocket, getting in her way with that tempting mouth, that velvet voice? It wasn't a crisis.

A hurricane wiping out New Orleans, now, that was a crisis. People not having enough food to eat, that was a crisis.

Abruptly she smacked herself on the forehead. Grocery shopping. After J.J.'s call and the change run for the gift shop, it had gone right out of her head. A peek in the refrigerator confirmed what she already knew—unless she did something drastic, like going grocery shopping at seven o'clock on a Friday night, she was stuck with a choice between a dried-out burrito or some wilted and slightly slimy-looking field greens.

One more grievance to lay at J.J.'s door.

She picked up the cordless phone and wandered over to the refrigerator, where she'd tacked up the take-out menus. Tomorrow. She'd go shopping tomorrow; for tonight, pizza would do. For tonight, food coming to her door was about the most civilized thing she could imagine.

An hour and a half later she'd changed her mind about the civilized part. She loved Renzetti's chewy, greasy pizza, but their delivery and timing skills always left something to be desired. Her stomach growled loudly enough to be heard over the stereo. If they didn't show soon, she'd go looking for them.

The doorbell rang. Lainie jumped to her feet and walked out on the landing. Going on two hours. This was enough to set a record. She stomped down to the street door. Whoever it was, if they didn't have a pizza in their hand, they were going to be sorry.

They did.

Or, he did, to be more specific. J. J. Cooper stood on her front doorstep, holding a steaming pizza box. The Fu Manchu now had a vaguely piratical look to it. His blond hair was even more disheveled than usual. With his earth-toned madras shirt unbuttoned over a T-shirt and shorts, he looked more as though he belonged in a beachfront Mexican bar after a long day of surfing than on her front porch.

Lainie pulled open the inside door and stared at him, arms folded. "What do you want?"

"I thought you might want your dinner."

"My dinner?"

"I intercepted the delivery guy on the front porch," he said, nodding at the taillights disappearing down the street. "You owe me fifteen bucks."

She opened the screen door and reached for the pizza, but he pulled it back. "Ah, ah, ah, package deal. I come with it."

"You're holding my pizza hostage?"

"I wouldn't put it quite like that. I thought you'd want to make a friendly gesture. You know, get to know the new guy on the street?"

"I know you already." Her mouth watered at the scent of hot pepperoni and cheese.

"You think you know me," he corrected. "I figure you're a little out of date."

"Well, we'll have to deal with that at some point." Lainie made another try for the box, but he just shifted it out of reach. She eyed him. "I could order another one."

"Sure, but you'll have to wait. This one's right here, and it's hot." He waved it in front of the door.

She took a blissful sniff. "Do I have to let you through the door? Can't I just give you a slice or two?"

"No way. You have to let me in *and* let me sit down long

enough to eat." He nodded down at his shorts, which hung from his hips with the weight of the beer bottles stuffed in the pockets. "I brought drinks, too."

She refused to be amused, Lainie told herself sternly, even as she pressed open the screen.

They sprawled on her streamlined gray couch, Death Cab for Cutie on the stereo, the remainders of pizza scattered on plates around them. J.J. took a sip of his beer and looked around the room. It had mottled grayish-beige carpet and walls of rental-property white. She hadn't given in, though. Instead, she'd livened things up with a purple floor lamp, a lime-green coffee table, and pillows in purple and bright pink and lime green. The overall effect was vivid, memorable.

Like Lainie herself.

Like the flowerboxes. "Did you plant the flowers downstairs?" he asked.

She gave him a puzzled look. "Elsie and the kids and I did it together. Why?"

"Just curious. They look good. This place does, too."

"And here you wanted me to move."

"It doesn't seem likely."

"No," she agreed.

Moving was a moot point, anyway. This was working. He was in Salem, she had let him in her house voluntarily—at least sort of. He figured it was progress. Persistence, that was the key.

"So what is there to do here?" he asked lazily, taking another swallow of beer.

"Nothing. Terminally boring. You might as well leave now," she added.

"Too late. I'm already here. Got to keep an eye on you."

"I don't need keeping an eye on."

He looked her over, in her shorts and skimpy top. "The pleasure's all mine, trust me."

Lainie snorted.

"What, you don't think I'm sincere?" he asked.

"I think you've been feeding women lines for so long it's second nature." She popped the last bit of pizza into her mouth. "God, that's good." She closed her eyes, chewing with a little moan of pleasure.

And opened them to find J.J. staring at her. "Remind me to bring you pizza more often," he said.

"You do that, you might actually start being welcome." She reached out for her beer. "So what does the ski team think of your little vacation?"

He gave her an amused look. "Vacation? I'm training five hours a day."

Her jaw dropped before she could stop herself. "Five hours?"

"Yep," he said, setting his plate aside. "Three with the trainer and two hours of weights at night. Oh, and an hour run in the morning," he added. "I guess that makes it six."

She stared at him. "That's nuts. I always knew you were a lunatic, but six hours a day? Nobody can keep up with that."

"It's not that bad," he said dismissively. "I mean, it's different kinds of training, targeted at different things."

"And PT for your shoulder?"

"Nope, the shoulder's pretty well healed. I got the release from the doctor last week. It still needs strengthening, but it's good to go."

"Congratulations. Does that mean you're heading out?" She should have been relieved at the prospect. So where did the sneaky wisp of disappointment come from?

"You're not rid of me yet. I've got a couple more weeks of training here before I hit the snow."

"Six hours a day," she mused, shaking her head. Even three or four hours was a lot. She'd had no idea he could be so disciplined. "So do they have you eating disgusting things like protein shakes and egg-white omelets? Did you break training tonight with the pizza?"

He shrugged. "The trainer sends me home with a box of stuff, I buy the rest. It's all balanced for protein and carbs, according to the nutritionist." When she made a face, he smiled. "See, I deserve sympathy, not sarcasm."

"Think of it as tough love."

"Zat so?" His eyes were speculative.

"Well, the tough part, anyway. Not the love part." Definitely not the love part. "Speaking of which, your bosses can't be thrilled that you managed to get yourself hurt playing around. Don't you have a contract that says what you can and can't do?"

"Not exactly. Anyway, I've got to train to stay in shape, so there's always a possibility something will happen."

She turned toward him, leaning one arm on the back of the couch and studying him. "You've never really gotten hurt, though, have you?"

"Not surgery hurt. Little stuff that healed on its own a couple of times. I've never had to go under the knife. Shoot, I think I'm the only skier I know who hasn't."

She remembered during the Olympics, hearing the commentators read off the seeming litany of injuries for each competitor. "Does it ever scare you, going down the mountain? Knowing what could happen if you make a mistake?"

He moved his shoulders. "The worst thing you can do is think about it. You do that, you start skiing scared. You get cautious and tense and you make mistakes."

"The science of not thinking?"

"If you like." His teeth gleamed.

"You've made an art of it." She'd always assumed it was

just J.J. being J.J. She'd never thought about the fact that his tendency to avoid thinking about the consequences was a habit born of professional necessity. "Do you ever think about what you might have done if you hadn't been a skier?" she asked.

He was silent so long she almost thought he wasn't going to answer. "I don't know," he said finally. "Nothing indoors, that's for sure. Work in my dad's construction company maybe. Work at a ski resort." His tone suggested that neither appealed very much.

"I guess it's lucky that skiing worked out."

"It's always been about snow and the mountain for me. I just can't imagine anything else. Anyway, let's talk about something more interesting than that." He reached out to play with the ends of her hair. "So what are you doing this weekend?"

"Don't you have moving in to do?" she asked, moving her head away. It didn't do to let her guard down.

J.J. shrugged. "I'm as moved in as I need to be. I was hoping for a friendly tour."

Sheer self-preservation had her rising. "You want friendly, I'm sure there are agencies you can call." Lainie picked up the plates.

"She cuts me without even a flinch," J.J. said, grabbing the empty beer bottles. "Here I am, new in town, and you won't even give me a break." He followed her into the minuscule kitchen.

"You've never in your life given me any reason to." She set the dishes in the sink.

"Spend some time with me and I will."

"Your problem is that you're terminally out of touch with reality." She turned to set the pizza box on the trash bin and found him right behind her. The breath backed up in her lungs. She kept her voice calm with effort. "I believe you're in my way."

"I believe that's intentional."

She swallowed. "I believe it's time for you to go."

"You really think so?" He reached out to trace his fingertips slowly down her throat. "I think it's still early."

Ignore it. "You're not going to kiss me," she said as much to herself as him.

His smile was slow and dangerous. "Oh, I think I am. Sooner or later."

Her chin came up at that. "Get out of my way."

"Spend tomorrow with me."

She blinked. "What?"

"You want me to leave, I'll leave, as long as you promise to spend tomorrow with me."

"That's blackmail."

"No, it's not, it's a simple deal. Either you spend the day with me or I kiss you, fate worse than death."

"Don't make me sound ridiculous."

He fought to keep from smiling. "I'm not. The choice is yours, anything you want to do. Just show me a side of Salem I haven't seen."

Arms crossed, she stared daggers at him as the seconds ticked by. Then suddenly her expression lightened. "Well," she said briskly, "then I guess it's time to call it a night."

"It's early," he argued, but moved out of her way and followed her to the door, knowing when to give in.

She unfastened the latch and turned to face him. "You want a side of Salem you haven't seen? Fine. Downstairs, tomorrow morning, seven-thirty."

"Seven-thirty? What, are you one of those sunrise watchers?"

"Don't want to go? Suit yourself."

"I'll go," he said hastily. "I just don't understand why you're so dead-set on starting at dawn."

"I'm not the one demanding to be entertained."

"You think getting up at seven-thirty is entertaining?"

"No one's making you show," she reminded him, and opened the door to wave him through.

"I know, I know. All right, I'll see you then. What are we going to do?"

She gave him a smile he didn't trust. "It's a surprise."

Chapter Seven

He'd forgotten how beautiful New England Septembers could be. Blue skies, balmy temperatures—sometimes the Indian summer was better than the real thing. It had been too long since he'd been at home for this part of the year, J.J. thought as he walked across the street to Lainie's house.

It had been too long since he'd had a home, period, not that his current rental was all that much to shout about. Then again, this time of year, he'd normally be staying in a rental condo somewhere, trying to remember which time zone he was in and waiting for the season to start, with its parade of hotels.

Which made him enjoy staying in one place all the more.

He vaulted up the porch stairs and rang Lainie's bell. He'd rung her bell a little bit the night before, he figured. That was the key, keeping her off balance so she didn't have time to come up with meaningless reasons why not. Given time, he knew he could convince her to take a chance.

He was pretty sure the result would be worth it.

Then the door opened and she stood there, and for a moment all he could do was stare. There was just something about her, something he'd never fully appreciated before. Somehow she was just a little more alive than anyone else around her. Something about her sparkled.

She stepped out the door carrying a canvas tote bag and gave him a critical scan.

"What?" J.J. glanced down at his cargo shorts and boots. When your thighs were four or five pant sizes larger than your waist, shorts were always the best option. He'd chosen the faded Clash T-shirt because he liked it, and because he figured that whatever they were doing outdoors wasn't likely to be a garden party. He'd chosen the work boots because he thought sneakers with shorts looked dumb. "Are we going to a wedding or something?"

She shook her head. "No, you'll do just fine."

"That's a relief," he said dryly. "So just what are we doing today?"

Lainie reached out and patted his cheek. "You racer types are so impatient."

He caught at her hand. He saw her eyes widen and darken, but he didn't let it go. "Not always. I'm willing to bide my time for things I want."

She opened her mouth to speak, but nothing came out for a moment. Experimentally, he gave a tug on her fingers to bring her toward him. Something like alarm flickered in her eyes. For a moment she swayed, then she tensed and set herself. "The deal was that I show you a part of Salem you haven't seen—"

"Or I'd kiss you," he finished. "Last night. I never made any promises about today." The hell with it, he decided and leaned in to brush his lips lightly over hers.

Her response surprised him. She didn't move, she didn't protest. But she trembled lightly, he could feel it.

He grinned. "Good morning, Lainie."

And for once she had no comeback. She swallowed. "I…we'd better get where we're going or we'll be late," she said faintly.

"I think we're already on the way," he said.

It was just surprise, she told herself, surprise and nothing more that had had her standing there like a ninny. It wasn't as though a guy—particularly J.J.—could poleax her with a kiss. And yet, that was exactly what had happened, wasn't it? It was one thing to be somewhat…discombobulated when a man kissed you senseless. In a situation like that, a woman had every excuse.

A chaste little peck shouldn't have stopped her in her tracks, though. It shouldn't have wiped every thought from her head except how soft his mouth felt, how warm, how real.

It shouldn't have made her crave more.

So what did it mean? she wondered as she directed J.J. through Salem, studying his profile covertly. What did it mean that she'd stayed up watching movies until almost three the night before because she'd been too keyed-up to sleep? What did it mean that her tossing and turning in bed had been punctuated by dreams of him?

He flicked a glance at her, and the heat of those blue eyes sizzled through her.

What it meant was that she darn well needed to watch her step.

"Park anywhere," Lainie directed J.J. as he drove down a tree-lined street in an older neighborhood. It wasn't the beachfront sunrise or dive breakfast he'd expected. Bemused, he pulled to the curb. It was easy enough—clearly they were in a neighborhood of homeowners, not renters, so the street wasn't bumper to bumper with cars. It was a step up from the neighborhood they'd left behind. The yards actually contained grass, not dirt and weeds, and the houses looked kept up. Small, maybe, but at least cared for.

Mostly, he corrected himself as Lainie started up the driveway of a cramped, shabby-looking house in a dispirited shade of green. It wasn't the sort of place to inspire comments about what a difference a coat of paint would make. It would take a lot more than paint for this one.

"Don't tell me you're house hunting," he said.

"Not exactly." Her lips quirked in what an uncharitable man might call a smirk.

And then he saw the sign and it all made sense. "Human Habitat?"

"Yep. Welcome to our house-wrecking party."

Around the lot, people milled, some with tool belts and hard hats, others standing around at loose ends. Enthusiastic but unskilled labor, he identified the latter. In the corner was the man who looked to be in charge, judging by the rolls of plans and the walkie-talkie phone hooked to his belt. J.J. didn't envy him his job.

"I thought Human Habitat was about building houses, or fixing them up."

"That, too."

He shook his head slowly. "Do you have any idea how much work this is going to take?"

"Days, probably." She gave him a brilliant smile. "You wanted a side of Salem you hadn't seen."

"Yeah, but I figured you'd take me on a haunted house tour."

"I thought I'd give you a chance to repay your debt to

society. Besides, you've never lived until you've taken out a kitchen window with a sledgehammer."

It was the weekend, for chrissakes. He'd been looking forward to relaxing, having fun, spending some time with Lainie, not working in the heat. He worked too hard as it was. "Well, I was—"

"Lainie!" high-pitched voices chorused and a confusion of bodies flew toward them. The tangle resolved itself before Lainie as Kisha, Tyjah, a taller, doe-eyed girl, and he wasn't sure who-all else.

Lainie didn't seem to care—she grabbed them all in a hug. "Hey, guys, you're here early."

"We've been here for hours and hours," Kisha informed her, then looked up at J.J. "I brought my sister, Latrice," she said with a nod toward the older girl. "Did you bring your sister?"

J.J. shook his head. "Sorry, I didn't know you'd be here."

"That's part of the deal," she informed him. "We get a new house, but we gotta help build it. Are you going to help build it, too?"

"Looks like you've already got yourself a house."

She gave a dismissive glance at the dilapidated structure and folded her arms like a union foreman. "That sad thing is just in the way. I'm gonna knock holes in the walls and we're gonna put up a new one, and it's gonna have white shutters and window boxes for Gran's flowers and I'm gonna have a bunny rabbit in the back named Bugs."

"That's a good name for a rabbit," J.J. said gravely. "So you're going to knock it down all by yourself? Don't you need a little help?"

"We need a lot of help." She eyed him. "That gonna be you?"

Lainie stood with crossed arms, studying him as though she knew just what he was going to say.

You won't even give me a break.
You've never in your life given me any reason to.
He smiled at Kisha. "I think it just might be."

It wasn't what was supposed to happen, Lainie thought as she watched J.J. tackle the brick fireplace, knocking a chunk of it loose with each well-placed swing of his sledge. She'd never for a moment expected that the good-time party boy would agree to spend his weekend doing volunteer work. He was supposed to take one look and run the other way. That he'd stayed had her shaking her head in bewilderment.

And wondering if she really knew him at all.

"Well, we're making a good start," a voice said from beside her, and she turned to see George from Cool Beans.

"With a foreman like you, how could we miss?"

"It's not the person who runs it, it's the quality of the labor." Hands on his hips, he scanned the living room, watching the group in the corner working loose the carpet, another team pulling out the windows, and J.J.

And J.J., she thought, watching the muscles ripple in his back under the T-shirt.

"So who's your fella?"

She blinked. "He's not my fella."

George gave her a long, amused look. "You so sure of that?"

She wanted to be, Lainie thought.

It wasn't the same thing.

"He's someone I grew up with," she said instead, and prayed George would let the topic drop.

"They build 'em tough up there in the north," George observed. A ripping sound had him turning to look at the carpet team, who'd finally succeeded. "We need to get everyone out of here so they can get the rug up," he said.

"Let's go grab your buddy and you can introduce me while you're at it."

She threw him a suspicious look. "What are you up to, George?"

"Nothing," he said innocently.

They picked their way gingerly across the living room to where J.J. stood swinging the hammer with a kind of exuberant glee. The thud of metal against brick punctuated their steps.

"Take ten, John Henry," George said.

J.J. stopped the sledge in midswing, his muscles standing out with the effort. Then he turned to them. There was something elemental in the way he looked, patches of sweat darkening his T-shirt as he held the forty pound hammer like it was nothing. Man and muscle, as it had always been, since the earliest days. He swiped at his forehead.

And if Lainie didn't watch out, she'd be the one breaking out in a sweat next.

"You want me off this?" J.J. asked.

George hooked a thumb at the carpet team. "I want you out of the room so these guys can finish the job. Take a break?"

"Works for me."

Outside, J.J. set down the sledge, wiping his hands on his shorts before holding one of them out. "J. J. Cooper," he said.

"George Metcalf." George squinted at him. "You look familiar. Do I know you?"

"You do now," J.J. said.

"Well, that's true. You live in Salem?"

"For the time being."

George nodded. "I run Cool Beans, the coffee shop downtown. Lainie's probably brought you in."

"Not so far."

"Falling down on the job, Lainie," George pronounced. "You're supposed to bring me new customers."

J.J. looked at her. "You holding out on me, Lainie?"

"Think of it as a pending education."

George led them over to the tiny garage where a sheet of plywood on sawhorses served as command central. His eyes twinkled. "Step into my office." He dug out some paper cups and a silver pump thermos and poured them all coffee. "You move like you know what you're doing, Cooper," he said, handing the cups to J.J. and Lainie. "You got experience in this kind of work?"

"My dad runs a construction company. I used to work for him, summers. Everything from gofer on up." J.J. rubbed at his shoulder absently.

"Oh, hell, J.J., your shoulder," Lainie blurted. Even if it was supposed to be healed, what had she been thinking, bringing him to a construction site? "How's it doing?"

"It's fine," he said too quickly.

George gave him a critical look. "Something serious?"

J.J. shrugged. "Nah. Dinged up my shoulder a little a couple months ago. The doctors tell me I'm good to go, though. The work probably helps it."

"Unless you do too much," Lainie said.

He gave her a mulish look. "It'll be fine."

He didn't like the idea of infirmity, she realized. He wasn't about to admit, even to himself, that his shoulder couldn't do everything it always had. Instead, he'd do extra to prove that it could, and never even acknowledge that in doing so, he could make it worse than ever.

"You know, I could use someone to run another crew," George said casually. "Leave fewer of these good people standing around, wondering what to do. You interested?"

"In supervising?"

"Sure. Watch other people work for a change. Unless you're too hung up on that sledge of yours."

J.J. hesitated and glanced at Lainie. In his eyes she read reluctance and discomfort. "Well, I'm not really a long-term—"

"Just for today," George said. "If you could run a fourth crew, we'll be done with the demo that much quicker. You could take the kitchen. It needs to be gutted—countertops, cabinets, appliances, everything. It'll go faster with someone who knows what he's doing. What do you think?"

Across the way in the backyard, Tyjah held a hammer with both hands and with great concentration pounded a dirt clod to dust. J.J. watched him for a minute, then he looked back at George. "I think I'm your man."

There was something immensely satisfying about knocking holes in a wall with a sledgehammer, Lainie thought as she slammed the heavy mallet with gusto. Especially when her emotions were all over the map. She'd known that she had something of an unhealthy attraction to J.J. If she were honest, that had been going on for years.

She'd never expected to like him.

I'm not really long-term...

It had never been a problem before to keep her distance, to maintain the scorn. Everything he was about made it easy: the partying, the women, the luxe life, the fact that his personal soap operas played out in the newspapers. Everything he was about made him the exact wrong person for any sane woman to be involved with, no matter how sexy that crooked smile was.

Always before, when she'd kept him at a distance, it had been easy.

It wasn't easy anymore.

"Remind me never to tick you off," J.J. said from beside her, where he was stripping away Sheetrock with a crowbar. From the house all around them came the sounds of pounding, the protesting screech of nails being wrenched loose, the whine of circular saws. "Of course," he added, tearing loose a slab of rock with a grunt, "now that I'm your supervisor, you have to be friendly to me."

"Aren't there laws against that?"

"What, being friendly?"

A snarky comeback was on the tip of her tongue, but somehow she didn't quite have the heart for it. "Thanks for helping George out," she said instead.

J.J. stared at her. Before she could react, he'd taken two steps toward her and pressed a hand to her forehead.

"What?" she said, face flaming.

"You feeling all right?"

"I'm feeling fine," she muttered, pushing his hand away.

"You've just never voluntarily said anything nice to me before. I figured you had to be delirious."

She glowered at him. "I was just about to say something nicer to you but I think I've changed my mind." She reached for her sledge.

"You're going to leave me hanging with that?" he protested. "Come on, at least give me something. Nobody drops a sink through the floor like I do, say."

That brought a smile, he saw. She glanced at the patch of shattered plywood at their feet. "That wasn't your fault. Tracy bumped you."

"Not only thinking about saying something nice to me but taking my side," he said with relish. "I think I'm making progress here."

"The only progress I care about is progress on the house," she said, glancing around at the gutted kitchen. She could almost convince herself that she meant it. Hollow thuds sounded from overhead as people walked on the roof.

"Do you realize we've been working more than eight hours?" J.J. asked, leaning against a stud.

Lainie shrugged. "The more we do today, the less we have to do tomorrow."

"Tomorrow?"

"We work the weekend. You can think of us while you're lounging around."

His Sunday plans had mostly focused on watching the game. On the other hand, suddenly that prospect didn't seem nearly so appealing. He'd enjoyed himself, he realized. Not just being around Lainie but all of it. Laughing with George, teasing Kisha and the other kids, working hard.

Doing something for someone besides himself.

"I'll be here," he answered.

"Here?" She blinked. "You mean working?"

"What did you think I meant?"

"I think—" She looked down at the floor, out into the dining room where a square of sunlight had just appeared from the roof dismantlers. "I think maybe I've underestimated you," she said slowly.

He grinned. "I told you I'd surprise you one of these days."

Chapter Eight

Lainie pushed open the door at Cool Beans. "Coffee," she announced, as the bell jingled. "For the love of God, I need—" And she stopped in her tracks at the sight of J.J. up at the counter, laughing with George.

"Hey, Lainie," George said, reaching automatically for a cup, "come on up. I'm just having a little confab with our newest team foreman."

J.J. held up his cup. "Great coffee."

"I know," she muttered.

His grin widened. "Cranky in the morning before she gets her fix, isn't she?"

George snorted. "You kidding? She's cranky any time of day without coffee. I think she mainlines it." But he held out a cup that she reached for gratefully.

"So, anyway," J.J. continued to George. "Here I am,

driving to the site with my overhead rack loaded with the PVC pipes. And I'm late—"

"Who woulda guessed?"

"Hey, I was sixteen. What do you want? Anyway, I'm blasting along. You know, back roads, early morning. But the closer I get to Montpelier, the deeper we get into the morning commute. And then I hit a yellow light that goes red just as I drive up to it, and there's a state trooper right there."

"Oops."

"Yeah. So I jam on the brakes. It's touch and go but I manage to stop, so I'm feeling pretty good. But then I see this shadow fall over the windshield and I realize that maybe I stopped but the pipes haven't. The whole damned load is still going. It hits the ground like pickup sticks out of a can and just keeps sliding."

George guffawed. "What did you do?"

"I had the statie right there giving me the hairy eyeball. What do you think I did? I got out of the truck and picked it up, pipe by pipe."

"Remind me never to put you on delivery duty," George said.

"Want to hear about the time I lost a couple of commodes, making a fast right?" J.J. offered.

"Definitely no delivery duty."

"Well, you helped us get down to bare slab." He set a blueberry muffin on the counter. "On the house, Cooper. Job well done."

"You never give *me* free muffins," Lainie muttered, "and I've been working Human Habitat for two years."

"Well, if you're going to pout…" George put out another muffin.

"I don't pout," she returned indignantly.

"Of course you do. You're pouting right now. Anyway, eat up, both of you. We've got a bare slab to celebrate."

It had taken time and work, but the Human Habitat crew

had finally pulled the old house down. Now it was time to start the real work—building it back up.

"Got the pressure-treated yellow pine and studs coming in this weekend," George was saying. "Lotta work to get done. I want to try to get the whole thing framed up this weekend."

"That's all?" J.J. snorted. "Why don't you add in getting it roofed over and sided this weekend while you're at it?"

"Hey, cold weather's coming. I want to get it buttoned up and into dry out as soon as possible."

"Okay, okay, I get you, but if you think you're going to get the whole thing framed up this weekend with your crew, you're going to be disappointed." J.J. mulled it over for a minute. "How about if I come work this weekend?"

"I never say no to a good volunteer." George turned to Lainie. "Best thing you ever did was bring this guy around."

An emotion she didn't quite recognize whipped through her. Irritation? Of course not, not at George. Frustration? Still didn't feel right, she thought. Jealousy? she thought, startled.

Jealousy.

Frowning, Lainie dropped a bill on the counter. "Thanks, George."

"You going?"

"Got to earn a paycheck."

J.J. grabbed his muffin hastily. "Wait. I'll go with you."

"No need to. I know the way."

But he was already on her heels as she went out the door.

It was silly. More than silly, it was childish to feel territorial about her coffee shop, but she was. Irritated at herself, she walked a little faster.

"What's the rush? Did you skip your workout this morning?"

"I've got stuff to do. It's only six weeks to Halloween, you know."

She'd managed to avoid being alone with him since that unsettling moment in the kitchen the previous weekend. The last thing she'd wanted to deal with was J.J.—or her feelings about J.J. But now he was showing up, everywhere, it seemed.

It wasn't just Cool Beans and George. She walked outside her house and he was there, showing Kisha and Tyjah how to get into a skier's crouch or fixing their porch rail. She showed up at Human Habitat and he was leading a team, she went to the farmers' market to buy vegetables and he was at the booths, joking with the vendors. He was everywhere, an outsider subtly shoehorning himself into her community.

Into her life.

And it made her feel like an immature jerk that it bothered her. Salem was just a passing phase for him. Right now he was at loose ends. It amused him to play big-time sports guy in the small town. And everyone was lapping it up—after all, it wasn't every day they got to hang with a famous athlete.

Although, he hadn't brought it up, now that she thought about it. Word had filtered around the Human Habitat site, but J.J. had downplayed it as much as possible. He hadn't told "World Cups I Have Known" stories when they'd all gone out for pizza at the end of demolition. Instead, just as he had with George a few minutes before, he'd put the focus on living in New England, telling self-deprecating stories of growing up in a small town.

Charming self-deprecating stories.

She made an impatient noise.

"You want to tell me what you're so ticked off about?" J.J. asked mildly.

"It's nothing to do with you."

"Tell me anyway."

Absolutely no way. She'd sound infantile. She *felt* infantile just thinking about it. She couldn't really be ticked off at J.J. She was mostly ticked off at herself.

"You know, I kind of thought we were getting somewhere last week. And then you started avoiding me."

"I always avoid you," she said automatically.

"I kinda started thinking that might change."

He wasn't joking, she realized, as they came to a stop in front of the museum. There was a slight, but unmistakable edge in his voice. And in his eyes she saw disappointment.

Disappointment? J.J.?

Lainie shifted. "Look, it's nothing personal. I've just been busy."

"Busy, tired. You can do better than that, can't you, Lainie?"

At the moment she couldn't, because she didn't even understand herself. She cleared her throat. "Look, I should really go in."

"I guess. I don't think we've finished this conversation, though."

"Probably not," she agreed. "But I have to get to work."

For a moment he just looked at her, and then something seemed to slip sideways.

Once, in college, she'd taken a road trip to San Francisco, going west of Albany for the first time in her life. Somewhere in Nevada, she'd looked at the land around her and with a dizzying abruptness understood down deep that she was on a different part of the globe. North was no longer Maine, it was Oregon. South was Los Angeles, not Manhattan and Baltimore. It was subtle and impossible to describe, but she could almost feel it as her internal grid shifted, momentarily filling her with an almost physical disorientation.

It was the same sensation that swept over her now.

Bewildered, she stared at J.J. She'd always known the geography of what they were to each other. Now, somehow, that had changed. She was in some new, unmarked place, and none of the usual landmarks were there to help her. "I should go," she whispered, but didn't move.

And as she stood there staring at him, he leaned in and pressed a kiss on her lips. It was a pressure, a warmth, no longer than the length of a heartbeat. It would have been almost friendly, if it weren't for the little whispers of demand laced through it. "You'll think of me, though," he said softly.

And she did. All day long, throughout the meetings, the phone calls to secure jugglers for the festival, throughout the games of phone tag with first one vendor, then another, Lainie thought of him. And every time she thought of the feel of his mouth on hers, she felt a little stir in her stomach.

Things were different. She didn't know when or how, but they were different, and if she didn't get them under control, she didn't know what was going to happen. She'd meant what she'd said to Caro. It wasn't just the women, not really. It was his entire world, the life he inhabited when he wasn't fooling around in Salem. A life that was a bit too fast—too temporary—to be sure about.

They had to talk. If they cleared the air, he'd understand that it was best they kept things from getting physical. He knew he was going back to racing soon. He was used to quick changes, to rushing from country to country, from relationship to relationship. From enjoying the moment to *really* enjoying it, then ending it with no hard feelings—or perhaps no feelings at all.

So it was that she found herself standing on the peeling brown porch of his house that evening, nerves jumping in her stomach. Taking a deep breath, she knocked. And while she waited, she rehearsed the words in her mind. *Too complicated... Too transient... Practically like family...*

Which wasn't the same as actually being family. Still…

There was no answer. Lainie knocked again, more loudly. No response.

J.J., it appeared, was out.

She wasn't about to admit to the sneaky little feeling of relief. Turning, she started back down the steps. She'd tried. Some other time, maybe. She could write him a note. Or maybe she should just leave and keep her distance, no matter what J.J. thought. It was what any sane woman in her spot would do.

And then she heard it.

Lynyrd Skynrd.

Reluctantly she turned and followed the narrow drive to the back of the house. Ahead lay his blue truck. Ahead of that, the open garage and inside, she saw, was J.J.

Hopping.

Bemused, she walked closer. He'd set up light rails about three feet high off the ground, parallel. From a flatfooted, standing start, he gathered himself and leaped over each, feet together, in a single explosion of power. Even with a running start, she'd be hard-pressed to do it. From a dead stop? No way. But J.J. just stood and leaped, stood and leaped, grunting with the effort but making it over each time. And each time, at the end of the row, he'd turn, and like a human metronome, do it all again.

Lainie watched, fascinated.

He wore only athletic shoes and a pair of workout shorts. His body gleamed with sweat. Below the shorts, his thighs swelled in a practically inhuman display. Above the shorts, his belly was corrugated with muscle, a set of six-pack abs that was enough to make any woman swoon.

Including her.

Six hours a day, he'd said, six hours of workout and

training. Exaggeration, maybe, she'd suspected at the time. She didn't anymore. Lainie shook her head as J.J. reached the end of the row and turned again, shuffling his feet until he was ready to jump.

It was more impressive than if he'd made it look effortless. It was the end of a long day. The exercise was obviously costing him, and yet he continued, making those agile, prodigious leaps, one after another, again and again.

She'd always wanted to class him as a lightweight, someone who'd been gifted with talent and coasted on it. But he hadn't, Lainie realized. J. J. Cooper, she had to reluctantly admit, had gotten where he was by hard work. Talent, too, sure, but much of it had been fueled by sheer bloody-minded determination.

She didn't want to care about him; she really didn't want to.

It was becoming impossible not to.

And at that moment J.J. looked over. "Hey." The smile that broke over his face didn't hold any mockery or challenge, only pleasure, and she found herself responding in kind.

"Hey."

He grabbed a towel and swiped his face as he walked up. "Don't let me interrupt you."

"That's okay, I was done," he said. "There's only so much fun I can stand." He raked his damp hair back from his face, and Lainie watched the muscles in his biceps and chest shift. It was one thing to know he was built. It was another to see it. Okay, so maybe there was more than liking going on.

That didn't mean she had to do anything about it.

"What brings you around?" J.J. pulled on a ragged T-shirt.

Dragging her gaze back up to his, she groped for coherent thought. "Oh. Well, I just…I wanted…"

"How about dinner?" he suggested.

"Dinner?" she repeated blankly.

"Yeah. I was just going to go grab something. You eaten?"

She shook her head. "I just got off work."

"Then come."

It was a casual invitation, even simple. Nothing was ever simple between them, and yet this sounded like no more or no less than it was. Just friends, going to eat. It could be the perfect location for The Talk, someplace out in the open where things wouldn't get out of hand. If he kept his clothes on, she could focus. "All right."

J.J.'s smile was bright and uncomplicated. "Great," he said as they walked across the parking apron to his back steps. "I've got to grab a quick shower. Wait for me?"

"Sure."

It was definitely a rental property, she thought as she wandered through the living room and listened to the water run through the upstairs pipes. Someone had obviously re-decorated in the seventies and the place still had the blue shag rug to prove it. The kitchen was resplendent with avocado appliances and antique-gold wall tile. Definitely seventies.

On the counter lay a newspaper clipping. The story featured a photo of J.J. after a race, his helmet on, his goggles up on his forehead, that effervescent grin shining out. "Local Champ Heads to Finish," the headline read. Reaching out, she picked it up and began to read, at first in idle curiosity, and then with a steadily growing anger.

In a sport where the average competitor is out to pasture by twenty-eight, thirty-three-year-old J. J. Cooper is a relic. The human body simply can't keep up with the demands of the World Cup circuit forever, not with the wear and tear of competing in one or two races a week for five months. This year's injury may simply be a har-binger of the end.

Meanwhile, the younger, hotter, more resilient racers are breathing down Cooper's neck, fighting for a share of the limited resources of the U.S. Ski Team. It's time that he passed the baton to them. Then again, given his current condition, the baton may be passed to them whether he wants it to or not.

Lainie snapped down the paper. A relic, indeed. She'd just seen that relic in action. Idiots.

At the sound of J.J.'s feet on the stairs, she moved back out to the living room.

He came in whistling, hair damp, smelling of soap. His royal-blue shirt made his eyes look incandescent. For a change, he wore trousers instead of shorts.

"Nice pants," she said awkwardly.

"Custom-made." He slapped his thigh. "Standard pants don't fit me."

"I can't think of anything standard that does," she said.

He didn't take her to a restaurant but to a narrow Irish pub tucked in at the edge of a residential neighborhood, blocks away from the fashionable wharf area. Dark wood, deep booths—above all it held a sense of comfort. They sat at a table butted up against a corner banquette and took their time, sharing shepherd's pie and fish with pub fries, picking from each other's plates and washing it all down with Guinness.

"Mmmmm." Lainie set her fork aside and dabbed her mouth.

"Good?" J.J. asked.

"I think I've died and gone to heaven."

"See how I improve your life?"

He sat around the corner of the table from her, which

meant that instead of a nice safe expanse between them, they sat practically elbow to elbow. It was the sort of table where couples held hands, leaning in to trade kisses and confidences.

And with the distraction of eating gone, it was far too cozy.

Time to change the subject. Lainie looked at J.J. speculatively. "So what would your trainers say if they found out you've gone off the wagon twice?"

"That I don't listen to those rules any better than I listen to anything else," he told her as the waitress who'd greeted him by name came over to clear their plates.

"Ah. A regular," Lainie observed. "And here you were bucking for sympathy over the egg white omelets."

"You asked me if they made me eat them. I told you my trainer gave me a box of stuff."

"And?"

J.J. propped his elbows on the table and leaned forward. "It's true, he does. And then I put it in a corner and come here."

Vintage J.J. Those who expected things from him were destined for disappointment. "You know, I should know better than to trust you," she said, amused despite herself.

He reached out to toy with her earring. "You can trust me to do lots of things."

"That's what I'm afraid of." She was afraid of more: the flutter in her stomach; the way the brush of his fingertips against her neck made every nerve ending come to alert.

The way despite all that, she sat there motionless.

She swallowed. "So how did you find this place? You seem to be a regular."

"Wandering around. I usually take different routes in the morning when I run, just to keep it interesting."

"Variety is the spice of life?"

"You're mellowing. A month ago, you would have told me it was inability to commit."

"Far be it from me to be predictable."

"That's part of what I like about you."

She shifted. Under the table her leg pressed against his, and immediately she flashed on the way he'd looked earlier, the power, the control, the bunch and ebb of gleaming muscle. He was so near, too near. It wouldn't take much, just leaning a bit closer and she could have her mouth on his; she could taste him, feel him, see where it would take them.

With a thump the waitress slapped the leather check cover on the table. Lainie blinked. She was out of her mind. Suddenly the warm, dim confines of the pub were fraught with danger. Time to go, she decided. "All set?" she asked abruptly, nodding at the check. "I'm ready to get outside."

"You don't want to hang out at the bar awhile?" J.J. asked, signing the slip. "There's usually a guitarist who plays on Thursday nights."

She rose. "I need some air." They'd come to the restaurant on foot; the walk back would be good for them both.

It had rained briefly while they'd been inside, adding a sheen of damp to the streets. The night air was surprisingly mild; in her short, flippy skirt and T-shirt she was more than comfortable. She swung her arms a bit, relaxing. Now that they were outside in the open air, she'd gotten her sanity back. She knew what the smart move was, and she'd stick with it.

"It's so nice to be outside at night and have it be warm," she said. "I hate the thought that winter's coming."

"It's a ways off."

"I know, I know. But it's out there."

"So's spring, on the other side."

She looked at him from under her brows. "Who are you, Pollyanna?"

"You're talking to someone who lives in the snow ten months out of the year. You've got to find some way to deal with it."

A car passed by, lights strobing through the night. "Do you like it?" she asked impulsively.

"Of course. I get paid for having fun. What's better than that?"

"Being born rich?" she offered.

"Nah. That just screws you up. Look at Paris Hilton. I think people need to have a purpose. It's how we were built."

She turned to stare at him. "Is this J. J. Cooper, Party Guy?"

"Work hard, play hard. If you work, you deserve it. There's no shame in relaxing."

And he did work hard, she knew that now. "So what happens when it all goes away?"

"What do you mean?"

"Skiing. Racing. I read…I saw the article." She broke off, wondering if she'd gone too far.

"You mean the one that's telling me to make reservations in an old folks' home?" He laughed, but it sounded a little forced. "They've been writing articles like that for the past five years. For some reason, it really pisses people off that I don't go by the rules."

"What rules?"

"Take your pick. Play it safe when you've got a lead instead of pushing it as far as you can. Pick just one discipline, don't ski them all. Retire at twenty-eight or twenty-nine. You know me, I've never been any good at doing what people expect."

"Yeah, I know you." And she couldn't imagine him without skiing as his life. "So you think you'll just keep going?"

He shrugged. "I don't know. I guess I'll figure it out when I get there." They turned onto their street, the houses growing smaller, shabbier. "The thing is, they're right, in a way. Sooner or later it is going to be over. And I don't know…"

"About what?"

They walked in silence for a while. "Anything," he said finally, his voice low and warm in the night. "My life has always been about the mountain. I mean, you don't realize, maybe, but I almost never get time like this. Except for about six weeks out of the year, my life is about the World Cup. It's always the goal, everything I do, everything I am."

"I thought the goal was to have fun."

His teeth gleamed in a smile. "That too. Winning is fun. Going fast is fun. But it doesn't just happen. You've got to work at it."

"People need to have a purpose."

"Exactly. The World Cup's the purpose. It's always been the purpose, the goal, ever since I was a kid. And now…" The smile faded. "Sooner or later it's going to change. It's got to."

"There's the ski lodge, the work with Gabe."

"I could do my part of it with my eyes closed. I mean, don't get me wrong, it's fun, but it's not enough." He paused. "And I don't know what is."

Her house was dark as they walked up. Of course, she thought, she hadn't left on any lights because she'd expected to be back quickly. "Are they right about the retirement thing?" she asked.

"Who knows? It's not like there's some expiration date. You go until it doesn't work anymore, or until it's no longer fun."

"What happens then?"

He was quiet for so long she thought maybe he hadn't heard her. "Your guess is as good as mine. I just don't want to be some has-been running around the circuit telling stories.

I've seen a couple of guys like that and they're pathetic. That's not what I want."

"What do you want?"

He looked at her, his eyes shadowed in the night. "You."

Chapter Nine

Lainie shivered, though the air was still balmy. "You don't mean that," she whispered, trapped by his gaze, unable to look away.

"I don't?"

"I can't be your way to kill time until the ski season starts."

"I didn't say you were. That's not what this is about." He stepped closer.

"What is it about?"

"You. Me. Something that's been a long time coming."

Intensity vibrated in his voice, determination flickered in his eyes. She felt panic, a sort of stunned resignation and, hidden underneath, somewhere down deep, a flicker of delight.

She swallowed. "We don't make sense together, J.J. You know that. You live a different life."

"And isn't that what you've always said you wanted? A different life? Aren't you even curious?" He reached out to trace his fingers along the neckline of her T-shirt where it dipped low. "I am."

Low and insistent as a distant drumbeat, desire began to thud through her. "It doesn't matter," she managed. "It can't happen."

His laugh was quiet, intimate in the night. "Oh, yeah, it can. Want me to show you?"

And then, before she could react, he slid his fingers around the back of her neck and pulled her to him.

Hot, urgent, demanding, his kiss was no more like the quick, friendly brush he'd given her that morning than a forest fire was like a match flame. It overwhelmed even as it scorched her, sending heat blasting through her veins. Always before, when she'd kissed men, she'd enjoyed the taste, the feel, the dance of tongue and lip. With J.J. there were no separate elements; everything was all bound up into an onslaught of sensation that was more force of nature than human touch.

In some part of her brain, she'd always known it would be like this between them: overpowering, devastating, uncontrollable. Anxiety crowded into her throat. But another part of her, a steadily growing part, wasn't alarmed at all. Instead, it was exhilarated, eager—and greedy for more. The excitement broke through the panic, broke through the control she'd imposed on herself, and suddenly she was diving into the maelstrom, tasting, touching, pressing herself heedlessly against him.

Now she wanted, and she took, nipping at his lips, savoring his flavor until she was giddy with it. Winding her fingers through his hair, she made a growling sound of demand.

The sudden impatience of her response stunned him. He felt her move, avid against him, pressing him back against one of the porch pillars. He fought the almost overpowering urge to simply lift that skirt and take her right there. This was the Lainie he'd wanted, the Lainie he'd always guessed was hidden away from him. She was flash and fire, heat and hunger. She was all he'd ever guessed she'd be and more.

"Upstairs," he said hoarsely. "Now."

Everest, J.J. thought, was not as lengthy a climb as the staircase to Lainie's flat.

"I don't remember it being this far before," he grumbled as they got to the first landing.

"Shhh," Lainie said, "you'll wake up Elsie and the kids."

"I'll be quiet," he said, and slid his hands up under her skirt, drawing a little yelp of surprise from her.

"Shhh," he cautioned, "you'll wake up Elsie and the kids." Although, at the moment he didn't give much of a damn about Elsie and the kids, because his palms still tingled from the surprise of the bare skin he'd found exposed by the thong Lainie wore under her little skirt. At the moment, rock hard and aching, he didn't give much of a damn about anything but getting her alone.

At the top of the stairs, in the little vestibule before her front door, Lainie stopped to open the lock. J.J. leaned in behind her. She felt a sudden breath of cooler air as he lifted her hair away, and then he nibbled the nape of her neck.

And her keys dropped from her suddenly nerveless fingers.

"I'll get them," he murmured, kneeling down.

Lainie trembled as she took the bundle back, trying to ignore the need that slammed through her. She'd just begun to clumsily sort through them when she felt the hot press of lips on her calf. She jumped and made a little sound.

"You'd better hurry," J.J. said, his breath warm against her skin as he worked his way up to the back of her knee, licking the tender skin there.

It took her far longer than it should have to pick out the right key. Blindly she reached back to touch J.J.'s hair. "I don't know how much longer I'm going to wait," he murmured. "I may just have you here." He slipped his hands up under her skirt, sliding them over the round warmth of her bare ass, framed by the thong.

"I thought about this at Gabe's party, you know," he murmured, tracing the back of her thigh with his tongue. "I looked at you in this little skirt and thought about how much I wanted to just flip it up and bend you over and—"

His mouth was hot against her bare ass cheek as he slid his hands up and down her thighs. The roughness of a day's beard provided a shocking counterpoint to the softness of his lips, the slickness of his tongue. She was on fire. "Tick, tick, tick," he whispered against her skin. "Turn around."

When she did, mindlessly, he pushed her skirt out of the way and kissed his way up, licking the fragile inner skin of her thigh. Lainie shivered and reached down to wind her fingers in his hair as he went higher. Then all she could do was fight for air in a sort of choking gasp as he pressed a hot kiss to the satin-covered mound at the apex of her thighs. She felt the heat of his breath through the fabric and bit back a moan.

"Time," he said softly and pulled the keys from her limp hand.

She was strung tight as a wire with need, breathless, shaking, barely able to let the front door close behind them before she seized J.J. and brought his face to hers to fuse their mouths together. Heat arced between them, searingly intense. There were no doubts now, no hesitation. She needed; it was as clear and as simple as that. She had to have.

His hand slid under her shirt to find her breast, sending a jolt through her. She could feel him hard against her leg.

And the thought that drummed through her was "I want."

"Now," she breathed against his lips, reaching for his belt buckle. There was no time for teasing and foreplay and all the rest. If she didn't get him inside her that instant, she was going to die.

As one, they sank down to the hallway rug. In a sort of delirious joy, she felt J.J. strip off her thong. Then he was on top of her, his erection thick and hard against her thigh, and tension coiled tight within her. When he rubbed the tip of himself against her cleft, she jolted in pleasure.

She could feel how wet she was as he ran himself over and over the hard little bud of her sex. She gasped for air. So hard, so silky, so slippery, each touch sent her twisting mindlessly against him.

And then he pumped his hips and plunged himself in fast and deep.

Lainie cried out as he filled her in a single surge. Bigger than she'd guessed, harder than she could ever have imagined. He stroked into her again and again until she almost didn't recognize the high-pitched whistling sounds coming out of her throat. And they, who had always been at cross purposes, were now one, moving together, gasping together, working toward the same urgent, glorious goal.

His eyes stared into hers, not relaxed and amused, for once, but narrowed in intensity. It was as though he could see into her, as though they were connected by much more than their linked bodies. He varied his rhythm, now speeding up, now slowing until she finally gave up anticipating and just wrapped her legs around him and held on, absorbing every sensation, feeling him drag her closer to orgasm with every fast, furious stroke.

When she got there, she didn't so much go over the edge as she was flung, gasping, jolting, feeling the explosive burst of sensation radiate out through her entire body. She cried his name.

And with a final groan, J.J. spilled himself into her.

"God." J.J. lay on his back, staring up at the hallway ceiling, waiting for his system to level.

"You can say that again," Lainie added feebly.

He'd thought about this in the past few weeks—longer, if he were honest—but he'd had no idea what it would really be like, to have her body taut and springy under his, furled tight around him, to feel her urge him on as her eyes went blurry and unfocused with pleasure.

On impulse, he reached out for her hand and brought it to his lips. "Sorry for not kissing you properly, but I'm not sure I have the strength to move."

"The spirit is willing but the body is weak?"

"Right now, the body is *happy*. So is the spirit."

"Glad to know you're satisfied."

"Oh, well, I think *satisfied* might be overdoing it. In fact," he added thoughtfully, "I think I'm a long way from satisfied."

"Oh, really?"

"Yes, really. If you've got a bed in this place, I'd be happy to demonstrate. In fact—" he turned his head to give her a wicked look "—once I get you naked, I'm thinking I'm going to spend a long time demonstrating."

"Mmmm, I like the sound of that," she said.

Somewhere in that breathless hour between night and morning, Lainie woke to see moonlight streaming into the room. She shifted, and in shifting felt the twinge of soreness between her thighs. Beside her, J.J. slept, one arm thrown over his head. He was indisputably there, and indisputably naked, meaning that she couldn't even for a minute tell herself that everything she remembered was just an astoundingly vivid erotic dream. It had really happened.

Hell.

She had to be out of her mind, Lainie thought as she looked at the profile of the sleeping J.J. Temporary insanity. After everything she'd seen, everything she knew about him, winding up in bed with J.J. was about the most idiotic thing she could have done.

And the most amazing.

She couldn't suppress a fatuous grin. She hadn't known what real sex was until just a few hours before. Even years after everything was all over, she would still fondly remember J.J. for showing her what her body was really all about.

Even after their affair was a thing of the past.

She stared at him, her smile dimming. Even sleeping, J.J. was a solo act, she thought, watching him. They'd been twined together when they'd fallen asleep, but once J.J. had made it to z-land, he'd pulled away, throwing off the covers that she'd bundled about herself. Symbolic, in a way, of everything they were about—separate lives, separate needs, separate experiences.

Hell.

Closing her eyes determinedly, she tried to drift off to sleep, but it wasn't happening. Not even close. Finally she gave up and stealthily slipped out of bed, grabbing her robe and padding noiselessly to the living room.

The light from the street lamps and the sliver moon streamed in through the windows. She had no idea of the time as she sat on the couch, only that morning lay in the distance. Moodily she stared out at the silent street.

It was far from the most intelligent move she'd ever made, but she'd done it. In all honesty, she wasn't as sorry as she might have been. Sometimes you had to throw smart by the wayside and just take a chance. The question was, what happened next? He'd be leaving soon for the racing season; he'd have to.

And she'd still be here in Salem.

The thing to do was keep it in perspective. If she started having expectations, she'd only be disappointed. *I've never been any good at doing what people expect.* J.J. wasn't about being tied to anything. Or anyone. He'd made that abundantly clear over the years.

She moved her head at the sound of a creak in the hall, and turned to see him there, in the doorway.

He was naked, his body washed by the outside light so that he looked like some kind of statue, sculpted and flowing. He studied the room. Studied her.

"What time is it?" he asked.

Lainie moved a shoulder. "I don't know. Maybe three."

"Didn't like sleeping with me in the bed?"

"I couldn't sleep. Did I wake you up?"

Her movement hadn't; her absence had. When he'd reached out to find cold sheets, he'd come looking.

He didn't answer her question, though. Instead, he crossed to the couch and sat beside her. She was curled up, arms wrapped around her legs, chin on her knees. Her silky robe had slipped off one shoulder.

"You look like you're way too deep in thought for 3:00 a.m.," he said.

"Not so much."

He reached out to pull her back against him. At first she resisted, but finally she relaxed, leaning back into his chest.

"What's going on?" he asked.

They'd had sex. Period. It hadn't meant anything, Lainie reminded herself. It never did to J.J. If she told him she was wondering what was supposed to happen between them now, she'd look like the worst sort of sap, the woman who mistook sex for something more. J.J. didn't do something more; he jumped into torrid affairs and got out of them just as quickly. She'd known that going in; if she hadn't been smart enough to protect herself, well, that was her own problem.

What shocked her was realizing that she would happily take the quick affair with him, just that, because she was not ready to have this over with.

She stirred. "Just thinking about tonight, I guess."

"What about tonight?" He tightened his arms around her.

"It was pretty amazing."

"I'll agree with that. That little number you did with the live python and the cowgirl outfit was something else."

She laughed and finally, finally, she was able to relax. One of his hands began sliding idly over her chest, tracing her collarbones, sliding down into her cleavage.

"So when do you leave?" she asked.

"Well, I have to go to Buffalo next week to work on my tuck."

She hadn't thought it would be so soon. The muscles tightened in her belly. "Work on your tuck?" she asked.

"Finesse the aerodynamics. They've got a wind tunnel there. You can lose a ton of time in downhill and super-G if you don't get your tuck right."

She nodded. "So week after next is it, then," she said, trying to sound casual.

"Not exactly. I'll only be gone a couple of days. Then the week after that I head to Aspen to get some slope time. I'll be there for maybe a week and a half."

"So, two weeks from now."

She could feel him smile. "Not exactly. I'll be back again. Then I go off to Austria to get serious about it. The World Cup season opener at Sölden is two weeks before Halloween."

"And then you really are gone."

He gave a quiet laugh. "Maybe. Hard to say. There's a two-

or three-week break between Sölden and when the season really starts. I can try to come home for a couple of days."

Good intentions. A woman could get in deep trouble pinning her hopes on good intentions. Better to focus on the here and now. "It's not a lot of time," she said. "I think we'd better make the most of it." And maybe, just maybe, she could burn out this sudden need for him.

His hand slid swiftly inside her robe to close over her bare breast, in a shocking rush of sensation. "Oh, I agree." He rolled her nipple between his fingers. "In fact, I think you ought to call in sick so we can make the most of it all day long."

She shifted and turned so that she lay over him, face-to-face. "I can't do that, but I do think we ought to take advantage of the time we do have." She felt him stir and harden against her belly.

"No argument here," he said hoarsely.

Chapter Ten

He'd never been much of an early riser. J.J. stifled a yawn as he scoffed a cup of coffee from George's thermos. If he saw the dawn, it was usually because he'd been up all night, not because he'd wrenched himself out of a nice, warm bed. Man, or at least J. J. Cooper, was at least partially a nocturnal beast.

Particularly on a Saturday morning.

But somehow, the past weeks, he'd come to enjoy dragging his sorry butt to the Human Habitat site each weekend. There was something immensely satisfying about it. Not the early rising—that part still sucked—but the work itself, the sense of contributing. All the itchiness he'd felt over not being at speed camp had abated. Some of it was about just knowing he was doing something meaningful.

And, of course, some of it was Lainie.

How the hell he'd managed to keep his hands off her for so many years, he'd never understand. Now the idea was ludicrous. He had only to look at her to feel the tug of want, only to touch her to feel the sharp spike of need. It might burn out at some point, but right now, in bed, they worked.

And out of it, he realized in a sudden blink of surprise. He felt good these days, really good. Maybe it wasn't just Human Habitat, and it wasn't just working the luscious Lainie over in bed. Maybe it was as simple as the fact that being with her didn't leave him time to brood over his future. He wanted to be more for her, and it took him outside himself. Maybe, he thought uneasily, it was just being with her, period.

He shook his head at himself. Nearby, on the grass, Kisha was turning cartwheels. Tyjah tried to copy her, but what he managed looked more like forward rolls. Latrice stood by watching, with the subdued resignation of the oldest child who winds up aged before her time.

Kisha executed another wobbly cartwheel and J.J. clapped.

She beamed. "Hi, J.J."

"Hey." He wandered over to them.

"Look at our house. It's almost done."

"Maybe not almost, but it's getting there." They'd framed the structure up the weekend before. Now they'd squared the walls and the roof was going on. As soon as he finished his coffee, he'd be back up with the roofing team, getting the plywood covering nailed down.

"Tall," Tyjah said, pointing at the roof.

On impulse, J.J. reached out for the three-year-old and hoisted him to his shoulders. "Nope, that's tall," he told a laughing Tyjah. "You're a big guy now."

"He's just a little kid." Kisha giggled.

"I'd be careful what you say to a person who's got high ground," J.J. advised.

"He can't do this." She turned another cartwheel.

"That's pretty impressive."

"I was s'posta learn to do a handspring but the Boys' and Girls' Center burned up."

J.J. frowned and put Tyjah down. "What? When?"

"Oh, forever ago," she said.

"In July," Latrice informed him, rolling her eyes.

Kisha stepped into a handstand. For a moment she held it, then she began to waver. J.J. moved quickly to catch her legs and steady her until she dropped them down and stood up. "Thanks." She bounced around, jumping on the grass.

"So you had to stop taking your gymnastics class because the center's gone?"

"Yup. We're supposed to go to Peabody, but that's a long way away and Gran's mostly too busy to drive."

"When are they going to build a new one?"

Kisha looked blankly at Latrice.

"There's no money," Latrice said. "Not now, anyway."

J.J. watched Kisha doing her cartwheels. "Did you take gymnastics classes, too?" he asked Latrice.

"I took painting," she replied.

"Painting, huh? Did you like it?"

Her eyes lit up. "Oh yes. I did a picture of our house and a picture of Tyjah and a picture of a sailboat." She smiled shyly. "I could show you sometime when you're visiting Lainie, if you want."

It was the longest sentence he'd ever heard from her. It was the first time he'd ever really seen her smile. Usually, she was a silent, serious presence watching over the exuberant Kisha and Tyjah. And now the center, the one place she didn't have to be responsible for them, was gone.

"How would you like it if we put up a new center and you could take classes again?" he asked impulsively. "Would you like that?"

"*Yeah!*" Kisha shouted, before her older sister could

answer. As for Latrice, she simply held Tyjah close and stared at J.J. with shining eyes.

Out of the corner of his eye, he saw Lainie walk up with Elsie. And he felt that same punch of anticipation that he felt whenever he saw her. Her hair was clubbed back in a ponytail. She wore jeans and a faded red T-shirt that he knew for a fact she'd spent no more than thirty seconds selecting that morning. How was it that she managed to look as artlessly sexy in it as any fashion model at some expensive shoot?

Lainie smiled at him, then glanced at the kids, jumping up and down and grinning madly. "What's going on?" she asked.

"Nothing. Latrice and Kisha and I were just having a little talk, weren't we?"

Kisha nodded with barely suppressed excitement.

Suspicion flickered in Lainie's eyes. "What are you up to, Cooper?"

He walked over and pressed a friendly kiss on her. "I'll tell you when I've thought it through. I need to get up to the roof now."

Lainie looked across the room, watching as J.J. used a framing square to mark a piece of wood, then slid it back into the pocket at the back of his tool belt with one hand, as he pulled out his hammer with another. There was a fluid grace to his movements, a confidence. When he picked a nail out of the bag that hung on his hip, he needed only two swings of the hammer to sink it entirely.

What was it about a man in a tool belt, anyway? J.J. should have looked bulky, stocky with his muscled thighs and arms, but somehow he only looked stripped down and powerful, as though his body were composed of the absolute essentials, muscle and sinew and bone.

George walked by, and J.J. flagged him down. Lainie

watched, at first casually and then with growing attention as J.J. spoke animatedly to a skeptical-looking George. When both of them started motioning and nodding, Lainie's eyes narrowed. Casually she stepped a little closer.

"...a few hundred thousand, maybe," George was saying.

"I've thought about that," J.J. responded. "I figure I can get some of my dad's suppliers to donate materials and we can do a benefit to raise the rest. I bet I could get Kurt or one of the other ski team guys to show, sign autographs, maybe get my sponsor to donate some equipment for auction. We do it right, we could have a new center up by spring."

A new center, she thought, knowing instantly what he meant. Knowing instantly the reason for the hero worship in Kisha's and Latrice's eyes.

"What do you want me to do?" George asked.

"Nothing, right now. Let me think about it, make some phone calls," J.J. said. "See if we get anywhere."

See if we get anywhere. A concept seven- and ten-year-olds didn't understand. Lainie looked out at the backyard, where Kisha was jumping around ebulliently.

And she stepped forward. "J.J., can I talk with you a minute?"

"Sure." J.J. glanced at George. "I'll catch up with you later on this, George, okay?"

"Works for me."

J.J. turned to Lainie. "What did you need?"

"Let's go outside."

He shrugged and followed her. "Why do I feel like I just got sent to the principal's office?" he asked as they stepped through the framed threshold of the front door.

At the edge of the yard beyond, Lainie turned to him. "I heard you talking with George about a center. A new Boys' and Girls' Center, you mean? Was that what you were talking about with Latrice and Kisha when I walked up?"

"Yeah, sure."

"What's George's take?"

"Wait and see, I think. I've got some ideas about how to pull it all together."

She frowned. "J.J., what are you doing? These are little kids. You can't go telling them you're going to build them a center, because they're going to believe you."

"Maybe they should," he said, an edge to his voice.

"Look, number one, you don't even know if the organization wants to reopen here. Number two, you need to get money—"

"Which I've already talked with George about," he interrupted.

"Number three," she continued, ignoring him, "you've got to coordinate the construction. And number four, you've got to actually build it. That doesn't mean George doing it." She fixed him with a stare. "He's already got enough projects. That means you. That's the way this organization works."

He shrugged. "Then I'll do it."

"How, when you're not even going to be around?" She tried unsuccessfully to temper her frustration. "I know you mean well—you always mean well—but you've got Buffalo, you've got Aspen, you've got Austria. Kind of hard to fit major construction in with all that, don't you think?"

"No, I don't. I can make some progress."

"J.J., you're talking about seven-year-old kids. They don't get *progress,* they only get *built* or *not built.* They've had a lot of disappointment in their lives, and I'm not going to stand by and see them hit with another one."

He felt the flare of anger. "They're not going to be disappointed."

"Yeah? You going to stick around until the place is done?"

"You know I can't."

"That's exactly what I'm talking about." She rounded on

him. "You don't know how volunteer projects work. There's never enough time and energy to go around. You leave, your precious center gets dropped flat."

"Why couldn't you take it on? You know they need it."

"Because they need a house more," she snapped. "J.J., you don't start stuff and leave other people to fix it. And you don't get people's hopes up and then disappear to go on about your life. It's not fair. It's not fair to them, to other kids who'll hear about it, to George, to everybody."

"I'll make sure it gets done." This time, he didn't bother to hide the irritation in his voice.

"You know, you don't have the best track record."

"What do you know about my track record that you didn't read in a tabloid?"

"Did you forget I grew up around you?" she demanded. "This is my community. These people matter to me. They're getting used to you, don't you understand that? You've become a part of their lives. They're starting to depend on you like you're going to be here in a month, when you and I both know that you'll be long gone. And if there's no one here to see it through, the center will be long gone, too. It's going to break their hearts, and these kids deserve better that that."

"I don't think it's the kids you're scared about," he shot back, "I think it's you."

The sound of hammering was very loud in the silence. Lainie stared at him, white faced. She moistened her lips. "This isn't about us." Her voice was barely audible.

"Isn't it?"

"No," she said more steadily. "I went into this with my eyes open. I know better than to expect anything. But they don't. And it'll be worse with the center. I'm just saying be careful with this. Be careful with them."

She turned to go back into the house, looking uncomfortably fragile.

"Lainie, wait, dammit."

"What?"

"Let's start this again." He took a deep breath, struggling with a roiling mix of anger, frustration and a sneaky little edge of guilt. "Look, I'm serious about this center. I want to get it built."

"I know right now you do. But plans have a way of changing. Just…just be careful, please. I know this is a lark to you, but it's not to them."

Hands on his hips, he looked off down the street. "Look, I know I haven't always been Mr. Straight and Narrow," he said slowly. "And sometimes that's gotten me in trouble. And, yeah, maybe when I was younger I went looking for that kind of trouble. But I'm not a screwup. I've never missed a race. I've never missed an event for my sponsor. The only person I could have hurt—really hurt—by my actions is myself."

"What does that—"

"This is different, okay? I know it. I'm not going to hurt these kids."

The expression in her eyes softened. "J.J., it's not that I think you're a screwup. I know that you're not. You've surprised me a lot since you've been here. You surprise me all the time. I just never know what kind of surprise it's going to be."

"That's part of the fun, isn't it?"

She gave him a brief smile. "Please don't lead them to expect something and then get back into racing and forget all about it. I just don't want to see anyone get hurt."

"No one's going to get hurt," he promised, pressing a kiss to her forehead. "I'll make sure of it."

"Okay, that's 150 feet," Caro read off to Lainie from the laser distance measurer. They stood on the town common, measuring off locations for the Halloween festival. A light breeze sent a few leaves scudding along. Overhead, some of the trees already showed the first signs of fall color among the green.

"A hundred and fifty feet," Lainie repeated. "Got it." She made a note on the clipboard she held and glanced up. "So what do you think about tattoos?"

Caro blinked and raised an eyebrow. "I'd say go find some sixty-year-old ex-Marine and take a good look at his arms and ask yourself if it's still as sexy as you think it sounds now."

Lainie rolled her eyes. "Not for me, for the Halloween carnival."

"You want to put a *tattoo* booth at the Halloween carnival? It's a family event, not a biker rally."

"A temporary-tattoo booth. You know, henna? On tonight, gone in two weeks?"

"Ah." Caro took a breath of relief. "Okay, for a minute there you had me going. Temporary tats, you could do. Although at that time of year, is anyone going to want to bare enough skin to make it worthwhile?"

"Good point. Maybe we should stick with face paint. I just wanted to try something different."

"Why am I not surprised?"

"Ha, ha," Lainie said. "So, okay, you want the food aisle along here, the souvenir and gift aisle opposite and the midway in the back."

"Right." Caro aimed her laser ruler across the common to one of the pillars on the perimeter and then stopped. "They called," she said in a low voice.

"Who called?" Lainie asked absently, scratching notes on her clipboard.

"Them. The museum."

"Oh my God, you mean the museum in New York?" Lainie snapped her head up to stare, clipboard forgotten.

Caro grinned. "I talked with the head curator for forty-five minutes."

"Oh, Caro, that's wonderful. This is so cool. How'd it go?"

"Perfect. Good chemistry. They want me to come down for an interview."

"An interview? Seriously?"

"Seriously." Caro's eyes flashed with excitement. "Next week. They're going to fly me in for an overnight interview."

"Wow, congratulations!" Lainie hugged her. "That's great."

"Tell me about it. I can't wait to get out of here."

"Come on, Salem's not that bad."

"Lainie, we're talking about Manhattan," Caro said, as though talking to a slow child. "You know, the city? Restaurants, music, shows? Clothes? I thought you were looking to get out, too."

"I was. I mean, I am," Lainie amended. "It's great, Caro, really great. We're just going to miss you here, that's all."

"Don't talk so seriously. I haven't gotten it yet."

Lainie gave her a smile. "You will."

No matter how much they needed to do site work, the main labor of pulling together an event like the Halloween festival lay in the endless phone calls to arrange work, check details, confirm participation. Lainie sat at her desk, going through the checklist she'd written up the night before.

All things considered, J.J. had been pretty patient with her working for most of the evening. Until he'd started licking his way up her thigh, anyway. A little flight of butterflies fluttered in her stomach at the memory. Things had smoothed out after their argument at the Human Habitat site. Trust him, he'd said, and she figured over the past two months he'd maybe earned that. It didn't mean she wasn't still nervous about it all, but she'd said her piece.

Now she'd wait and see what happened. Maybe he had changed, and if he had, she approved of the new J.J.

She approved very much.

He'd left for Buffalo just that morning. Only hours before. Already it seemed too long. Sighing, she looked back down at her folder and flipped through to find a printed estimate.

A slip of paper fluttered out.

I'm missing you.

The writing was J.J.'s. She stared at the scrap of notepaper with a smile. Only that morning, they'd been wrapped together in bed, naked. Only that morning, they'd showered, making love amid the soap and steam and hot stream of water….

The sound of voices in the hallway broke her out of her reverie. She blinked and went back to work. Sitting around moony-eyed wasn't going to get the Halloween festival together. She gave her head a shake and flipped through for the printed schedule she'd made notes on.

Another slip fluttered out.

I'm thinking about you.

A little giggle slipped out. Who would have thought that J.J. was a romantic? A fun companion, sure. A stupendously talented lover, no doubt. A romantic? She shook her head. He simply continued to surprise her.

She dug deeper in the stack and saw another sheet.

I'm wanting you.

And she reached for the phone. She didn't have to look up his cell phone number but dialed it by heart, listening to the tones signifying a ringing phone five hundred miles away.

"Hello?"

"I'm missing you, too."

She could hear the smile in his voice. "Hey, sweet girl."

Sweet girl. She couldn't tamp down the little surge of pleasure.

"So you're missing me?" he asked.

"Uh-huh."

"Are you prepared to demonstrate it?"

"Just what did you have in mind, Speed?" she drawled in her best Mae West voice.

"Phone sex?" he asked hopefully. "You know what your voice always does to me, and any bumps in my speed suit will create drag."

She suppressed a snort of laughter. "Well, as much as I'd like to help you stay as aerodynamic as possible, I can't do anything for you right now. But if there's anything else I can do…"

"Oh, I can think of a whole lot of things. I'll show you when I get back tomorrow. You did read the third note, right?"

"Of course."

"That's a guarantee. Anyplace, anytime."

"Talk is cheap," she sniffed.

"Not when you can back it up. Hey, I've got to run. I'm up in a couple of minutes. I'll call you tonight, okay?"

"Okay. Be good."

She could hear the smile in his voice. "I'll be great."

She slid the receiver back into its cradle and just stared into space, a ridiculous smile plastered all over her face.

It was the noise that always surprised him. When the giant turbines of the wind tunnel cranked up, they roared. Louder than a thousand freight trains, louder than a shrieking storm, they howled in his ears, even through his helmet.

J.J. moved into his tuck and held it as the wind whistled

by, buffeting him. With a hiss, the narrow ribbon of white smoke released, the white smoke that would show observers where he was creating drag.

I'm missing you.

He forced the thought from his mind. Now wasn't the time to think about Lainie. When he was doing testing that cost the ski team a bundle, he probably owed it to them to concentrate. It was just damned hard to keep her off his mind.

He tensed against the wind flow, imagining himself heading down the *piste* at Sölden. In just weeks, he'd be there, racing on his favorite mountain, looking for the first win of the season.

Too bad Lainie couldn't be there with him.

"Head forward a little, J.J.," said the voice in his ear.

When he obliged, he felt a lessening in the resistance. Like he was feeling a lessening resistance from Lainie. In the tunnel, less resistance meant a smoother profile. With Lainie, he wasn't sure what it meant. Then again, he wasn't sure what he wanted it to mean. There was something between them, that much he knew. Where they went from here, he hadn't a clue, but just because he was leaving town didn't mean it was over.

Maybe the thing to do was to get her to come to some of the races. If she were there with him, she wouldn't get as freaked out about the lifestyle. She might even start enjoying it. He could show her places on the off days, Innsbruck, Torino, Lyon.

"You're stiffening up, J.J.," said the voice. "Relax back on your heels a little."

When in doubt, relax. Maybe he needed to just step back and let things flow for a while until she got used to the idea. Try to get her to one race, maybe. Show her that he could ease off on the party thing. Show her that she could depend on him.

"That's perfect, J.J. You're good to go," said the voice in his ear.

Good to go. It was the best news he'd gotten in a while.

Lainie sat on her couch in jeans and a light sweater. The Indian summer heat wave was over; an evening chill had begun lingering in the air in the evenings. The weather was fitting—she'd been so focused on planning the Halloween festival that in her mind it was already late fall. She found herself almost surprised to see the leaves still green on the trees. It seemed that they should have been awash in color. It felt like it was already time for Halloween.

And the start of the World Cup season.

She looked around the empty room and sighed. Always before, being alone had been good. It had been what she liked, a luxury after the craziness of growing up with four siblings. She'd never missed company. She'd never found herself at loose ends.

Not the way she was now.

It was hard to say when it had happened, but somewhere along the line she'd gotten used to having J.J. around. She sighed again. She'd schooled herself to expect nothing, but it was getting harder and harder. Each time he did one of those startlingly sweet things like leaving the notes, another chunk of her armor fell away.

And a little more anxiety crouched in her throat.

Sweet girl.

It was a risk to get used to the sweet things. She knew he cared, but she just couldn't see how they could make it work. Right now, she and Salem were his substitutes for the life he knew, a way to feel on solid ground. She was very afraid, though, that it wasn't anything more.

He'd fled mundane, everyday life when he'd been fourteen,

to go off to ski academy and, eventually, the travel and excitement that was the World Cup. That was the life he'd known for fifteen years. That was the life he obviously loved, one that took everything he had. Once he was back on the slopes again, racing and winning, Salem wouldn't matter anymore.

And neither would she.

Lainie blinked fiercely and swallowed. All she could do was enjoy the moment and focus on anything besides what came next. After all, who could say what came next for any of them? So what, if two months from now, J.J. would be in Europe. Who knew where she would be? Maybe it was time to get serious about looking for work. Caro wasn't the only one who could change jobs.

Maybe it was time.

The doorbell rang. Lainie frowned at the little jump of excitement in her stomach. It was scary how conditioned she'd become. A caller at night had come to mean J.J. Not this night, though—he was still in Buffalo, not due to return until morning.

Scolding herself for being foolish, she still sprang up from the couch and hurried down the stairs. She might as well get it over with. The sooner she dealt with her caller, the sooner she'd get back to…what, staring at the walls and trying not to go nuts?

Shaking her head at herself, she went down the short hallway to the front door. Twisting the knob, she opened it wide.

And there, waiting for her, was J.J.

Nothing he'd ever seen or felt was as right as watching Lainie open the door to him. He saw her eyes light up and suddenly he felt the same way he did when he skied off a knoll that launched him into the air, the punch of adrenaline, the great gulp of oxygen, the soaring sense of being able to do more and better and faster.

The sense of everything being right in the world.

And then she was in his arms, soft and fragrant against him, fitting so right, tasting of promise and pleasure, and suddenly he felt as if he could just hold on to her forever.

Suddenly he was home.

Chapter Eleven

It must have taken time to open the door, to get upstairs to her apartment, Lainie thought hazily. She remembered none of it—all of it was parsed out in desperate kisses, in the immediacy of J.J.'s arms hard around her. And still, standing in her bedroom, they were too far apart, separated by the barrier of clothing.

It didn't matter that cloth tore as it came off, ripped by their impatient hands. It didn't matter that they never made it to the bed. The only thing that mattered was slaking the burning desire they had for each other.

It was hard and fast and furious, heedless, desperate.

And even then, it wasn't enough.

"I thought you weren't coming home until tomorrow," Lainie murmured against J.J.'s chest, feeling the measured, hypnotic stroke of his hand on her back.

"I thought maybe I needed to see you sooner."

"I like the way you think." And at some point, *she* was going to have to think about that little leap of excitement she'd felt when she'd seen him. and about when "just an affair" became something altogether more serious. "So are you home now for a while?"

"A few days. The rest of this week, anyway. Gabe's wedding. Then I go out to Aspen to get some slope time. I've got a lot of prep work to do. Sölden is only three weeks away."

"Right. Sölden." And the tension gathered, for all that she tried to wish it away.

J.J. seemed to sense it. "Relax. We'll deal with it when it happens." He pressed his lips against her hair. "I can think of a whole lot of other things I'd like to do first."

"I know one thing that comes first. Gabe's wedding."

"Yeah? What about it?" He traced his fingers slowly down her back again, so lightly that she could barely feel them.

Lainie melted against him for a moment before stirring. "Well, we've got to figure out how to handle it."

"I didn't think it needed handling."

"Of course it does. You're talking about people who have known both of us our entire lives. If we show up as a couple, they're going to ask questions. What are we going to say? Or do we just drive up separately?"

She could feel his brows lower. "Why the hell would we drive up separately?"

"Oh, maybe because otherwise people are going to think we're together? I mean, what else are they supposed to think?"

"We *are* together."

The words stopped her for a moment. It felt too good to hear them, especially when she could practically still feel him inside her. But she had to keep it in perspective. She couldn't let herself hope for too much. She sat up. "We're not together, J.J. This is just something we're doing for now."

"And you have a reputation to protect?" he drawled, and reached out an arm to tumble her back against him.

"Stop it," she yelped.

"Not a chance. Just in case you're confused, I'm going to show you how together we are."

He bent to fasten his mouth on her breast and pleasure flowed through her, thick and hot. She shouldn't lose track like this, she thought, they needed to talk. But he caressed her nipple with lips and tongue, scraping it lightly with his teeth. When he ran his hand up her thigh to find her where she was slick and wet, she jolted. How on earth could she be ready again after the hours they'd been through? How was it he knew just how to touch her?

Practice, said a mocking voice in her head and she gathered her wits together.

"J.J., no." This time she managed to sound serious enough that he raised his head to look at her, hands stilled. She waited a moment for her heart rate to level before she went on. "Look, I don't want this to turn into something where we've got everyone watching. Can't we just keep it between us?"

"Why, are you embarrassed?"

"No. I just don't want to be under a microscope later on."

"Later on?"

"If something happens."

"You mean when something happens."

Something cooled in his gaze. "Sounds like you've got it all planned out."

"No, I don't. I'm just trying to use some common sense. You're going to get skiing again, and you'll be back to living the World Cup life. Salem, me, we only make sense now

because you're here. And anyway, you told me yourself that
you only spend about six weeks a year stateside. That sounds
pretty done to me."

"So maybe I come home more often. There are races over
here. Shoot, you could even come to Europe. You'd like it."

"So, what, I can be this year's girl?" This time she did
move away, reaching for her robe.

Something in his expression hardened. "You are never
going to cut me any slack, are you?"

"It's not a question of slack. It's a question of dealing
with what is."

He rose and yanked on his jeans. "Maybe 'what is' has
changed. You ever thought about that?"

"J.J., for fifteen years, more than fifteen years, you've
lived your life a certain way. You don't change that overnight,
even if you want to. I don't see why you're getting upset that
I want to play it low key. Can you honestly say that you're
doing any of this for the long haul? Salem? Human Habitat?
Us?" she challenged him.

"How am I supposed to know?" he burst out in frustration. "It's only been a week or two. What's wrong with just
seeing what happens? Dammit, Lainie, I care about this. I
care about you."

"And I care about you," she snapped back.

"Isn't that enough for now? Look, just come over for
some of the races. You've always wanted to see Europe.
Take a month off, a year. We can hit all the places you've
wanted to go."

For a moment she could see it, wandering through Vienna,
Salzburg, hand in hand. "I don't have that kind of money,"
she reminded herself as much as him.

"So what? I do."

"I can't let you keep me," she said, shocked despite herself.

"Why not? You let me take you out to dinner. You'd let me take you away for the weekend."

"Supporting me is something different." And the idea of throwing everything away, to depend utterly on J.J. and what the next day held was terrifying. "J.J., I've got a life here, a career. I can't throw that away on 'let's see what happens' with you. I've seen what happens."

"Dammit, why won't you believe in me?" he demanded.

"J.J., I've had a lifetime of watching you," she returned. "It's easy to be someone else here. It's a different place. Over there who knows what will happen?"

He blinked, studying her for a moment. "You're afraid," he said slowly. "That's what this is all about. You're scared to take a chance."

She opened her mouth to deny it and stopped. "I'm just trying to get by," she said instead. "I'm trying to be smart. Like you said, it's only been a week or two." She walked over to put her arms around his neck, resting her forehead against his. "Look, I don't even know what we're arguing about. It's good right now, J.J., really good. All I'm saying is let's not pretend it's more than it is. It's just…right now." She raised her head to look at him. "Fair?"

He didn't look happy about it, but finally he nodded. "Fair. Then you'll at least think about coming to Europe?"

She sighed. "Let's wait until Halloween's out of the way. After that we'll see."

In the end, they arrived at the nearly empty parking lot well before the eventual tide of friends and family. When they walked in together, only hotel employees were around to notice, Lainie saw with a little tingle of relief.

The venerable old hotel looked more beautiful than ever, with its soaring ceilings, gold-leafed pillars and broad swaths of windows. Outside, the mountains rose all around. Inside was luxury, fantasy, a reminder of a gentler time.

"What a place to get married," Lainie murmured.

"I bet they got a great deal on the rental."

For a few minutes they just wandered, strolling through the lobby, climbing the sweeping grand staircase to admire the view from the top, tiptoeing into the dining room with its salmon-colored walls and ornate chandeliers. Finally they stepped outside to stroll down the broad veranda that ran along the east wing of the hotel for what seemed like a mile before making the turn around the end and sweeping along the back side. Hanging baskets spilled over with the last of the year's crimson and purple petunias. White wooden chaise lounges that would have looked appropriate on the deck of the Queen Mary back in the early 1900s lined the inner side.

It was so open and deserted, out in the midday air, that she didn't protest when J.J. took her hand and kissed it.

"It's all so gorgeous," Lainie murmured, looking out over the woods with their bridle trails. A stream wound between the forest and the almost unnatural green of the golf course, spanned periodically by curving white footbridges. In the background, over it all rose Mount Jefferson.

They followed the veranda as it curved around the glassed-in semicircle of the conservatory. Inside lay a fantasy of flowers and greenery and white wicker, of Grecian pillars draped with plaster garlands. At the front of the room stood a temporary arch wound with flowers.

And before it, Gabe.

Lainie pulled her hand hastily from J.J.'s.

"I guess we've found the wedding," J.J. said and opened the door that led inside.

Gabe looked as if he'd been born wearing a tux. With his dark, polished good looks, he could have made a successful career as a model. With his air of command, though, Lainie could never have imagined him in such a passive job. He needed to be running empires—or a resort the size of a small city, like this one.

As they approached, he gave J.J. a narrow-eyed look. "You two are here early."

"We thought you might need help." Hastily Lainie took her garment bag from J.J. "I mean, I did. Who knows what Speed, here, thought."

"People seldom do," Gabe said, with an edge to his voice.

"Where's Hadley?" Lainie asked.

"Upstairs in the Presidential Suite with her mother and sisters. Fifth floor. They said for you to come on up when you got here."

"I should go, then." She'd half turned toward J.J. for a kiss before she caught herself. When she turned back to the lobby, she found Gabe's eyes on her. "Well." She cleared her throat. "I'm off. See you both later."

"Am I going to have to kick your butt?"

Gabe and J.J. stood out on the veranda outside the conservatory, leaning on the rail, watching the smoke from the cog railway train as it made its way up the mountain.

"One, you couldn't," J.J. said. "Two, you'd mess up your tux. Three, what for?"

"Lainie."

J.J. looked at him. "I don't think so."

"And that's because you're not going to treat her like one of your groupies, right?"

J.J. stifled the little surge of irritation. "Look, despite what everyone seems to think around here, I am not in the habit of lying to people or pretending to be one thing when I'm something else. I'm an adult. Lainie's an adult. Together, we're going to act like adults, which—believe it or not—I'm perfectly capable of doing."

Gabe raised his eyebrows. "Well, certainly that would be a welcome change of pace. Because if you do end up dumping Lainie for Miss Lillehammer 2003, there's going to be a whole line of people back in Vermont looking for a piece of your worthless hide. Starting with me." The smile left Gabe's face. "You'd better take this one seriously."

"I do," J.J. blurted before he even knew he was going to say it. Interesting. Where, exactly, that had come from, he hadn't a clue. Even more interesting, the more he thought about it, the more it felt right. "I'm not just doing this to keep busy. I care about her."

More than cared, he realized suddenly. A lot more. Shock rolled over him.

Gabe gave him a sharp stare and then he began shaking his head, a reluctant grin spreading over his face. "Well, I'll be damned."

"What?"

"Mr. Saturday Night finally got caught."

"I'm not caught. I'm…I don't know what I am," J.J. muttered bad temperedly.

"Neither does anyone else, which is why we're all worried." They stared out at the grounds for a while, watching a couple play tennis on the clay courts.

"Look, you're right, you're both adults," Gabe said finally. "But she's like a kid sister to me. I just don't want to see her hurt."

J.J. sighed. "I know. Look, I don't know what's going to happen—that's up to her as much as it is to me—but I guarantee, I'm going to do my damnedest to take care of her."

"Gee, mister, you're such an inspiration."

"That's why I'm your best man." J.J. looked at him and

hefted his garment bag. "Which, I guess means it's time to get into this monkey suit and marry you off."

"I can't believe I'm this nervous." Looking distinctly queasy, Hadley Stone pressed a hand to her stomach. She was ravishing in an utterly simple, beautifully cut white silk sheath that probably cost the Earth, her pale hair adorned with flowers.

Lainie frowned in concern. Across the room, Hadley's frighteningly thin mother twittered about the hairdresser and makeup artist who were working on Hadley's twin sisters, whom Lainie had entirely given up keeping straight. They looked so much like Hadley, the same wheat-colored hair, the same fragile-looking bone structure they'd all inherited from their mother. But there the similarities ended. They were spoiled, self-absorbed and unerringly skillful at sucking up all of their mother's attention.

And on this day of all days, the focus should have been on Hadley.

"You could try some ginger ale," Lainie suggested. "That's what my mom always gave me when I was sick."

"Ginger ale sounds good."

"No ginger ale," Irene Stone called from across the room. "If you spill it, you'll stain your gown. Club soda only."

"*Motherrrr,* this hairstyle makes me look twelve," one of the twins whined.

Lainie glanced questioningly at Hadley. "Club soda?"

Looking distracted, she nodded.

Lainie crossed to the minibar and got the sparkling water and a glass for Hadley, who sank down on the dressing chair.

"Hadley, you stand up or you'll wrinkle that gown," Irene ordered.

Hadley stood. Her hands, Lainie saw, were trembling.

"If it helps at all, Nick's wife, Sloane, was a nervous wreck before their wedding," Lainie said casually.

"Really?"

"Big-time. She couldn't stop crying. Every time we got her makeup on, we had to start all over."

Hadley frowned. "Second thoughts?"

"Not even. She was just, I don't know, overwhelmed that it was really happening, I guess."

"But she's so strong. She looked completely together at the ceremony."

"Yep." Lainie waggled her eyebrows. "Amazing what a shot or two of good Kentucky bourbon will do."

Hadley stared at her. "You're kidding."

"Do I look like I'm kidding?" Lainie winked and showed her the bottle of vodka she'd palmed from the minibar. "Sometimes a woman's got to do what's necessary. It won't stain your clothes, either," she added in a whisper as she poured it into the glass.

Hadley grinned and sat down.

"Hadley Stone," Irene began.

"Mother, it's my wedding day and I'll sit if I want," Hadley interrupted calmly and took the glass from Lainie and raised it. "Here's to good times," she said and drank.

"What a handsome group of boys you all are." Molly Trask stood back, camera in hand, and beamed.

"Ma, please."

"Hush, Jacob. I see the three of you together little enough, especially dressed up. And J.J., too. Now stand together and smile. Ready?" She started to take the shot and then stopped, blinking a little. "Oh, you all look so grown-up."

"We are grown-up," Jacob growled, yanking at his collar.

"Will you take the picture so that I can get out of this damned jacket?"

"Now you've gotten your tie all messed up. Celie, can you do anything about him?" Molly asked over her shoulder.

A sloe-eyed beauty with a dark, Louise Brooks bob stepped forward to straighten his tie. "Listen to your mother, Jacob," she advised. "I'm betting she can take you down in two, if you're not careful." She stood on tiptoe and kissed him on the lips.

J.J. grinned. He'd never figured on Jacob Trask for getting married, let alone to a little pixie who came up to his chin. Of course, this particular pixie looked as if she could take him in two also. Although, judging by the totally enamored look Jacob gave her as she walked away, she probably wouldn't ever have to.

And then he realized that Jacob was looking back at him from a distance of approximately five inches. Or not looking, precisely. Glowering. "What are you grinning at?"

J.J. smiled even wider. "It doesn't work anymore, Jacob. Once you lost the beard, you stopped being scary."

"Yeah," said Jacob's brother Nick from the other side. "Now you're just another pretty boy. It's about as frightening as being glared at by Justin Timberlake or something."

"It's been a while since I pounded you, hasn't it?" Jacob said pleasantly.

"Jacob, behave yourself," Molly scolded. "Nicholas, stop teasing your brother. Honestly, the three of you act like you're ten sometimes."

"What'd I do?" Gabe protested. "I'm just an innocent bystander."

"You were biding your time," she said severely.

"At least this evening," Nick whispered in Gabe's ear, then smiled for the photo.

* * *

It was magical, as weddings should be, all lily of the valley and white lace, perfume of flowers and liquid sound of the harp. Overhead, trompe l'oeil vines encircled the parabolic cutout in the conservatory ceiling. Underfoot, the carpet was spring green. A little buzz went through the room as the twins and Lainie started up the aisle in their gauzy tea-length dresses.

Gabe stood up at the front by the arch of flowers, looking nervous, just as a bridegroom should. Next to him was J.J., relaxed and easy. Of course, J.J. would be relaxed in front of a firing squad, Lainie thought. She'd never seen him any other way than easy, even before the one race she'd seen him in, a qualifier for the Junior Olympics. Smiling, he leaned over to Gabe and muttered something too low to catch, earning a laugh.

She wondered if it was different for him these days, now that the stakes were higher. Somehow, she doubted it. When it came to how he thought he should live life, J.J. wasn't one to compromise. If he wasn't enjoying things, he wouldn't do it. Although, even for him, there were exceptions.

After all, he *was* standing there in a tux.

With his hair only slightly less disordered than usual, he looked completely delicious and utterly uncomfortable. The things we do for love, she thought. Then his eyes locked on hers and the breath backed up in her lungs. There was some special intensity to his gaze and he watched her as she moved to her place. And every male Trask in the bridal party turned to stare at him.

All but one.

Because, suddenly the music of the harpist changed. Suddenly the air was charged with breathless anticipation, and Hadley appeared under the archway that led out to the lobby, on the arm of her father. She was radiant, suffused with joy to the point that she glowed.

Lainie glanced over at Gabe, who stared at his bride like a man poleaxed. It was amazing, Lainie thought, watching Hadley walk up the aisle. A year before, Gabe hadn't even known she existed. Now she was his world. How things could turn on a dime, irrevocably.

And without intending to, Lainie looked beyond to lock gazes with J.J. Reaction slammed through her system, as surely as though he'd touched her. How your life could just change in one day.

Irrevocably.

Chapter Twelve

J.J. stood in the start house, waiting for the pips that would tell him when to go, the familiar prerace tension tightening his gut. Frigid air, glacier pure, knifed into his lungs. The sun shone down out of a perfectly clear sky, revealing every ridge on the icy snow of the course. He shifted restlessly.

He was ready for this one, God knew he was ready after all the hours, the days, the months of training. All he wanted to do was get out on the course and feel the speed.

And win.

"You will." The soft voice made him jump and he looked over in shock to see Lainie standing beside him, her eyes alive with promise.

"What are you doing here?" he asked.

"Go fast," she whispered, and leaned in to kiss him.

And took him to that place where all that mattered was the

contact, the heat. Her mouth was soft and mobile against his, making everything else recede until all he was aware of was her, all he wanted was her.

The pips interrupted them then, almost unnaturally loud in the cold. And then they got louder and louder, never stopping, never quieting until they were shrilling in his ears.

The shrilling turned into ringing as J.J. came fighting up out of sleep. He groped on his bedside table for the cold metal of his cell phone and flipped it open. "'Lo?" he mumbled groggily.

"What are you doing out there, sleeping half the day away?" demanded a male voice.

"What?"

"Jesus, listen to you. Wake up."

J.J. looked toward the still-darkened windows of his hotel room. "Why? The damned sun isn't even up yet," he growled.

"Sure it is. It's lunchtime already."

"Not where I am. Why are you calling me this early?" he demanded grumpily.

"Do you always talk to people you don't know like this?" the voice asked.

"Madsen, only you would be this much of a pain in the ass," J.J. shot back. Kurt Madsen, J.J.'s teammate from the U.S. Ski Team and Olympic medalist in the combined downhill and slalom. "It may be lunchtime where you are, but that's because you're in Innsbruck. I'm in Aspen."

"So?"

"So it's not even four-thirty in the morning."

"It's the perfect time to get up to train."

J.J. let his head fall back against the pillow. "There was a reason I stopped rooming with you on the circuit."

"Yeah. I got married. Otherwise, you'd still be relying on me to get your sorry ass out of bed."

"You're enjoying this."

"If I enjoy it, who do I hurt?" Madsen asked, his voice ripe with laughter.

"Me."

"And that's bad, why?"

There was a moment of silence before J.J. sat up in resignation. "Okay, I'm getting out of bed. You satisfied?"

"Hey, you were the one who called me."

"At daytime in your time zone. Any reason you couldn't do the same?"

"Because this is more fun."

"Sicko," J.J. muttered.

"So what's this all about, anyway? Your message wasn't very clear."

J.J. flipped on the light, his brain slowly coming up to speed. "The Salem Boys' and Girls' Center burned down last spring. I'm trying to help them build a new one. I'm organizing a benefit to raise money."

"Salem where? Is there a Salem in Vermont?"

"You're a regular laugh riot, Madsen."

"So my wife tells me."

J.J. gave a jaw-creaking yawn. "No, Salem, Massachusetts. I'm living there right now. Their center burned down and the kids don't have any place to play."

There was a silence.

"Madsen, you there?"

"Yeah. I'm just getting all choked up by how adult you've gotten all of a sudden," Madsen said sorrowfully. "The man who used to party all night in Val d'Isère has gone to organizing bake sales?"

"Benefits," J.J. corrected.

"What's next, quilting?"

J.J. scowled. "Look, I'm serious. It's a good cause and I

could use some star power. In your case, low-wattage star power, but still… Can you do it?"

Madsen chuckled. "Of course I'll do it. If nothing else, I get to come laugh at you. When is it?"

"It's next Saturday."

"Next *Saturday?* Hell, J.J., that's the week before Sölden. What are you doing worrying about charity stuff? That's an off-season gig. We've got a race."

"Because they don't need the center off season, they need it now," he replied, an edge in his voice. "These kids don't have anywhere to go, they're missing out, big-time. It's important, Kurt. I want to get the money together so we can build the place by spring."

"What do you mean, 'we'? You're going to fly home between races and hammer nails?"

"If that's what it takes. First, we've got to buy the nails, and that means pulling off this fund-raiser. Look, we've got a Port-a-Slope coming in, my sponsor's put up some equipment to be raffled, but we need names to really draw people. Will you do it?"

Madsen sighed. "I'll catch hell from Doug and the rest of the coaches for coming over when I ought to be practicing," he predicted. "So will you."

"What else is new? You've got enough brownie points built up to pull it off. But if you can't be there, can you at least give me something to auction off?"

"Like what?"

"I don't know, like your gold medal."

"No problem, I'll get right on that. Anyway, who said I wasn't coming? I'll be there. Of course, you do realize you'll get maybe a dozen people showing up for this if you're lucky, right? Outside of the Olympics, people could give a hang about ski racing."

"This is New England. I think we'll get more than a dozen, especially if we advertise it right. We've already got the word out in fliers and in the papers, and I've got my ski rep working on the ski stores and resort areas."

There was a short silence. "You're really into this, aren't you?"

"It gives me something to do," J.J. said uncomfortably, rising to walk to the window.

"What you're *supposed* to be doing is training and getting slope time out in Aspen."

"Where the hell do you think I am? I'm just making some calls in between training runs."

"It's not enough, J.J." Madsen paused a moment. "Look, the coaching staff is already ticked that you hurt yourself playing around. Guys like us have to watch it, my friend, because the bright young things are breathing down our necks."

"So, what…I'm not allowed to do anything but ski?"

"If the U.S. Ski Team has anything to say about it, yeah. And if you *do* do something outside of that, you'd better make sure you kick ass on the *piste*."

"Yeah, yeah, I got it. So you're going to be there?"

Madsen let out a breath. "Yeah."

"What'll you tell the coaches?"

"That I need to go donate a kidney to my cousin."

"They're gonna love that."

"I thought you wanted me there."

"I do, I just don't want you getting crap from Doug over it."

"Hey, I'm still turning in A-team times, and in between they've got me mentoring the new guys. Like you said, I have brownie points. It's you I'm worried about. You don't sound right."

"What does that mean?"

"I don't know. You sound different, like you sound in the summertime. Like the World Cup is really far away. It's not, dude, it starts in three weeks and you need to be ready. You've got to get dialed in."

J.J. flipped aside the curtain to stare outside at the light reflecting off the snow-covered hillside behind the condo. He'd spent six hours on the slopes the day before. "You finished with the lecture, Mom?"

Madsen blew out a breath of frustration. "I don't know why I bother. You don't listen anyway."

"Yeah, but I appreciate the thought. And the wakeup call."

"Hey, I've got to get my entertainment somehow."

"I guess." J.J. let the curtain fall closed. "Thanks for agreeing to do this, Kurt. I owe you one."

"Actually, you owe me more. Remember that twenty euros that you borrowed from me in Val Triest?"

"So? When I hit Sölden, I'm buying."

"Last one down the mountain always does."

"Then I guess that means you're buying." J.J. yawned again. "Hey, take it easy. And, Madsen?"

"Yeah?"

"I *am* going to kick ass on the *piste*."

J.J. ended the call and walked into the bathroom to pull on his sweats. He and Madsen had come up through the ranks together, a couple of raw-boned teenagers straight out of high school ski academies. They'd grown up fast in the crucible of the World Cup circuit, going from fighting just to finish in the top twenty to becoming standard fixtures on the winners' podium.

And now, however much they might be at the tops of their games, the warning light was beginning to blink for them both. Madsen was right about the hot young guys, J.J. thought as he headed down to the workout room. And the coaches always gave the benefit of the doubt to those hot young guys because they were the future of the team; J.J. and Madsen were its present and past.

Of course, Madsen had a future—the coaches weren't just hooking him up with the young skiers to make him feel good. Kurt Madsen had a gift for helping guys get faster, and J.J. could see him sliding right into the U.S. Ski Team coaching staff. As for J.J., well, given his tendency to break every rule, he suspected that to most of the coaches, the idea of him joining their staff would come under the heading of signs of the apocalypse.

So what came next? He had the director of ski position at Gabe's resort, but that was hardly a full-time job. The prospect of going home to join his father's construction business didn't appeal at all. Whatever it was, it had to matter.

He'd seen what happened to guys when it didn't.

Sitting down on the mat in the workout room, he began to stretch. That was the thing about life on the World Cup circuit—everything was focused toward one goal. The idea of living a life where nothing really mattered, well, it might be a nice break for the short term, but after six or eight months of just flopping around, it would make him crazy.

Life wasn't supposed to be meaningless. He wasn't built for that; he was built to accomplish things, whether they were World Cup wins or whatever came next.

Unfortunately, he wasn't at all sure what that might be. He didn't know where things went next, but one thing he did know—he sure as hell had better get started figuring it out.

Of course, he ought to be used to not knowing where things went next, because he sure as hell didn't have a clue when it came to Lainie. They hadn't talked much since Gabe's wedding. It had never seemed the right time and if he were truly honest with himself, he didn't know what he wanted to say anyway.

This is serious, he'd told Gabe, and he'd meant it. But he'd also meant it when he'd said he hadn't a clue what happened next. Always before, it had made him feel choked when a woman had expectations of him. With Lainie, it pissed him off that she didn't.

He was different and she was part of why. The problem was getting her to see it.

The only thing he really knew, he realized as he rose, was what to do when he strapped on his skis and hit the *piste*.

And maybe that was where he needed to go right now.

"Your bouncy jack-o'-lantern split a seam?" Lainie frowned into the phone. "You can fix it, right?"

"Well, here's the thing," the contractor said. "The split's too big to fix so we got to get a new one. But there's a month waiting time from the manufacturer, see?"

"I see," Lainie said with a sinking heart. "What you're telling me is I need to go somewhere else." A mere three weeks before the festival, and with Caro down in Manhattan for her job interview. Perfect.

"I guess it depends on how much you're set on a jack-o'-lantern. It's a specialty item, you know. Now, we got a bouncy rocket ship we could send instead. Red and blue, doors on both sides. Nice fins. I even got a blow-up Buzz Lightyear I'll throw in free."

"It's a Halloween festival," she enunciated.

"So? No reason you can't use a rocket ship. Kids, now, they don't care so much. They got imagination. The bouncing's the thing."

"A bouncy rocket ship."

"Maybe you get some kids dressed up like astronauts. Look, I know it's not what you asked for but it's what I got."

Lainie drummed her fingers on the desktop. She could call around for a replacement vendor, but this close to the festival, she had a pretty good idea that her chances of finding a good replacement would be about nil. She sighed. "Okay, give me the bouncy rocket ship."

"Smart move," he approved. "You're gonna love it."

Her phone flashed. "I've got another call, I've got to go."

"I'll send over the paperwork."

She switched lines. "This is Lainie."

"And I am forever grateful," J.J.'s voice said.

"Hey, you." The grin spread over her face before she could prevent it.

"Hey, yourself."

"So how's Colorado?"

"Snowy, mostly."

"What a shock," she said dryly.

"It was for me. So how are things going?"

"Let's see, I just had to trade out my bouncy jack-o'-lantern for a bouncy rocket ship." She pursed her lips, waiting for his response.

"A bouncy rocket ship?"

"For the festival. You know, those big inflatable things that kids jump around in?"

He cleared his throat. "A rocket ship for a Halloween festival?"

"I was hoping it wasn't quite as bad as it sounded."

"Well, ultimately, who cares? They're kids, they'll jump around and have fun."

"That's what the vendor told me."

"I'll jump around with you and have fun, if it helps."

Her lips quirked. "I'll bet you will. So just when are you going to show up again, anyway?"

"I've been gone too long, haven't I?"

"Well, a week and a half is a while, but I've taken up with the mailman." She grinned.

"The mailman, huh?" He paused. "Hey, wait a minute. I've seen the mail carrier on our street and she's a woman."

"Oh, then I guess you're missing out," she said, her tone innocent.

"No fair doing it if I can't watch. First thing tomorrow, I'm flying out to hide in your closet."

"I'd rather see you hide in my bed."

She could hear the smile in his voice. "That can be arranged. I get in Friday night for the benefit. Want to come pick me up?"

"I'll be there with bells on."

"Don't forget the mail lady," he added.

Lainie looked across the packed ballroom at the Seven Gables Inn, frankly amazed at the turnout. A scritching noise had her glancing to her right to see a wildly grinning Latrice ski down the Port-a-Slope. To the left, a series of glossy booths displayed the latest snowboards and ski equipment. On a table in the center, a large glass urn watched by security was steadily filling up with cash. Straight ahead, an auctioneer stood on a podium, auctioning off memorabilia.

J.J. had gotten it right, she thought. Somehow, he'd known what to offer and how to market it. For a small admission fee, people had been able to meet the two Olympic stars, buy raffle tickets for ski goods and lift tickets, try the latest equipment, and, like Latrice, try skiing down an artificial slope.

How he'd managed to pull it off in the short time he'd had, she'd never know. His cell phone bill had to be terrifying. But it wasn't just the planning effort. He and his colleague, Kurt Madsen, had made the event work. They'd laughed and joked, signed autographs, posed for pictures.

Working her way through the crowd of people, Lainie walked behind the table where J.J. sat, scrawling his signature on a program.

"You're my hero," she said.

"Always nice to be someone's hero. What do I owe that to?"

She waved at the room. "Everything. All of it. You really pulled it off."

His smile held surprised pleasure. "I didn't do it alone, trust me. George helped, and my ski rep and—" He broke off, eyes narrowed.

On the podium, the auctioneer held up a square of white. "Come on, folks, let's get it up above twenty-five. This is the bib that J.J. wore in the clinching race for the World Cup overall, year before last." He waved the Tyvek bib. "How about thirty? Thirty dollars, anyone?"

J.J. gave an incredulous look. "What the hell?" he demanded. "Excuse me." In a few swift steps, he'd reached the podium and hopped up on top. "Thirty bucks?" he repeated in disbelief. "Thirty? That's a tank of gas, folks. You're looking at a memento of the first overall World Cup win by a U.S. skier in twenty years. This is history."

Around the room, heads turned to watch him. People who were focusing on other activities began paying attention.

And J.J. thrived on it. "Okay, so maybe you're not a big ski racing fan and you don't care, but you know what? Buy it anyway and put it on eBay. Buy it and take the tax write-off. This isn't about the bib, folks, it's about building this center. That's what counts. Come on, what more do you want? What have I got over there, a hundred? Okay, a hundred. That's more like it."

The bidding climbed to a hundred and fifty, then two, then stalled at four.

But still J.J. wasn't satisfied. Microphone in hand, he stalked the podium like a restless tiger. "Come on, people. Don't you want to give these kids somewhere to learn and grow and play? Do you want the country to be run by idiots when you get old? Do you? Well, neither do I. That means we need get out and support this. That means we need to build them a new center. Come on, what are you willing to pay?" he shouted.

It was like mind control, Lainie thought. Suddenly energized, people were raising their hands, pushing the bids higher and higher until they topped out at something over $5,100. For a numbered piece of Tyvek.

But that wasn't it, she realized. It was $5,100 for J.J., pure and simple.

It was the last item of the auction, and people began to filter out of the room. He'd done it, she thought jubilantly. He'd convinced people to come, he'd talked the sponsors into donations, coordinated it all and made it happen, right down to the auction.

Lainie pushed through the crowd of people to find him and pressed an exuberant kiss on him. "I can't believe you pulled this off."

"Hey, I want you to meet Kurt."

"Who?" Lainie turned to see a tall, strapping blond with a vaguely familiar face.

"Lainie Trask, Kurt Madsen. Kurt won a medal at the Olympics last spring."

"I think I remember hearing something about it," she said dryly.

"Kurt, this is Lainie Trask. My girlfriend."

Lainie snapped her head around to stare at J.J. so quickly it about threw her neck out of joint. Girlfriend?

J.J. just gave her an affable grin and nodded toward Kurt. "Kurt and I go back a ways."

"Nice to meet you, Kurt," she said faintly, shaking his hand.

"Pleasure's all mine."

"I would have introduced you before but the putz got here late," J.J. added.

"Hey, I didn't spend six hours on a plane to get abused."

"Sure you did. Anyway, watch out. Lainie works at the witchcraft museum. Don't tick her off, she might put a hex on you."

Kurt gave an amused look and eyed J.J. "So you're from Salem, here, are you, Lainie?"

"Yes, I am. Why?"

"No reason. Just clears up a few things," he said genially. *"J.J.!"*

They looked up to see Kisha and Latrice running across the floor toward them, with Elsie and Tyjah in their wake.

"Hey, guys." J.J. hoisted Tyjah up. "Aren't you supposed to be working on your house?"

"I got to ski!" Latrice announced, beaming.

"So did I," Kisha said. "It was so fun. Can we have one of these at the Boys' and Girls' Center? Then we can go ski and stop giving my gran gray hair." She wound her hand around J.J.'s.

Elsie came up behind them, flushing. "Don't you listen to what this child says."

J.J. grinned. "Well, we're hoping to keep your hair brown, Elsie. We'll get you your center, I think."

"Are you going to get it done by the costume parade?" Kisha demanded.

Lainie put a hand on her shoulder. "That's only two weeks away, hon. I don't think even J.J. can build things that fast."

"J.J. can do *anything,*" Kisha said.

"Maybe not that," Lainie replied. "We're having the costume parade at the high school gym."

Kisha wrinkled her nose. "It smells like dirty socks."

Lainie laughed. "You're right, it does. We'll have to try to do something about that."

"What's the costume parade?" J.J. asked. "Do you march?"

"It's a costume contest," Lainie told him. "We used to hold it in the center before it burned down."

"Are you going to be at the costume parade, J.J.?" Latrice asked softly.

"Yeah, you could judge," Kisha said. "You'll pick all the best costumes."

"We shouldn't ask Mr. Cooper to do something like that, Kisha." Lainie studied the girl's shining eyes uneasily. "He'll be over in Europe."

"Where Europe?" Tyjah asked.

"A long way away," Latrice told him with a superior tone. "Too far to come back from."

"I think Mr. Cooper could make it back for Halloween. In fact, I'm sure of it," J.J. said easily.

Madsen gave him a sharp look.

"We'll find judges," Lainie hastened to say. "You need to focus on your racing."

"It's no problem," J.J. assured her. "We can make it another fund-raiser for the center. I can sign autographs. Let me talk to George about flyers."

Her first thought was that it was impossible. But he'd pulled off the benefit, she reminded herself, and she'd thought that was impossible, too.

"I'm going to have the best costume ever, wait and see," Kisha said.

"What are you going to be?"

"It's a secret," she told him, grinning. "You'll see at Halloween."

Lainie cleared her throat. "Isn't that going to be a problem with your schedule?"

J.J. shrugged. "Relax. After Sölden, we get three weeks off before things start up for real."

"Doug's probably going to want you to stick in Innsbruck," Madsen murmured.

"I can deal with Doug," J.J. told him and kissed Lainie. "Don't worry. I'll ski Sölden, come home for your festival and costume parade, and then head out. It'll be cool."

Chapter Thirteen

The first practice run was always the most important part of race preparation. Sure, J.J. knew the mountain, he'd been skiing it for most of the decade and a half he'd been on the circuit. Year to year, though, subtle changes took place. The first practice run was where he figured them out. The first practice run was where he found his line.

When he got the nod, he pushed out of the starting gate at a measured pace. This one wasn't about time, it was about reconnaissance, looking for any new idiosyncrasies that he needed to take into account. There would be time for break-neck speed later; now he needed to relearn the course.

If downhill was all about speed, and slalom was about weaving through the pattern of gates, then giant slalom was a hybrid of the two—part speed, part technical skill. The giant slalom morphed the frenetic rhythm of traditional slalom into a more measured oscillation—if anything that happened at sixty-plus miles an hour could be called measured. It started out like a downhill, then whipped between a series of fifty or so gates separated by a hundred or more feet.

In any kind of slalom, the skier was at war with the course designer. The fastest way down the mountain was a straight line. Slalom gates forced the skier off that straight line. The challenge became getting down as quickly as possible while weaving back and forth; the straighter the line, the shorter the time.

That made giant slalom and its steeper sibling the super-G, in particular, a delicate balancing act. Skis went fastest when they were floating flat on the snow, minimizing friction. Straightening the course required digging in the edges of the skis to carve a tight line around the gates, though. But not too tight—unlike slalom, where the gates consisted of single poles that a skier could ski practically on top of and knock out of the way with his shins, giant slalom used double-poled gates. With two poles jammed close together in the snow and bound by a wide swatch of plastic, a giant slalom gate could rip you right off your feet if you got too cute. Mildly embarrassing, potentially hazardous and guaranteed to tick off the coaching staff.

Racing giant slalom became a process of finding the float, finding the edge, finding the float, finding the opposite edge, getting close to the gate but not too close, pitching your body for the turns and staying in your tuck the rest of the time.

And doing all of it faster than the competition.

All in all, a satisfying challenge, and one J.J. excelled at. Sölden had been good to him over the years. He'd taken second in the season opener the year before. This time around, though, second wasn't going to be good enough. This time around he had something to prove.

This year, he was going to win it.

* * *

"Weren't you just in here?" George stared at Lainie over the counter of Cool Beans.

"An hour and a half ago."

"And that's not enough for you?"

"The coffeemaker at work is broken. Come on, George, baby, I need my fix," she begged. "I'm hurting bad."

"Hmmph. 'Fix' is right. You had an extra large this morning with a shot of espresso. That should have lasted you all day."

"It's a nutritional thing. I have a caffeine deficiency."

"A caffeine deficiency?"

She gave him a bland look. "Caffeine's an essential nutrient."

"Do tell."

"At least it is for me. I'm ordering stock for the store. Come on, George, you don't want me to order sixty cases of witch museum tilt pens just because I'm half asleep, do you?"

"Tilt pens?"

"You know, the ones you tip up and down that show the witch being dunked in the well."

He eyed her. "Sixty cases?"

"It'll be on your conscience."

He shook his head and turned to the coffee machine just as bell at the front door jingled.

"There you are."

Lainie turned to see Caro, who was practically vibrating with suppressed excitement.

"Hey, Caro, what's up?"

"I got it!"

"Oh my God, the job? You got an offer? When?"

"Yesterday, when I was out. We spent the whole day negotiating price and they just faxed the official offer." She danced a little jig. "I'm going to Manhattan!"

Lainie threw her arms around her. "Oh, Caro, that's amazing. I'm so happy for you."

"I can't believe it. It's like it just dropped into my lap."

"It didn't drop into your lap. You worked for it and made it happen."

Caro drew back and studied her. "Speaking of making it—"

The front door jingled and they both turned to see a group of their colleagues coming in.

"Look, I'll tell you all about it later. How about dinner?"

"You know it. My treat."

Caro shook her head. "No way. This treat's mine."

"Number nineteen, Hermann Leipzig, Austria."

There was a cheer from the crowd, and flashbulbs popped. The bib selection party at a World Cup race was a major event. It was like a whole different world from the U.S.

In Europe, especially in Austria, World Cup skiing was a mania. Being a racer was the equivalent of being an NBA star in the United States. The fans were everywhere, the media was relentless. In the U.S., J.J. could walk through airports or down the street without being noticed too much. In Austria or Switzerland, every few feet, it seemed, someone asked for an autograph.

It was almost enough to go to a guy's head, and maybe it had for him early on. Of course, all he'd needed to do for a dose of reality was fly back home. Lainie, for one, always made sure she punctured any lingering bubbles of self-importance he'd had.

Lainie. It seemed so incongruous to think that his tart-tongued sparring partner was now the warm, silky woman in his bed. Gabe's cousin, the one he couldn't charm, the one who challenged him head to head. Well, she still challenged him, but now in a different way.

And he was damned if he knew what to do about it.

He missed her, suddenly, with an almost physical ache.

The skiing felt right to him, never better. He loved it, loved flying down the mountain, beating the hell out of his muscles with run after run. It was the nights that were the hardest. It was in the evenings, when the women crowded around, that the life in Salem that had started making sense to him seemed so strange and faraway. That was when he wasn't exactly sure how he fit in his own skin.

But he couldn't worry about that now. He was here and had a race to win. A whole series of races.

"Number twenty, J. J. Cooper, U.S."

The perfect spot. The course would be swept clean of loose snow by the early skiers but not too choppy. He resisted the urge to pump his fist. Instead he walked out on the stage amid cheers. The bib girl, a ravishing blonde with knife-edged cheekbones, took her time sliding it over his head.

"Good luck."

"Thanks, I need it."

"I do not think so. Perhaps I will be here to help you celebrate," she said and gave him a heavy-lidded smile of promise.

Flashbulbs snapped. J.J. gave her a brief, noncommittal nod and turned to walk off the dais. Even a half year before, he would have taken her up on her invitation in a heartbeat.

He liked to think he was finally getting smarter. He needed to focus on his job, not on accidental encounters.

And not on what he'd left back home.

In the front row, a fresh-faced beauty who couldn't have

been more than sixteen flashed him a smile along with her cleavage. J.J. blinked in disbelief.

On her forehead, in marker, was written "I love you, J.J."

Definitely a different world.

Lainie gave a dubious glance at the five-inch balloon of the wineglass. "You ever notice how the larger the wine-glasses get, the smaller the amount of wine they put in them? What's up with that? Do they think we won't notice?"

"Maybe they figure you'll be too intimidated to say anything."

Lainie snorted. "As if." She raised her glass. "To the Museum of Antiquities and Caro Lewis, the best boss in the world."

Caro made a mock frown. "I'd rather be known as the best friend in the world."

"That, too." Lainie tapped her glass against Caro's. "To Caro Lewis, best in show."

"Now there we go." Caro sipped and then raised her glass again. "To Lainie Trask, great friend, great assistant curator." She tapped her glass against Lainie's. "And currently a woman with a decision to make about her life."

Lainie swallowed her mouthful of wine and shook her head. "I don't want to talk about J.J. tonight, okay? Off-limits."

"Who's talking about J.J.?" Interest sparked in Caro's eyes.

Lainie flushed. "It's nothing."

"It doesn't sound like nothing if you're connecting J.J. with decisions about your life. Did something happen?"

"No," she mumbled. "He's just gone back to Europe to start racing."

"Ah."

"Yeah, ah."

"What does he say about it?"

"That he's only going to be gone for a week, that he'll be back and stay until mid-November."

"And then he's gone for good."

"Yeah. For good." Lainie lapsed into silence, staring moodily at her wine.

"You weren't expecting anything else, right?" Caro asked carefully. "Wasn't that what you told me?"

"Sure. It's just been fun while it's lasted."

"Well, does it have to end just because he leaves? Can't you keep going?"

"I suppose. He says he wants to, but things will be different once he gets over there. I can't see how it won't. I mean, he's the big celebrity, everybody wants a piece of him. Maybe he's not even the same person as he is here. And we'd never see each other."

"You could go there," Caro pointed out. "Just think, you might wind up on the cover of a European tabloid. J. J. Cooper's latest squeeze."

Lainie snorted. "My life's ambition. Besides, it costs a lot of money to get over there."

"And I suppose you wouldn't want Mr. Megabucks to pick it up."

"Would you?" She raked her hair back with both hands and stared at Caro. "He asked me to quit my job, travel with him for the season."

Caro's eyes went round. "Seriously? Wow. You'd see some great places. You'd love Europe."

"Come on." Her voice was impatient. "Are you going to tell me even for a minute that you'd quit your job and let some guy keep you? Even if I were married to the guy, I couldn't do that. And we're not married. I don't know what we are," she muttered.

"It would be a risk."

"There are risks and then there's just foolhardy. There's no way a relationship could possibly work under that kind of pressure. That's not fair to either of us."

"You're probably right," Caro admitted. "It's not possible, but it's still a fun thought."

"I don't think I can handle any more fun right now," Lainie said.

Caro twirled her wineglass thoughtfully. "He might have really changed. People do, you know."

"It's true, they do. And I hope he's one of them, but I just don't know." She sighed.

"So where are things now?"

"Day by day." She took a breath. "I haven't told him yet but if I can scrape together the money, I think I might go over for one of his races, see what it's like. See what *he's* like when he's not here." Saying the words made it all more real. She felt as if she were balanced on the edge of a cliff, preparing to leap out into the void with only a fragile pair of wings to sustain her. If it worked, it would be exhilarating beyond her wildest dreams.

If it didn't…

Lainie gave her head a shake. "Enough talk about J.J. Tell me about your hot new job. When do you go?"

"A month, probably. Maybe longer," Caro said. "I need to give the folks here enough time to find a replacement. And I need to hire an assistant at the new job. I don't suppose you'd be interested, would you?"

"What?" Lainie asked faintly.

"They're letting me bring on an assistant curator." Caro's eyes brightened in excitement. "I told them about you. I have to do due diligence and interview several candidates, but they've given me the authority to hire you if you want to come on board."

"Me?" Lainie squeaked. "To Manhattan?" Living in a city. *The* city. A chance to live the glamour life she'd always dreamed of. "You know my degree's in fine arts, right? I'm not trained in antiquities," she felt duty-bound to point out.

"That's all right. We'd be working under my friend Julia, the head curator. Our job would be logistics, coordinating exhibits, that sort of thing. You're perfect for it. We work so well together, I can't imagine working with someone else."

Manhattan, Lainie thought as it sank in. To live at the hub of the universe. She wouldn't be traveling Europe like J.J., but she'd be doing something, finally.

"Now, you don't have to decide right away," Caro cautioned. "Think it over for a week. Decide if it's right. If it's not and you want to stay here, I'll recommend that the board consider you for my position." Her sunburst smile broke out. "But I'm hoping you'll jump ship with me."

From small town to big life. From a limited job to one that could really take her somewhere. A chance to live her dreams.

With or without J.J.

J.J. stood and watched the World Cup official inspect his skis, checking the length, the materials. Next to him, Martin, the rep from his ski sponsor, hovered protectively. Ski reps were the racing equivalent of golf caddies—indispensable to the success of a skier. They persuaded their companies to develop the custom skis that a racer needed, and J.J. was more demanding than most. If there was a reason outside of luck and bloody-minded determination that J.J. was on top, it was Martin.

"Not so rough," Martin muttered in his Danish-accented English, watching the two strips of laminate as though they were his children. Martin guarded J.J.'s skis jealously, turning them over to the technicians to wax and maintain, shepherding them through the race process, handing them off to J.J. at each race proudly and almost reluctantly.

And sometimes dolefully collecting them splintered and delaminated at the end.

The official gave a decisive nod. *"Ja,"* he said shortly. "Is good."

Like an overprotective mother, Martin leaned in to gather the skis to him. "So. I will meet you at the start house," he said briskly as he zipped them back into their carrier.

"Oh, I can get them," J.J. said for the sport of it, reaching for the handles.

Martin snatched them away. "Hands off, barbarian. You would bang them around. Worry about skiing and—how you say? Leave the rough stuff to me?"

J.J. grinned. "And leave the rough stuff to you."

Chapter Fourteen

Lainie couldn't believe she was spending a perfectly beautiful Saturday morning watching television. Actually, she wasn't so much watching television as presiding over a meeting of the Salem chapter of the J. J. Cooper Fan Club. Elsie and her family, George and his wife and daughters, the collection of people sprawled around her living room, nibbling on chips and waiting for the show.

"It's starting," Kisha whispered to Latrice. The three kids sat on pillows on the floor, squirming impatiently.

Catchy theme music came on and the camera panned over a snow-covered mountain and a timbered village so quaint that Lainie almost expected to see Heidi and her goats come walking by.

"Welcome to Sölden, Austria, and the kickoff event of the 2006-2007 World Cup season," said the voiceover. A commentator appeared in a heavy coat and toothy grin. "I'm Bill

Reynolds, here with former World Cup racer John Carstairs."
He turned to a younger guy standing next to him in a parka.
"This is the start of an exciting year, isn't it, John?"

Whereas Reynolds had the fleshy look of a football hero
gone to seed, Carstairs appeared wiry and lean, even
bundled into a ski jacket. "That's right, Bill. World Cup is
really the peak of ski racing. The Olympics are kind of like
baseball's All-Star game—they get a lot of attention but
they don't count like the World Cup season. The racers
who win medals at the World Cup championships—or
better yet, win the World Cup overall title—are at the top
of their sport."

"And we've got J. J. Cooper coming in fresh off Olympic
gold last spring and second in the World Cup overall last
year," Reynolds said, "so he'll be the one to beat."

Suddenly the screen changed to show J.J. stretching, up
on the mountain. A cheer went up from the people in the
room. "Knock 'em dead, J.J.," George called.

The sight of J.J.'s face hit Lainie with an almost physical
impact—the blue of his eyes, the taut line of his jaw, the sharp
focus of concentration in his expression. The easygoing beach
boy was gone, replaced by the gladiator. His speed suit
showed the rock-hard swell of quad, bicep, deltoid, as though
he'd been stripped down to muscle and sinew. The machin-
ery of a winner.

"Speaking of Cooper, he's looking stronger than ever."

"You got that right," Carstairs said. "He missed some of
his summer training because of a shoulder injury, but if his
practice times are any indication, it didn't slow him down."

The network guy glanced down at his notes. "He's got a
reputation as a racer who enjoys the parties and his personal
life as much as he enjoys racing. Do you think it's a
problem?"

Carstairs grinned. "It hasn't been so far."

"But he's thirty-three now and he won't recover from the nightlife like he once did. Is age a factor?"

"It can be," Carstairs admitted. "Most racers, downhill racers especially, are done by thirty."

"You retired at twenty-seven, didn't you?"

"Correct. J.J.'s in superb physical condition, but it's got to be catching up with him, and Hermann's been logging phenomenal times in practice."

George put his hands around his mouth. "Go home, Hermann," he yelled in high good humor.

"Yeah, go home, Hermann," Kisha added enthusiastically.

Lainie closed her eyes briefly.

"That's the Austrian, Hermann Leipzig, also known as the Exterminator," the network guy said. "He took third place in the World Cup overall last year, right on Cooper's heels. Outside of Cooper, he's one of the few racers who does all five events, right John?"

"Right. Most racers either choose the speed events, like downhill, or the technical events, like slalom and giant slalom. The fact that these two race both just tells you how amazingly talented they are."

"Which one's better?"

"Hermann's a force of nature," Carstairs said admiringly.

"And he's six years younger."

"And he's six years younger, but J.J.'s got six more years of experience on every mountain in the circuit going for him. He knows Sölden like the back of his hand."

"So who do you like for it?"

Carstairs broke into laughter. "You aren't going to get an answer out of me. I'm going to let the mountain decide."

"It's gonna be J.J.," George said. He started clapping and the kids joined in. "J.J., J.J., J.J., J.J."

* * *

J.J. stood in the start house, listening to the grunts and thuds of Hermann Leipzig psyching himself up for the run. Everybody had their own method, and the stocky Austrian's was noisier than most. Actually, J.J. had skied directly before or after Hermann so many times that the noise actually triggered his own race mentality. Pavlov's dog, or, rather, Pavlov's ski racer.

J.J. took a breath and closed his eyes, relaxing. Some racers focused, stringing themselves up tight as a wire. He preferred to be as loose as possible and rely on all the practice and groundwork he'd put in. He put his faith in muscle memory, the fact that once he got skiing, his body knew what to do before he commanded it.

He knew the course. He'd trained exhaustively earlier in the week, he'd inspected it again that morning. His skis were tuned, he was ready. And when he stepped into the gate at the start house, conditioning would take over and he'd be as focused on the course as he knew how to be.

The pips sounded, and with a roar, Hermann pushed out onto the course.

Applause and the flat clatter of cowbells sounded further down the course. Up at the start house now, all was quiet. J.J. stepped into place at the gate and let out a long breath, imagining the course, imagining how he'd ski each foot of it. He knew where he was going. He knew what he had to do around each gate.

Then the first pip sounded and *wham,* he brought it all back to the snow before skis.

It made her think of a spring uncoiling. One instant J.J. was motionless, the next he was exploding out of the start gate, slamming his poles into the ground, pushing off with his skis, getting every bit of speed possible before he sank down fluidly into his tuck.

The room around Lainie erupted in cheers and clapping.

It was a grade she'd be nervous about walking down and he shot down it fearlessly, doing his best to go faster, crouched the way she'd seen him practice so many times. Now it was the real thing. Now he was using the muscles he'd trained in all the brutal hours of conditioning. Now he was doing what he was meant to do.

He whipped into a turn, his whole body slanted nearly horizontal against the slope of the mountain, his edges digging in. She could see his legs shake, see the skis bend and flop with the force of his passage, and yet he looked somehow perfectly relaxed, at home.

And plastered across his face was an exuberant grin.

"We know that Hermann's time is the one to beat."

"That's true, but wow, J.J.'s looking good," Carstairs said enthusiastically. "Look how he came off that jump and found his line right away. I think he's going to at least keep up with Hermann."

"We'll know when we see the split time coming up. We'll be able to see if—"

"Look at that split!" Carstairs' voice rose. "Four tenths of a second ahead. That's *huge*."

George whistled.

On the screen, J.J. flew down the course, rhythmically carving his way from gate to gate.

"He's got a different style from Leipzig," Reynolds said.

"Absolutely. You can see it in the way he's skiing. Hermann's very mechanical, very technical. J.J.'s like a savant. He's just got this natural feel for the course. Oh, *wow!*"

Lainie caught her breath as J.J. cut too close to a gate and smacked it with his shoulder.

"See," Carstairs was saying, "that would have spelled disaster for most guys, out of the race, but J.J. just comes back. He is such a gifted athlete."

"He's lost time, though. He's behind Leipzig, and even Anders in third."

"It's not over yet," Carstairs said excitedly, abandoning his pose of neutrality. "Watch him, he's carving his line perfectly. That is so clean."

"Come on, J.J.," George bellowed.

Lainie's fingernails were embedded in her palms but she didn't notice. All she could do was stare at the screen, at the black square of the clock where the numbers ran up alarmingly quickly. All she could do was watch, willing J.J. to win.

"This is perfect technical skiing. Look at him, he's gaining back time." Carstairs' voice rose.

"But does he have enough of the course left?" The commentator echoed Lainie's thoughts.

On the screen J.J. whipped through the final curve of the course and drew down into the tuck he'd perfected so fanatically. The clock raced along, nearing Leipzig's time, nearing it.

And stopping abruptly as J.J. flashed over the finish line.

Lainie jumped up, whooping. Her living room was bedlam, full of cheering, clapping, whistling.

"He did it!" Carstairs' voice was jubilant. "He beat Hermann!"

On the screen, J.J. was slowing abruptly as he skied in an arc around the apron at the bottom of the course, hands down, standing as casually as though he were at a bar, waiting for a drink, not skiing along at maybe thirty miles an hour. He pushed up his goggles, looking for the clock.

She could see the moment his time registered, see the flash of uncomplicated joy on his face.

Excitement bubbled through her. He'd shown them all, everyone who said he was too old to compete. He'd come back from injury and triumphed.

"Let's go down to Bonnie Plummer, who's with our winner. Bonnie?"

"Thanks, Bill." A perky redhead in a green woolly cap stood beaming next to J.J. "I'm here with J. J. Cooper, who just came back from the edge of disaster to take the race from Hermann Leipzig. J.J., what were you thinking about in the last half of that run, after you had trouble?"

He looked, Lainie thought, like someone had plugged him into a wall socket, crackling with energy, eyes almost incandescently blue. "I don't know, you don't really think. Not when it's like that. When it goes like that, you're not thinking, you're just doing."

"In the zone?"

He gave a manic laugh she'd never heard before. "Yeah, in the zone."

"How do you feel about this year?"

"Like I want a lot more days like this." Someone handed him a glass of champagne and he drained half of it in a swallow.

"What about the future? You won the downhill gold at the Olympics and second overall in last year's World Cup, but you're already several years past typical retirement age. What happens next?"

He laughed at her as though she were a circus clown. "I'm thinking about right now. Who cares about the future? Right now, I feel like I could ski forever."

"And you look like it, too. Congratulations, J.J. Back to you, Bill."

The camera panned to the awards dais, where officials were announcing the winners. A blond Valkyrie draped the medals about the neck of each racer, giving a cursory air kiss over each cheek after she did. Leipzig looked distinctly grumpy, Lainie noticed.

Then they announced J.J.'s name and the crowd went crazy, cheering, ringing their cowbells and blowing horns. J.J. walked across the podium grinning, both hands in the air. There was something about him, that same otherworldly spark that celebrities had. And in that life, that continent, he was a celebrity. She'd always known it at some level, but she'd never really understood it until now.

On the dais, the trophy girl put the medal around his neck. And instead of giving him the air kisses, she pressed her mouth to his.

Hard.

The air went out of Lainie's lungs in a whoosh. The crowd erupted in even more noise, if that were possible.

Her living room went dead silent.

When J.J. stepped back, he raised his hands in the air again, the bouquet of flowers in one hand.

George cleared his throat. "Now there's a job," he said in a falsely hearty voice. "Women grabbing you and kissing you."

"Hush," Amanda, his wife, hissed, elbowing him.

Lainie leaned back on the sofa, fighting to catch her breath, fighting to act like everything was normal. It wasn't the woman, she didn't think. It was clear that he'd been surprised by the kiss. Whatever else he was, J.J. was honorable. She didn't think he'd hit the Continent and just started catting around, not while they were ostensibly involved. It wasn't that that was upsetting her, she didn't think.

Because she was upset, she couldn't deny it. "Anybody want more chips?" she asked, and rose to walk to the kitchen.

Once there, she stared out into the street. It was just seeing him in this totally different environment, seeing him be someone else, someone very far away from her, and not just in the sense of miles. It was a life that had nothing to do with anything she knew…where goddesses kissed him on the lips. Nothing to do with the way she lived.

His life centered around working unimaginably hard—and playing hard when he wasn't. There was no room for anything else, especially for a guy like J.J., who was at a place where he needed every bit of effort he could bring to bear on his training to keep himself at peak. This was a J.J. she could admire. This was a J.J. who lived in a world that had no room for her.

It was ridiculous to feel jealous, she told herself. It wasn't the kiss—although it was a *long* kiss, okay, from a ten-foot-tall blonde with cheekbones that could cut diamond. It was…everything. Without being conscious of it, she began to pace. It wasn't the kiss—but it was the kiss. It probably happened to him a lot. He inhabited a world that was foreign, and not just because it was on a different continent and three thousand miles away.

It was more like a million miles away. There was no way her life could keep up, no way anything she had to offer could possibly be big enough. And she was an idiot to ever think that what was between them could be more than a passing fling.

She heard a cell phone ring, out in the living room.

"Hey, Lainie, I think this is you," George called.

She walked out to get it, flipping it open. "Hello?"

"Lainie?" It was J.J., talking amid cacophony. "Hey, sweet girl, how are you?"

And how was it that despite everything she was feeling, hearing those words from him could still make her melt? "Congratulations."

"Thanks."

"We saw it all on TV. You were amazing."

Someone whooped near the phone and she heard J.J. grunt. "What?"

"I said you were amazing. You almost went down and it didn't even faze you."

"Hey, you gotta put it out there if you want to win," he said, in the same singsong tone he'd used with the television interviewer. From somewhere nearby him, Lainie heard the sound of a cork popping. "How are you?"

"I'm doing fine. Everybody was rooting you on today." Behind her, George and the kids stomped and cheered.

"Great. Hey, I'll take some of that," he said to someone in the background, and broke out into laughter.

"Everyone misses you here." She paused. "I do, too."

"Hey, what'd you say, babe? This connection really sucks. I'm not getting you at all."

She was very afraid that was exactly the problem. "Look, I'll let you go celebrate. Call me when you get back."

"Look, how about if I call you when I get back?" he said. "Maybe then we'll get a better connection."

Maybe then, Lainie thought as she hung up.

Chapter Fifteen

The wheels of the plane hit the ground with a jolt.

"Ladies and gentlemen, we'd like to welcome you to Boston." The voice of the flight attendant came over the intercom. "We will be taxiing for the next several minutes, so please remain seated with your seat belts securely fastened until we are at the gate."

Boston. J.J. stared out the window, across the blue glow of the runway markers to where the terminal blazed light. Boston had always meant he was back in the United States, but it had never felt like home before. Home had always been another hop up to the Montpelier airport; Boston was just a way station. Somehow, though, this time it was different. This time Boston meant Lainie.

It had been two days since he'd talked with her. Too long, way too long. Of course, it had been his fault. He'd forgotten how frenetic and insular the World Cup atmosphere could be. Between time zone differences and the packed schedule, it was like being sucked into an alternate universe. Communicating with the outside world was strange; reentry was usually stranger, a combination of jet lag, physical exhaustion and social burnout. Somehow, he always felt like he was coming back from farther away than just another continent. It felt more like coming back from another planet.

Of course, this time around, he'd felt that same sense of dissociation when he'd landed in Innsbruck. Nothing in Sölden had felt quite right, either. Sure, he'd gone to a party or two, but mostly he'd spent the time waiting to leave. It had felt familiar and yet somehow wrong, like walking through his old elementary school.

The only thing he was sure of was that he missed Lainie. He missed the sound of her voice. He missed the feel of her against him.

He missed her.

At the front of the cabin, a curvy dark-haired flight attendant beamed at him from her jump seat. J.J. just waited for the ping that indicated the plane was well and truly stopped. The instant it sounded, he was on his feet, pulling his duffel from the overhead bin and moving forward to the exit door.

The flight attendant rose. "Congratulations again on your race, Mr. Cooper. Are you visiting or do you live here?"

"It's home," he answered, shifting impatiently.

"I hear it's a fun town. I've only ever been here on layover. I bet a guy like you knows all the best places to go."

It took him a minute to recognize the nature of the smile she gave him, the interest that lingered in her eyes. He blinked as the door went up. Things really had changed, he realized. There had been a time not so long before that he'd looked at every flight as an opportunity to enhance his social life.

Now all he found himself thinking about was Lainie. He

glanced at his watch. In forty-five minutes he'd be in Salem. In fifty, he planned to have her in his arms.

"Enjoy the city," he said to the flight attendant and vaulted out into the Jetway, focused, as always, on speed.

Lainie stood in a lamplit street in the old quarter of Salem, a flickering lantern in her hand. She wore a long grayish-tan skirt with the traditional white apron and cuffs of the puritan costume, a cloak slung over her shoulders. Her hair was braided into a demure twist on her head and covered in a mobcap.

She'd always loved doing the ghost walks, but this time around it was hard to muster up much enthusiasm for it. She hadn't really felt right all day. If she were honest, she hadn't been feeling right since the last time she'd talked to J.J., two days before.

She felt so distant from him, and it wasn't just that it had been a week and a half since they'd seen each other. Things felt off, with no way to fix them.

And under all of the uncertainty, she missed him fiercely.

For now, though, she had a job to do, she reminded herself, turning to give the tour group a smile.

"Our next stop is Templeton House. In 1710, Isaiah Templeton, a widowed merchant, lived in this house with his daughter, Hannah. Isaiah had lost his wife at Hannah's birth, so he was highly protective of her, especially when it came to any men who might take her away from him.

"And then one afternoon, she came down to bring Isaiah a message at the wharves and ran into a dashing young sea captain, Abel Vance. Hannah and Abel fell in love, nearly at first sight, or so their letters show," Lainie said, warming to her tale. "Soon after, Vance asked Isaiah for her hand.

"But Isaiah wasn't about to let his daughter marry a sailor, a man who would take her far away from Salem. So Hannah and Vance made plans to steal away and marry. A storm came up on the night they were supposed to leave, though. A falling tree limb woke Isaiah so that he overheard Hannah tiptoeing down the stairs. And he guessed what was going on. He pulled out his pistol and locked her in her bedroom, and went in a fury to find Vance.

"The young captain was standing at the wharf where he'd promised to meet Hannah. Historical records show it was pouring that night. Vance would have been drenched, barely able to see through the sheeting rain when Isaiah walked up to him and put a musket ball in his heart. A sailor who saw it said Vance dropped like a stone."

Lainie raised the lantern and led the group around the side of the house, where windows and a widow's walk looked out over the harbor. "Then Isaiah turned to go back home, but all that was waiting for him was heartbreak. Hannah had tried to escape to warn her lover, you see."

Lainie pointed to the slate-blue house. "Look at the upper window. Hannah had opened it. They think she was trying to climb from the parapet outside to the widow's walk, maybe hoping to escape to warn Vance. But between the rain and the wind, she slipped and fell to her death in the courtyard. And Isaiah found her there, bloody and broken."

Lainie raised her lantern so that it cast light over the front of the house. "People say that during a full moon, you can sometimes see a woman in the window. And if it is very, very quiet, you can hear a man sobbing in the courtyard when you pass by."

Lainie turned back to the tour. "And now, it's time to—" The words stopped in her throat. At the back of the pack of people stood J.J., hands jammed in his pockets, eyes silvery in the moonlight.

And adrenaline vaulted through her system.

He was here, just feet away, wearing that special smile that was just for her. He was J.J., not the ski racer on the TV. She stared at him, drinking him in.

The need to touch him was almost unendurable.

Lainie knew she finished the tour because they walked up to the wrought iron gates of the witchcraft museum courtyard, but she didn't remember a moment of it. She must have told the stories, because people smiled and nodded, but she hadn't a clue. All she could concentrate on was J.J. All she could think about was him. After all the miles, all the days apart, he was here. And all she could do was want him.

The hairs on the back of her neck prickling with awareness, Lainie led the way into the courtyard. "Well, that's our tour." She turned to smile at the group, her heart hammering. "Thank you for joining us. There's hot cider inside the museum if you'd like to go in and warm up."

Normally, she'd go in and socialize with the people from the tour, help the staff hand out cider and cookies.

Not tonight. She'd waited as long as she could. She wasn't about to wait any longer. Expectantly, she turned to scan the courtyard. For a panicked moment she didn't see J.J.; then she caught sight of him standing outside the gates. She walked over, conscious of every muscle and tendon moving in her body. She intended to say something casual, to play it cool. She saw the crooked smile on his lips.

And the next thing she knew, she was in his arms, her mouth fused to his.

Touch morphed into heat, heat morphed into hunger. Through the alchemy of desire, they were no longer J.J. and Lainie, but something together. And all the uncertainty she'd felt for days dissolved in the hard reality of his touch.

It wasn't fair that it felt so right. It wasn't fair that even as she was losing him to his real life, she found herself needing him more and more. She knew how far apart they were, but it couldn't stop her from responding to him. It couldn't stop her from wanting.

She pressed herself closer to him and sighed. "It's good to see you," she murmured.

"It's good to feel you," he replied.

She laughed. "When did you get in?"

"Oh, about forty-five minutes ago."

"To your house?"

"To Boston." He slipped his hands beneath her cloak. "I came straight here."

She caught a breath. "Lucky me."

"No," he said, his lips hovering a hairsbreadth from hers, "Lucky me."

"I'd have put down a couple of hundred bucks against you knowing how to turn on the stove, let alone cook," Lainie mused as she stood behind J.J. and watched him stir eggs in a skillet.

A pair of sweatpants hung low on his hips as he stood at the stove. "I'm not sure that scrambling eggs counts as cooking, but I'll take the hundred bucks in trade, as long as it winds up being some sort of sexual favor."

"You haven't had enough?"

He turned and swept her to him. One minute she was blinking in surprise, the next he was kissing her thoroughly, his hands roving over her until her knees dissolved into water. "Does this feel like I've had enough?"

"I guess not."

"Dinner first, round two after."

"I think we're more like up to round five or six. And can you call it dinner when it's 2:00 a.m.?"

He divided the eggs onto two plates and added toast. "I can

call it anything I want. I'm cooking. Besides, it's dinnertime somewhere in the world."

"Hawaii, maybe."

"I'll add pineapple." He picked up the plates. "Into the living room, it's more comfortable. So what's been going on? I tried to catch you yesterday but I kept getting your voice mail."

"I went to see my parents in Burlington."

"I didn't know you were going up there."

"It was a spur-of-the-moment thing." Because she had to get out of town, away from thoughts of J.J. "You must be excited about how the race went."

"It was a sweet win. I've been waiting on it for a while." He handed her a plate.

"Back in the saddle, so to speak?"

"We'll see how the season goes. I felt strong out there, but it's the first downhill that'll really show where things are."

"So, what…giant slalom is an old man's sport?"

"Easier than downhill, anyway."

"Isn't almost everything?" She forked up a bite of eggs.

He hesitated. "What did you think of the race?"

"We had fun watching."

He shot her a look. "We?"

"Elsie and the kids and George and his family came over," she said, her voice elaborately casual. "Didn't I tell you?"

J.J. closed his eyes briefly. "So, I guess you saw the awards ceremony."

"Part of it."

Better to tackle it now, he thought, no matter if she'd seen it or no. There was nothing to be gained by keeping his mouth shut. "The part where the trophy girl planted one on me, that part?"

"Yeah." She looked at him. "That part."

"It probably looked bad. It was just something that happened. It didn't mean anything. You should know that."

"I didn't figure it did." She looked down at her plate a moment. "It bugged me. I know it shouldn't have, but it did."

"I kind of thought it might, especially with everyone watching."

"I don't care about people watching. I only care about you and me."

"Nothing happened," he said.

"I know," she told him. "It was just hard. It was like you were some celebrity I didn't even know." She shook her head. "One of those things that goes with the territory, I guess."

That made him angry. "What territory, mine?"

"Mine, in getting involved in this—" she moved her shoulders "—whatever it is." She rose, carrying the plate, and headed for the kitchen.

"Lainie." He caught up with her. "Nothing happened. I didn't ask for it."

"I know. I believe you." And it was driving her crazy that she couldn't make it stop bothering her. "But that's kind of beside the point, isn't it?"

"What is the point?"

She stared stubbornly at the worn linoleum on the floor. J.J. reached out and tipped her chin up so that she had to meet his eyes.

"It's the lifestyle you lead," she said. "You're in the spotlight. It's wilder than here, I know. I just wasn't expecting the whole kiss thing. Or how it made me feel." She spoke slowly, choosing each word with exaggerated care. "It caught me by surprise."

"You know, I thought about you over there. A lot."

"J.J., you don't have to throw me a bone to make me feel important." Her reply was impatient. "It was just a little weird, that's all. Nothing I won't survive, nothing that I'm blaming you for."

"Then why do I feel like it?"

She leaned against the kitchen counter and gave him a steady look. "It wasn't the kiss. Well, maybe it was. I didn't like it. I didn't like it at all. But that's part of your life, just like the women they showed with your name written on their foreheads. You live in a world where stuff like that happens."

"Only sometimes. Less often than you'd think."

"But often enough." She bit her lip. "I looked into tickets, before the race," she blurted.

He stared at her. "Did you buy any?"

"Not yet."

He tried to imagine what it would be like, waking up with her, getting a kiss for luck before the race. What would it be like, flying down the mountain to her, knowing she was there, waiting at the bottom? His feeling that parts of his life weren't meshing anymore would finally abate. He caught at her hands. "Come over. I really want you there."

She swallowed. "I'll try."

"Don't try, do it."

"I will. Just maybe not right away. I might be starting a new job soon. Moving takes money and time."

"Whoa, back up," he ordered. "Moving? You have a new job?"

"Might," she clarified. "Caro offered me a job in Manhattan."

J.J. blinked. "Caro, your boss?"

"She just got a job at the Museum of Antiquities there. She's allowed to hire an assistant. She wants it to be me."

"Excellent! Congratulations. Although you don't sound all that happy about it."

Lainie hesitated. "I should be. Living in Manhattan, working at a world-class museum…it's what I've always wanted."

"But maybe not what you want now?"

She turned back to the living room. "It's a way to move

up. I'd be in a better job, making more money and living in a city, finally. *The* city."

"I keep hearing a *but* in everything you say."

"I don't know if there's a *but,*" she flared. "If I'm smart, I'll take it."

He nodded. "Have you told anybody here yet?"

"Not yet. Caro just asked me last week. I said I'd let her know by Friday. She says if I don't take it, she'll recommend me as her replacement when she gives notice next week."

"So either way you win."

"Maybe. No guarantees. If I stay here, they may still decide to hire from outside, no matter what Caro says. But I'd be an idiot not to go with Caro." She paced across the room.

"When would you leave?"

"I don't know. A month, maybe."

He drummed his fingers on his thigh. "It won't be the same," he said abruptly.

Lainie turned to look at him. "What do you mean?"

"You not being here. It won't be the same."

She snorted. "Why do you care? You'll be long gone."

"I won't be gone. I'll just be away."

"Away? That's not gone?"

"Gone is permanent. Away is just being out of town for business."

"A seven-month business trip?"

The flicker of humor in her voice gave him hope. "It doesn't matter how long I'm gone. What matters is that home's here."

"Eastmont's still there. Your condo is still up by Gabe's ski lodge. You've always got a home to go to."

"I suppose. Although, you know," he said thoughtfully, "Manhattan could be cool."

Chapter Sixteen

A faint breeze rattled the last of fall's leaves. Overhead, the full moon poured down silver light over the Salem town common and the torches and jack-o'-lanterns of the Halloween Festival. People streamed in from all directions, the children running to the midway rides, or dragging their parents along by the hand.

A couple of teenagers dressed in full Goth regalia wandered by.

J.J. leaned in toward Lainie. "Marilyn Manson has a lot to answer for."

"And I don't even think they're in costume," she said.

"I still say you should have rented the tavern wench outfit."

"You just wanted to see me in a low-cut blouse."

"Guilty as charged." He pulled a strip of red tickets from his pocket. "I got ride passes in case you want to go on the Tunnel of Love and fool around." He leered at her.

"You men. You're all sex maniacs."

"That's not what you said this morning when you put my—"

"There they are," a voice boomed.

Lainie jumped and turned to see George and his wife and daughters headed toward them.

"Well, hey," she said. "Welcome to the festival."

"Nice job, Lainie," George said, looking around. "You really outdid yourself this time."

Music played from outdoor speakers. The mouthwatering scent of fried something-or-other drifted over to them from the food aisle. Opposite them, the crafts booths glittered with silver and gold jewelry, blown glass and dream catchers. Next to where they stood, the fountain was covered with two hundred jack-o'-lanterns. Lainie knew; she'd helped place every one of them.

"Hey, we saw you win your race last weekend," George said to J.J. "Nice going. I guess you're a pretty famous guy."

J.J. winced. "I don't think famous is it," he muttered.

"Congratulations," the eldest daughter, Ginny, said shyly. She'd met J.J. several times before at the Human Habitat site, but she'd never gotten over her awe.

J.J. winked at her. "Pretty easy when everyone else slows down. I just put a little glue on their skis and they stick to the snow."

"You never," she said, but laughed and relaxed.

How did he do it? Lainie wondered. Somehow, he always managed to put people at ease. Charisma, she decided, but it was more than that. There was something genuinely well-intentioned about him. He didn't always manage to execute on those intentions, but he was good where it counted.

"Well, I promised a couple of young ladies that I was

going to take them on the Tilt-A-Whirl and win them pink teddy bears," George said, "so I'd better get to it."

"Knocking over milk cans?" J.J. asked.

George nodded. "I've been practicing my fastball for weeks. I'm thinking of going out for spring training with the Sox."

"Don't hold your breath on that one," Amanda said behind her hand.

"Hush, wife. Show some respect," George grumbled, and herded them all off to the midway, the girls laughing.

"You want me to win you a pink teddy bear?" J.J. asked as they ambled past the game booths.

"Only if you carry it for me."

He eyed her. "You want me to walk around carrying a pink stuffed animal?"

"If you truly cared about me, you'd do it," Lainie told him and leaned in to linger over his mouth. "Pretty please with sugar on top?" she whispered.

Half an hour and thirty bucks later, she was the proud owner of a plush magenta bear with button eyes.

"You could have bought one for less," J.J. grumbled.

"If you'd paid more attention in phys ed, it wouldn't have taken so much to win one."

"Yeah, yeah, yeah. Okay, you got your stuffed animal. What next?"

"Corn dogs," Lainie replied promptly.

"*Corn* dogs?"

"Corn dogs. It's a fair. You have to get a corn dog."

"No wonder you didn't want dinner. Forget the mystery meat. I say we go get a steak."

"How could you think about a restaurant when you could have this?" she demanded, waving a hand at the food aisle. "You've got every option you could want, gyros, lemonade, fried dough, cotton candy… This is America."

"I knew there was a reason I spend so much time in Europe," he muttered.

Ignoring him, Lainie bought two corn dogs at the brightly striped booth and handed him one. "Look, any man who subsists almost entirely on burgers and pizza has no business looking down on a corn dog. Have you ever had one?"

He held his up and inspected it dubiously. "No. I'm happy to keep my streak going. How about if you have both of these and I get a regular hot dog?"

Lainie shook her head briskly and walked over to the condiments. "Take a chance, J.J. Slap some mustard on and try it. If you hate it, I'll eat yours." She squeezed a line of mustard onto the corn dog she held and traded him, then stood watching expectantly.

Grumbling, he took a bite and chewed. And tilted his head consideringly.

"So?" she asked.

"Not bad," he admitted.

"It's better than 'not bad,' and you know it." Lainie pumped mustard onto her corn dog. "God, I look forward to this every year."

"They always have them?"

She looked at him like he had two heads. "Of course. I make sure of it."

"The perks of coordinating the festival?"

"Exactly." She licked some mustard off her dog and caught J.J. watching her. Taking her time, she ran her tongue up the length of the dog and swirled it around the tip. She gave him a bawdy leer. "There are other benefits, as well. Did I mention that corn dogs have a well-known aphrodisiacal effect?"

"It's working on me," he said.

* * *

"Who knew there were so many kids in Salem?" J.J. marveled, looking across the festival grounds at all the costumes.

"You might as well start studying up on what's out there for the costume parade. You've got your basic store-bought model." She pointed at a passing PowerPuff girl. "Or the rentals." She pointed out a boy dressed as SpongeBob, complete with oversize cartoony-looking shoes. "The ones that are really great, though, are the homemade ones." A broad grin spread over her face as she scanned the crowd. "Like this."

"Lainie! J.J.!" Kisha and Latrice ran up with Tyjah.

Tyjah wore a plastic ghoul mask and a diminutive cape. Latrice was dressed as Pocahontas. Kisha, though, was a sight to behold. She wore miniature long underwear, dyed blue-black, with a white bib tied over the top. Dangling around her neck was a ribbon with a circle of cardboard, spray-painted gold.

"Great costume," J.J. said, grinning broadly.

"I'm you." Kisha proclaimed.

J.J. handed the stuffed animal to Lainie and swept Kisha up. "You're better than me."

"Elsie, you outdid yourself," Lainie said.

"Girl wouldn't stop talking about it. Been driving me out of my skull for weeks."

Tyjah pulled at Elsie's hand. "Rocket," he begged, looking beyond the midway to the resplendent bouncy rocket ship.

J.J. glanced at Lainie and let Kisha down. "Looks like it's a hit after all."

"I guess so," Lainie said.

"I wanna go on a ride," Kisha pleaded.

Elsie looked at the midway and shook her head. "Crazy children. Well, take your brother to that rocket thing first.

Then you can each go on two rides apiece." She rummaged in her purse for her wallet.

J.J. pulled the long strip of tickets from his pocket. "Or you could take these."

Kisha and Latrice went round-eyed at the prospect, and Tyjah reached out. "Hold on, you three," Elsie ordered. "Those are their tickets."

"We've gone on all the rides we're going to," J.J. said. "They're just going to go to waste." He tightened his arm around Lainie. "I'd rather walk around with my girl."

A corner of Elsie's mouth twitched. "I can see that. Well, thank you."

"Thank you, J.J.," the children chorused.

"Now listen, you three, I don't want you going on any rides alone," Elsie ordered.

Kisha bounced up and down. "I wanna go on the Zipper."

Latrice stared at the colorful fluorescent tubes outlining the narrow cars that spent nearly as much time upside down as right way up and shook her head. "Uh-uh."

"Please?" Kisha wheedled.

"No way."

"But I wanna go," she said again.

On impulse, Lainie stepped forward. "I'll go with you."

J.J. raised his eyebrows. "You know what you're in for?"

"Come with us," she invited with a smile. "Now's your chance to live life on the edge, Speed."

The children ran off ahead, and Elsie gave them a resigned look. "Those children will be the death of me yet," she said resignedly, but her eyes were fond and her voice soft as she followed them.

The ride was just the kind that Lainie loved. Clanking and noisy, pulse pounding, it scared her silly and left her grinning.

Then again, Elsie and her family always left her grinning.

"You've got a fan club," J.J. told her as they walked away from an adoring Kisha.

"I think you're the one with the fan club, judging by Kisha's costume."

J.J. looked embarrassed, she was delighted to see. "She's just at that age."

Lainie snorted. "Are you kidding? Around you, every female's at that age."

J.J. caught her fingers in his, and they walked hand in hand down the bazaar. A group of teenagers pushed by, laughing hysterically. In the bandstand, a live group played a cover of "Monster Mash." Moonlight streamed down around them. From the picnic tables, George and his family waved.

And suddenly it hit her. This would be the last time she'd be at the Halloween Festival in her town. Manhattan probably had street fairs, but not like this. This was the last one she'd be able to look at and have the satisfaction of knowing she'd brought it to life. It would be the last one where she'd know half the people there.

It would be the last one where she belonged.

Lainie stopped. "What's wrong?" J.J. asked, but she shook her head blindly, unable to talk. In a year she'd be in New York, at a party or a restaurant, or perhaps just sitting home in her living room—with her two or three dozen roommates, judging by Manhattan rental prices.

A wave of sadness hit her and for a moment she just leaned against J.J., pressing her face to his shoulder. "I don't know how I'm going to leave this," she said in a low voice, not trusting herself to say more.

J.J. pressed his lips to her hair. "You never really leave any place. The places you've been, the places you've cared about stick with you." It was something he knew better than most.

"It won't be the same."

"Nothing ever is." Suddenly J.J. loosened his arms. "Come here a sec." He took her hand and led her over to a nearby jewelry booth.

"What?"

"This." He reached out and picked up a necklace of moonstone and silver. The stone glowed white and mysterious, as though lit from within. Fluid and somehow warm, the silver chased around it. He pointed to the full moon, shining above them. "To remember tonight, always."

Something twisted inside her.

She didn't want to leave, she realized with sudden clarity. What she wanted was there, in Salem. With the museum. With J.J.

And in a blinding flash of emotion, she knew.

She was in love with him.

When it had happened, she couldn't say. Somehow, even as she'd been doing her damnedest to keep him at a distance, he'd managed to work his way into her heart. In the end, all her strategies, all her plans meant nothing. She'd fallen for him completely.

She watched him pay for the necklace, trying to understand what had happened, fighting the impulse to start knocking her head against the trunk of a nearby tree. She couldn't help thinking it had all the earmarks of disaster.

What's wrong with just seeing what happens? She raised her hand to the moonstone.

What had happened was that she'd fallen in love.

Two months ago she'd have seriously considered getting a lobotomy before letting herself fall for J. J. Cooper. Two months before, she'd have been certain how things would inevitably play out. Now, though, she was no longer sure. The J.J. she'd come to know was a different person than she'd always thought. He was caring, romantic and unfailingly generous.

This J.J. was someone special. This J.J. was worth taking a chance for.

But this kind of chance? Being in love with him? *Telling* him she was in love with him? Her stomach roiled at the thought. She had to be out of her mind to even think of it. She knew better than to do it, she so knew better.

She'd never had any patience with foolish women. But she'd never had any patience with people who were afraid to live, either. Whether it was riding the Zipper or being the first out on an empty dance floor, she'd always believed in taking chances. She'd always believed in trying. Why, now, was she so afraid?

Because it was her heart at stake.

"You're awfully quiet," J.J. said as he walked up, sliding his wallet in his pocket.

"Just admiring my necklace."

He studied her until she flushed. "What?"

"Just admiring your necklace, too," he said. "So what do you think, have we done the festival?"

Lainie kissed him. "I think we should go home."

There was moonlight there, too, streaming in through the windows as they undressed. There was the soft whisper of the wind outside. And there was that breathless moment of pure pleasure when J.J. pressed her down into the soft mattress, his body stretched along hers.

They came together in heat, in passion. In tenderness. Naked except for the moonstone, she leaned over him and stared into the face that had imperceptibly become an essential part of her life. The knowledge beat in her heart and pulsed through her veins. And hovered at the back of her throat.

Strokes and caresses, the whisper of skin on skin.

Whatever might happen in the future, there was the now, when their mouths were so close they inhaled each other's breath. Wherever this thing went, there was this moment, when the barriers were all but gone. It wasn't about need, somehow, but some final connection, like the last piece being added to a puzzle. When he slid inside her, it felt so exquisite that she wanted to weep.

"Thank you," she whispered.

"For what?" he asked, his eyes silvered by the light.

"For the necklace." She kissed him. "For giving me surprises." She kissed him again. "For making me feel like this."

"You're beautiful," he said softly. With deep, powerful strokes, he quickened inside her, drawing her deep and hard against him, bringing her up slowly and taking her over with him.

And somehow the words she'd resolved not to say just spilled out.

"I love you, J.J."

The sound seemed to echo in the quiet of the room. At first, he thought he must have imagined the whisper as his body clenched against hers in the final throes of passion. In the next heartbeat, though, he realized he hadn't.

And in the one after that, he wondered what the hell to do.

It wasn't the first time he'd heard the words from a lover. None had ever heard him say them in return, though. He didn't believe in "I love you" as a rote call and response. The way he figured it, those words were too important to say unless you felt them through and through, unless you were absolutely sure you meant them.

And J. J. Cooper had never been in love. Like, sure. Lust, definitely.

But never love. At least, he didn't think so.

The thoughts flicked through his mind in seconds. Then he saw Lainie staring down at him, horrified.

"Wow. That's…amazing," he said uncomfortably.

The horror gave way to embarrassment and annoyance. And hurt, he realized. She slid off him and moved to rise, but he caught her.

"Let me go."

"You're not going anywhere," he said. "Let me finish."

"You don't have to, J.J. Forget you heard it. It was a dumb thing to say. I just…got caught up."

"No." He felt the little flick of anger. "Don't pull back on me."

"I don't think I'm the one pulling back." Her voice was cool.

"Dammit, Lainie, you can't just drop something like that on me out of the blue and then get ticked because I don't have an immediate response."

"Pardon me for not giving you more time to prepare," she said tartly, sitting up. "It wasn't like I planned to say it."

J.J. reached out to turn on the light. "Look at me." He sat on the edge of the bed beside her, his gaze unwavering. "That's a wonderful thing for you to say. And…yeah, I wasn't ready for it."

"Let it go, J.J.," she said impatiently, and moved to rise again.

He pulled her back. "Just hold on, okay? You owe me that."

Unwillingly she turned. The flush that still stained her cheekbones added guilt to the uncertainty and tension that had settled in his gut. She was hurting. He had to get this right.

And he had to figure it out in a hurry.

He swallowed and took both of her hands in his. "Lainie, I care about you, more than I've ever cared for any woman, ever. But I've never said 'I love you' to anyone." He studied their tangled fingers. "I do not want to screw this up. I want to get it right. And part of that is not just saying the words because I think you want to hear them." He raised his chin and met her gaze, his eyes unwavering. "I've got to be sure about it. Just give me some time. All right?"

He held his breath and after a long moment, she reached out and turned off the light. "All right," she said in the dimness and lay down silently.

J.J. lay down beside her and gathered her to him, inhaling her scent, feeling her breath sigh out.

But he didn't think either of them was going to get much sleep that night.

Chapter Seventeen

The shrilling phone dragged J.J. into consciousness. Only moments before, it seemed, he'd drifted off. He had a second to register that Lainie was already up before he dug out his cell phone and flipped it open to silence it.

"Yeah?" he said bad temperedly.

"Hey, man, you awake?"

It was Kurt Madsen, calling from Innsbruck. And there wasn't even the remotest ghost of humor in his voice.

"What's going on?"

"Doug's looking for your hide, that's what's going on. He got back last night from his trip to headquarters and he was seriously pissed that you weren't here."

"He'll get over it," J.J. mumbled, lying back down on the bed.

"No, he won't get over it, J.J. Get working on a story for him, because you're going to need a good one."

"Can I use your cousin and the kidney?"

Madsen blew out a breath of frustration. "It's not a joke this time. He can suspend you, you know. And I know you don't need the money but you're going to need the races or your sponsors will drop you flat."

"Look, Doug went to Aspen, I went to Massachusetts. I'm just taking a couple of days. I'll be back."

"If you're lucky," Madsen said quietly.

"What's that supposed to mean?"

"Just be careful, J.J. I know you won at Sölden, but that didn't buy you any more rope—it's starting to look like you're all out of it. Watch out."

"All right." Even he could hear the irritation in his voice.

"I don't know why I bother," Madsen said with a sigh.

J.J. closed his eyes. "I'm sorry. Look, thanks for the heads up, Kurt. I mean it."

He ended the call and put the handset down thoughtfully. So Doug was on the warpath. It wasn't that unusual a situation—so why was Kurt concerned enough to call?

The phone rang again, this time with the digits that he knew meant the head coach of the ski team was on the line. J.J. swore under his breath and pressed the receive button. "Hello?"

"Two-tenths of a second, Cooper."

"What?"

"Two-tenths of a second. Less time than it takes your heart to beat. That's how much Rob Munro missed winning by, last week."

J.J. frowned. "Rob Munro…isn't he that kid who came up last year?"

"Listen to the smart guy. Yeah, he came up last year on the C-team. This year he's on the A-team, and his practice times are as good as yours. Better, in some cases."

"Doug, listen—"

"No, you listen," Doug snapped. "I told you to stay in Sölden for two weeks after the race to do speed runs. You remember that conversation, Cooper?"

"Yeah."

"You want to tell me why I came back here and found you gone?"

"You never asked me whether I could stay. And I never said I'd do it."

"Oh, I forgot. Classic J.J.—just keep your mouth shut and go off and do whatever the hell you want."

"Doing whatever the hell I want won me the opener," J.J. reminded him, an edge in his voice.

"I don't give a damn what you won. Because Munro's going to win, too. And so is Peter Hardesty. While you've been partying, they've been coming up and working hard, and they're standing by to replace you, Cooper."

J.J. swung up and sat on the edge of the bed. His behavior wasn't that unusual. So why was Doug so bent out of shape? "Look, I'm not trying to be a pain, Doug. I just had something I needed to do stateside for a couple of days. I'll be back Wednesday and do all the speed runs you want."

"The hell you will. You'll be back tomorrow morning."

"I can't. I've got something I've got to be here for."

"Yeah, and you've got something you've got to be here for. It's called a job."

"I'm going to—"

"I'll tell you what you're going to do," Hoover interrupted. "You want to stay on this team, you're going to get your butt down to the airport and get on the first flight to Innsbruck you can find. And when you get here, you're going to drive to Sölden and get your butt on that slope. *Capisce?*"

Mentally J.J. gauged his chances. There was a time he'd

have just said to hell with it and done what he wanted. That time wasn't now, though.

He sighed. "Capisce," he said.

"Morning." Lainie smiled as J.J. walked into the kitchen and tried to relax. He'd dressed, she realized. Then again, she had, too, when she'd gotten up. Somehow she'd needed that little extra bit of confidence. "Want some coffee? I've got scones, too."

"That would be great," he said as he sat.

She busied herself filling mugs and setting out the raisin-studded triangles. "They're George's, although they're a couple of days old, so they may taste like sawdust. I've got jelly if you like or orange juice."

She was babbling, she realized with a pang. In all the twists and turns their relationship had taken, she'd never felt awkward with J.J. Annoyed? Yes. Amused? Often. But never awkward. To feel that way now just strengthened the sense of foreboding that had settled over her as soon as she'd opened her eyes that morning, a gut-level certainty that her revelation the night before had pushed the relationship off course in a way it wasn't going to recover from.

Tapping his fingers restlessly on the table, J.J. stared out the window. When she sat, he turned to her. "There's a problem," he said abruptly.

That much, she already knew. "What's going on?"

"I got a call from the head coach of the ski team. He wants me in Innsbruck tomorrow."

"They're going to make you fly over for a day?"

"No." He hesitated. "I have to fly out tonight and stay with the team for the duration."

"But," she said blankly. "Tuesday is Halloween. The costume parade, the fund-raiser for the center."

"I know, but I'm going to have to skip it."

"I don't get it. They just called out of the blue and demanded you show up?"

He gave a pained look. "They told me when I got to Sölden. I'm AWOL. I didn't say anything because I figured it wasn't a problem, I could get out of it. I always have before."

"And let me guess, this time you couldn't." The kids, she thought with a quick twist of anxiety. "J.J., we talked about this. You promised. People are counting on you."

"You don't need to tell me. I feel like hell about it."

"And?"

"What do you mean, *and?*"

"What happens next?"

"I guess you'll have to find someone to fill in for me."

"And what about the autograph signing?"

He groaned. "Ah, hell."

"Yeah, hell. Dammit, J.J.," she burst out. "Didn't you ever think of making sure you can make good on a promise before you actually make it?"

"I meant to."

"Sure, I've known you practically your whole life, remember? It's always like this. You always mean well. And then things go wrong and you figure it's no problem. It'll be all right with a little J. J. Cooper pixie dust and a grin, right? Well, I don't have any pixie dust to fix the mess you just created." Irritation bloomed into anger. "You may be running off to the land of J.J. groupies, but I'm going to be stuck here dealing with the real world once you've gone. I'm the one who'll be telling Pete at the muffler shop that he donated flyer costs for a fund-raiser with no special guest, and telling a bunch of kids who worship you that you can't be there for them."

"You think I don't know that?" J.J. demanded. "You think

they don't matter to me? There's nothing I can do, Lainie. It's my job."

"No, it's your life. It's your whole life in a nutshell. And that's what it is—nuts. And so am I." She rose abruptly and paced away.

It hurt, God, it sliced through her. Despite everything she'd known, she'd taken a chance on him. And all her worst fears had come to pass. Here was the J.J. she'd always known, completely unchanged, the J.J. who didn't keep his promises, who skated through life to his own soundtrack—and if you didn't dig the music, that was your problem.

And if you fell for him and gave him your heart, that was your problem, too.

"I can't do this," she said positively.

"What?"

"This." She flung her hands up. "You. Me. It doesn't work, J.J."

"Because I'm missing the costume parade?" He gave her an incredulous stare.

"Because of the world you live in. The way you live. Your life doesn't make sense to me. Your world, your glam thing doesn't work."

"Glam thing? Lainie, what is this? Until five minutes ago, we were working just fine."

"Fine? Says the guy who doesn't even know how he feels about me? Speed, how was this working just fine?" Her short laugh held no humor. "Come on, admit it, this was all just place-holding for you, something to do while you were bored, before you went back to jet setting."

"Wait a minute, you were talking about leaving, too," he said hotly.

"Yeah, well, I changed my mind. This is what I want, J.J. This is the life I want. And it doesn't fit with yours."

"I'm not going to bc living that life forever."

"Oh, come on, I saw you at Sölden. You're hooked on it like a junkie. You're going to be racing World Cup until they cart you off the mountain."

"Are you not getting this?" His voice rose. "Lainie, I'm thirty-three. Why do you think Doug can strong-arm me? I'm at the end of my career and I don't know what the hell happens next. I've got this season, maybe one more and then it's over."

"So, what, we've been your dress rehearsal? Try it and see if you like it? A test-drive? That's not the way it works, J.J. It's not just about you. You're supposed to be with people because you care about them, not because you want to try them on like a new pair of ski boots. You can't just jump into people's lives when it's convenient. You're supposed to be there no matter what. But that's not what you do," she finished. "That's never been what you do."

"Just like believing in me is what you never do. Ever since I got here, you've been busy telling me where I fall short, setting standards. You want me to change but you won't believe that I have."

She looked at him tiredly. "J.J., I tried believing, remember? And look what it got me. I'm not so sure I'm all that hot to believe anymore." She pressed the heels of her hands to her eyes for a moment, then lowered them. "Look, I've got to get dressed and over to the festival. Why don't we just let it drop, all right? You took your test drive and it just didn't work."

Anger sparked in his eyes. "I took a test-drive? From where I stand, it looks like you've spent the whole time looking for an excuse to bail. Last night, you love me, today I'm a jerk you can't wait to get rid of." His jaw tightened. "Maybe you're right about ending this. I'm sick of talking to the air. You don't like my life? You don't like my job? Too bad. Because I do." He stood. "You know, you're something special, Lainie, but you're too damned much work. You ever get your head on straight about this, come look me up. Maybe we'll talk. But I'm not holding my breath."

And he turned around and walked out.

Chapter Eighteen

She didn't cry. Maybe she swayed a little when she heard the door slam behind J.J. Maybe her hand shook as she dumped out the coffee and food she suddenly had no taste for. The bitterness of disappointment lay like ashes in her mouth. But she didn't cry.

Instead, she finished cleaning up the kitchen and went to her bedroom. She had to get ready for the festival. The yoga pants and T-shirt she'd drawn on when she'd risen were comfortable, but not exactly appropriate for work. Time to get ready to go.

She faltered a little when she walked in and saw the sheets and coverlet still rucked up from the night before, saw the dent that remained in the pillow from J.J.'s head. She made herself move on, though.

There was no point in dwelling on it. Bad enough she'd been such a sap as to fall for him when everything she'd learned over the years had taught her better.

She wasn't about to let him make her ache.

Instead, she stripped the bed briskly, throwing sheets and spread and mattress cover onto the floor. The thing to do was clean up, get rid of all traces of J.J. and go on with her life. She piled the bedclothes together and picked up a pillow to strip it.

It smelled like him.

She froze, holding the pillow in her arms as she'd once held J.J. And a wave of misery surged over her.

From the beginning, she'd known what the end would be; she just hadn't known the how.

And she hadn't known how much it would hurt.

It was as though some merciless machine had sliced into her and ripped loose something that was woven into the fiber of her being, making it impossible to think, impossible to breathe. For a moment she simply stood and shook.

But with sheer will, she held on. *Put it away. Don't think about it.* Over and over she repeated it to herself like a mantra, as she showered and dried her hair, as she put on her makeup, as she drew on a sweater and skirt and shoes. Over and over, she repeated it to herself and gradually she got control.

It would get easier with time. She just needed to get through these first few hours.

Finally she stood at her bureau, studying her earrings, trying to choose which to wear. She was the kind of person who kept solo earrings even when she'd lost their mates, out of some optimistic hope that the missing piece of jewelry might someday appear. It happened just often enough for her to keep her faith.

Pairs, reuniting. *Put it away. Don't think about it.*

Instead she strapped on her watch, smoothed back her hair. And then she glanced down and saw the small, polished serenity stone J.J. had given her when he'd first shown up at the museum. *Beginnings*, read the word etched into its surface.

It was that, finally, that made her weep.

* * *

J.J. considered himself a philosophical man. You did what you could do and let the chips fall where they may. Things didn't always work, but as long as you knew you'd done your best, there was nothing to regret.

Why, then, couldn't he feel that way about what had happened between Lainie and him? Why couldn't he stop wanting to put his fist through a wall to get rid of some of the frustration and loss? So she'd never believed in him from day one. So she'd never given them a chance, despite how good they were together. So she'd thrown it all away out of sheer stubbornness. He should forget it and move on. A smart man eventually stopped beating his head against a brick wall.

And yeah, maybe he'd been partly to blame. He tended to bite off more than he could chew; he always had. Mostly, he managed to get everything handled. It was his bad luck that one of the times he hadn't, had provided Lainie with the excuse to bolt. *Your life doesn't make sense to me. Your world, your glam thing doesn't work.*

Glowering, he shoved a pair of jeans in his duffel with unnecessary force. From the time he'd shown up in Salem, she'd assumed the worst about him. He should be happy to be walking away.

He'd get to Innsbruck, rent a fast car to drive to Sölden and get himself on the slopes. And at night, maybe find some diversion with a lovely lady who'd take his mind off his troubles. If he was going to be hit with his reputation, he might as well enjoy it, right?

Scowling, he yanked open his bureau to grab a couple of T-shirts. He'd enjoy it, all right, and wipe Lainie Trask right out of his head.

Witches and ghouls, Elmo and SpongeBob. The children stood in a ragged line, clutching their pumpkin-patterned carrier bags and shifting back and forth in excitement. A sort of giddy glee hung in the air as Lainie moved up and down the line, adjusting hats and cloaks, wiping noses. Finally the doors to the gym opened and the competitors walked in.

The Salem Costume Parade was under way.

As with the best of contests, it was designed with pomp and ceremony and lots of prizes, so that nearly every participant walked home with something. Any other year, Lainie would have been thrilled. Any other year, it wouldn't have seemed flat and gray and uninspired.

J.J. should have been there, the thought came unbidden. He'd have made it into an event, getting on the microphone and whipping the audience up into a frenzy. He'd have made every child feel special as he stuck the participation ribbons on their chests or hands or whatever he could reach under the costume.

But J.J. was in Austria, back in his life.

And she was here.

Put it away, don't think about it. Now was not the time to go into one of those funks that swept over her without warning. She wandered back into the hallway, leaving the group inside to their cookies and punch and candy corn. A few minutes to herself to get her head together and she could go back inside and join the party.

"You miss J.J., don't you?"

Lainie looked up to see Kisha standing there, a ribbon on her chest. "Hey, sweet girl, what have you got?"

"I won the prize for best home costume."

"And you deserve it. You win all kinds of prizes in my book," Lainie told her.

"I wish J.J. could be here."

It was what she'd dreaded from the moment he'd told her about the cancellation. "I do, too, honey. I know he loved your costume. And I know he wanted to be here. He just couldn't." And she realized as she said it, that it was true.

Kisha nodded gravely. "I know. I was sad, but mostly I miss him. When's he coming back?"

Lainie bit her lip. "I don't think he is, sweetie. I think he's gone for good."

"He can't be gone," she objected. "He's s'posta teach me how to ski. He said it's going to be my Christmas present."

J.J. had said lots of things, Lainie thought. "It might have to wait, honey. J.J.'s got important things to do right now."

"He'll be back," Kisha said confidently. "He wouldn't forget about us."

And Lainie found herself wanting to believe it.

Skiing was what it was all about. He rose at dawn and hit the slopes, flying down the mountain over and over again until the coaches were telling him he'd had enough.

Of course, he'd never been one for listening.

The skiing saved him, he thought as he stood in the start house. When he was on the mountain, fighting the g-forces, feeling the wind, it kept his mind from running down the same profitless paths. Partying was an empty effort that he'd abandoned the first time he'd tried it. The thing to do was just keep working.

"You want to come back to the real world, there, Cooper?" Doug asked.

J.J. jolted a little and looked down at the snow covered slope that fell abruptly away from the start house. "I'll show you real world," he said, and moved out of the gate, pushing aside the slender pole that started the clock running.

The sudden rush of speed, the drop was a shock to the system. The snow fences were a blur in his peripheral vision. They'd never seen him so focused, the coaches all said, and

Doug was congratulating himself for finally establishing discipline. J.J. didn't bother to tell them the reality—that it was self-defense, the only way he knew to get Lainie out of his head.

The turn came before he'd set himself, so that his skis scooted across the ice-covered snow for a moment as he struggled to stay up. Quads trembling, adrenaline saturated, he fought the g-forces. At ninety miles an hour you didn't mess around. A man who thought about his girlfriend—ex-girlfriend—when he ought to be thinking about the treacherous angles and curves, the jumps that appeared almost without warning, deserved the flashing chaos of a fall.

He hit the inside of a gate so closely that he brushed it with his shoulder. That was what he needed to do, focus on the curve, the gates, his tuck. Forget thinking about Lainie, forget what might have been.

If only she'd believed in him, even once. Sure, he'd made mistakes, but that wasn't the real problem. The real problem was trust, and if there wasn't trust there, how could there really be anything else? How could she sit there and tell him she loved him when she never really even believed in who he was? More than three weeks had passed since the scene in her apartment and the question still dogged him.

Only half-focused, he missed his line, cutting in a little too close on the next gate. And like a giant hand, the red fiberglass and plastic flung him back to go spinning spread-eagled down the slope, tumbling, grinding his face into the snow and ice.

It was, he thought as he got up, a pleasant break compared to what the rest of his days had been like since he and Lainie had split. Then again, you could only split up with a person when you'd been together in the first place. Whether that had been the case, he couldn't honestly say. They'd been side by side, certainly, but together?

And then he remembered the way it had felt that night he'd

returned from Buffalo and he'd held her in his arms. Together? The hell they hadn't been.

The lanterns from the ghost walk were back in the museum storeroom where they belonged. The grass on the common gradually filled in, obscuring the dents that served as mute reminders of the festival. At a glance it was impossible to tell that anything had ever been there.

Just as at a glance it was impossible to tell that J.J. had ever been a part of her life.

It was just standard post-Halloween letdown, Lainie told herself impatiently. It was an occupational hazard. After all, you couldn't devote months of energy to pulling off the festival, the galas, the myriad parties, without the events themselves seeming to become memories far too quickly.

Then again, post-Halloween letdown usually lasted a couple of days. When it stretched out into weeks, even she had to acknowledge that it wasn't just Halloween.

It was J.J.

Memories of him turned her every step around Salem into a ghost walk. She stood outside her house, and the memories were there. She saw Kisha, Latrice and Tyjah at the Human Habitat site and the memories were there. She went into Cool Beans, the memories were there.

But most of all she lay in her bed at night and the memories were there.

During the day she could mostly keep the misery at bay. It was at night that the ache for him came to crouch on her chest like a physical thing, making it impossible to sleep. It was during the night that she wondered if she'd made a big mistake.

She missed him. She found herself turning on the television to see if she could catch a glimpse of skiing, reading through the sports section to find mention of his name.

Put it away. Don't think about it. At least there were some things she could rely on, Lainie thought as she listened to the jingle of the door at Cool Beans, inhaling the scent of coffee. It smelled the way it had always smelled, looked the way it had always looked. George walked in through the swinging door from the kitchen, carrying a tray of scones.

"Hey, Lainie."

"Hey, George, how are you?"

"Better than you, it looks like." He handed her mug. "Hey, everything okay?"

"Of course. Why do you ask?"

"I don't know, you look tired or stressed out or something. Hey, you want to come over to our house and watch J.J.'s race tomorrow?"

"The one in Val d'Isère?"

"Yeah. I figured you'd want to see your guy."

"J.J.'s not my guy."

"He was. He should still be." George gave her a level stare. "He's one of the good ones, Lainie. I know he screwed up—"

"And left us all hanging," she put in.

"Yeah, and left us all hanging, but he's come through more often than he hasn't. Come here." He waved her behind the counter. "I want to show you something."

"But your customers—"

"They can wait."

She followed him through the kitchen and into the tiny, chaotic room he called his office. It was more of a closet, really, stuffed with a desk that held pigeonholes, a low shelf and a computer.

"Take a look at this." He waved her over to the thick folder that sat on the desk. "I got it in the mail a couple of days ago."

She reached out to flip back the cover and saw a sheet of

paper with J.J.'s chaotic writing. Notes on how to get a zoning variance, she saw. Setting it aside, she found an invoice for a set of basic plans. There was more: a computerized list of materials suppliers; beneath that, a letter from a lumberyard in Peabody pledging to donate three thousand board feet of lumber.

It was planning material for the Boys' and Girls' Center. A comprehensive plan, she realized as she leafed through the stack of photocopied sheets. It had to have taken hours to put together. "J.J.?" she asked.

George grinned. "Pretty wild, huh? It's kind of messed up because I've been going through it but take a look at this." He rummaged through the pile and pulled out a thick sheaf of papers fastened with a binder clip. On the top was a letter with the Boys' and Girls' Center logo on it. It was from the center's coordinator, Lainie saw, thanking J.J. for his efforts. "Our board of directors has reviewed your proposal to rebuild the Salem facility and we'd accept your offer to act as general contractor on the project, with a target completion date of August 1 and an operating budget of $250,000, thanks to your fund-raising efforts."

It was dated the previous week.

Lainie stared at the sheet. "J.J.'s going to build the center?" she asked faintly.

"Appears that way. We're going to do a site review while he's home at Christmas. He's got a bunch of construction companies lined up to donate materials. A couple of his sponsors are throwing in some money, too."

He'd intended to do it from the beginning, she realized, and even with what had happened between them, he hadn't stopped. *He wouldn't forget about us,* Kisha had said. She'd know it, she'd been right.

Because she'd believed.

Lainie realized she'd been an idiot. She'd been an idiot and she had to fix it.

She snatched up her purse. "I've got to go."

"Hey," George protested, "where are you going?"

"The airport."

Chapter Nineteen

There was nothing quite as beautiful as early morning in the Alps, J.J. thought as he slowly skied through his inspection run for the downhill at Val d'Isère. He'd skied in New Zealand, Chile, Japan, Canada and the United States. Gorgeous places, all of them, but nothing like the corniced Alpine peaks.

The wind kicked up, dry and cutting as a knife. It was cold and getting colder, with clouds scudding in. Never a good thing for a race—the light from overcast had a way of flattening out the look of ruts and rises, making the course harder to see.

He cruised down a steep section and off a knoll, then brought himself to a stop. Scanning the slope, he found the exact line that he wanted to take down the next transit. Step by step, he worked his way back up the mountain until he was once again poised at the top of the jump. This time, he crouched down in his tuck and looked for the landing spot he'd chosen.

It was a matter of figuring the right takeoff angle, finding the landmark to focus on. Downslope, he spotted a tree with a dead branch, right in the direction he needed to be facing. Committing it to memory, he let himself come off the knoll to try the landing.

In his practice runs, he'd aim for that tree. When it came time for the race, he'd have it committed to muscle memory. By then, he'd no longer be thinking, he'd be operating on instinct.

Too bad life didn't have inspection runs. He could have used one with Lainie. Not to say that he wasn't still ticked at her, but there were things he could have done better, too. It had taken over a month for him to really admit that. There were things he could do better in his life all the way around.

Unfortunately, if you screwed up in a race, you could always say "next year." With Lainie, it didn't look like he had that option, he thought as he skied over the finish line.

With Lainie, finished was finished.

Lainie stepped out of the Jetway and into the color and noise of the Lyon airport. Sleep on the flight had been impossible. Now, she was simultaneously exhausted and wound tight with nerves. When she'd left, it had all seemed simple— find J.J. and make things right.

Now, in the harsh light of morning, she wasn't so sure. It had been over a month since she'd seen him last, over a month in which they'd exchanged not a word. He'd been on their side of the ocean for races in Colorado, but he'd never called, never even e-mailed her.

Maybe it had all been easy for him. Maybe he'd gone on with his life without a hitch. Maybe, a sneaky voice said in her head, he'd even been relieved. Certainly that would fit with the J.J. she'd known. And she'd made it so clear that she was done, how could she blame him for believing her?

The answer was, she couldn't. Shaking her head, Lainie threw her satchel over her shoulder and headed toward the passport check line. She couldn't blame him. On the other hand, she could blame herself if she never even tried. She had to say something, if nothing else, to clear the air. Maybe that meant they would just be friends who could run into each other and be cordial at mutual events. She'd smile, she'd be friendly, ask how he was doing.

And try to pretend seeing him didn't feel like swallowing ground glass.

She blew out a breath of impatience. This wasn't her, this helpless, maudlin thinking. So what if there was only a chance? She'd make it work, the same way taking a chance at the museum had worked.

Anyway, she was only thinking this way because she was tired and jet lagged. What she needed to do was get out of the strange suspended reality of the airport and on her way. Once she got doing things instead of just sitting around waiting, she'd feel better. There was a car waiting for her at the rental desk; she'd have to get it and then deal with the adventure of driving to Val d'Isère.

Assuming she could figure out where the hell it was.

The fallow time between the practice runs and the actual race was always the hardest time for J.J. He was dialed into the course, he wanted to be out on it, not eating and sitting around, trying to find a worthwhile, or at least interesting, way to make the two-hour window pass by.

It was activity, movement that kept him focused. It was activity that kept him from thinking about Lainie.

He'd done his best to make her reconsider. He'd done his best to convince her to take him seriously, to give them a chance. She'd said she loved him, but what was love if not faith? What they'd had together was worth checking out. Who knew what it might have turned into? You didn't close the door on that, you put time and effort into it, didn't you?

Then again he'd had plenty of women tell him that very thing over the years. Mostly, he'd gotten involved with women of like mind, women who'd pretty much wanted what he wanted—a fun companion, a warm body at night, someone who quickened the pulse when they appeared. Sometimes— all right, more often than not—he'd let things go on a bit longer than they should have so that the woman got a chance to get tired first and be the face-saving initiator of the breakup.

There were times even then that he'd had to be the one to end it, usually with the regret of hurting someone. On one or two occasions, though, he hadn't really been a hundred percent sure it was the right thing to do. No, the relationships hadn't felt right, there had been problems that wouldn't go away. And yet, enough about them had worked that he'd wondered whether that woman was The One. Had he just been running away? Shouldn't he have stuck around and tried to work it out?

But relationships weren't supposed to be that hard, were they? If you had to work and slave to make a relationship go, didn't it follow that maybe it was the wrong relationship, the almost-but-not-quite right one?

Then again, Lainie had taken work, but being with her had felt good. Not walking away when they'd had things to discuss between them had felt like the right thing to do. Despite their conflicts, it had never felt any way but right, at least not until everything had blown up at the end.

He moved his head to ward off the thought as he pulled his plate toward him. There wasn't any point in focusing on a problem when there weren't any answers, and there weren't any answers here.

He wasn't sure there were any answers anywhere.

* * *

Compared to driving in Boston, getting out of Lyon was a breeze. The neat young woman at the rental car agency had given Lainie a map and detailed directions to Val d'Isère.

"How long to drive there?" Lainie asked.

The agent frowned. "Oh, perhaps two hours. Only…"

Now it was Lainie's turn to frown. "Only what?"

"It is snowing later today, you see. Perhaps fifteen or twenty centimeters. More in the mountains. You must arrive quickly, before they close the roads. There are chains in the boot."

Snow in the mountains. Snow for J.J.'s race. Did that mean they'd cancel it? Did that mean it was dangerous?

The highway was open, dotted with nimble, compact models of cars she'd never seen before. Ahead, the Alps knifed upward, all sharp crags and sudden escarpments, dizzyingly steep and looking close enough that she could reach out to touch them. Compared to them, the smooth, regular mountains of New Hampshire were like her frumpiest aunt alongside a legendary Hollywood beauty, with a face all angles and drama. Lainie kept stealing glances as she drove. Clouds obscured the tips, clouds that would be fog up at the top.

Where J.J. was.

Where she was going.

J.J. was still at the bottom of the mountain when the first skiers started coming down. Given that he was bib number twenty-eight, there was no reason to hurry. With the two-minute start intervals, he wouldn't be going for nearly an hour, and there were only so many places to hang out at the top of the mountain. No sense in standing around the swirl of tension that was the start house for any longer than was necessary.

Motion caught his eye and he watched Kurt Madsen rocket

around the final turn onto the terminal slope and speed over the finish line. Fast, he thought. Really fast. When the time flashed up, he saw just how fast it was.

Kurt grinned as he pushed his goggles up and skied to the edge of the crowd on the apron. He leaned over to kiss a blonde woman wearing a white sweater and a scarf printed in scarlet and green bands. Madsen's wife, at the bottom for every race. Rain or shine, good season or bad, Suzanne Madsen was always there for him. Rain or shine, good season or bad, Madsen ended every race with her.

The way it could have been with Lainie.

The thought ambushed him. Madsen's happy domesticity had never seemed like something to envy before. After all, a wife meant you were tied down. A wife meant the end of partying, and even if the wife didn't, the kids that inevitably followed sure did. Not that J.J. hadn't always expected to have a family.

Some day.

What would it be like to come down the mountain, knowing every time that someone would be there waiting for you? Someone who didn't care how many points you'd made for the team. Someone who didn't want to heckle you about the fact that you'd hooked a gate and been disqualified. Someone who cared only for you.

Suddenly it didn't seem stifling. Suddenly it seemed immensely appealing, companionable, comfortable. The way lying in bed with Lainie after making love felt comfortable. For him, affairs had always been about the fire and heat. What would it be like, though, to have the fire and heat and also the quiet comfort?

What would it be like to have Lainie?

He shook his head and willed the thought away. Not a question to ask anymore.

Why not?

He had a race to run, he reminded himself, a race he needed to win. This wasn't the time to think about Lainie. Eventually he'd stop missing her so damned much. He had to. It wasn't possible to go on feeling so carved up over maybes and might-have-beens. So they'd had something good going. The operative word was had. Sometimes things didn't work out no matter how much you wanted them to.

And he needed to forget just how much that had been.

It wasn't a highway, Lainie was convinced, it was a trail for mountain goats, the shaggy kind that spent their days hopping from precipice to precipice. At times the road had threaded down the center of one or another U-shaped valley, steep mountains to either side but smooth driving. And then, without warning, she'd head up through one of these narrow passes that made her glad she had chains, however squirrelly the car felt on the road. She squinted into the thickening snow, threading her way slowly through it. And cursing Murphy and his stupid law.

Of course it had to be snowing now, of all times. Of course she'd had to sit, crouched down on the side of the road, putting on the chains with frozen fingers under the sharp eyes of the French highway patrol. Then the snow had only been falling in flurries. Now it was coming down as though it meant it.

All she wanted to do was get to the race. It wasn't that much to ask, was it?

The French policeman had told her the journey to Val d'Isère was easy enough—drive the highway and watch the signs. Of course, the highway was a bit more of a challenge than she'd bargained for, and she was scared to death that she was going to drive right by the resort. He'd assured her she couldn't miss it, though, and she trusted him.

She just needed to get there and find J.J. Nothing else

mattered. Once she'd accomplished that goal, she'd figure out what came next. And if that meant driving down the mountain and flying home, at least she'd know she'd tried.

The time outside the start house during a race was usually J.J.'s time to chill. This time around, he was impatient, eager to get on the course. When he started the race, he wouldn't be consciously thinking about Lainie because he'd be in the zone, flying along, the trees, snow fences, cameras, fans, officials all turning into a blur with the only reality the way his skis were running, floating free over the *piste*.

The clouds hung down over the highest peaks of the mountain, turned to mist just a bit higher up. Snow fell around him. Down in the valley, he could just glimpse the village of Val d'Isère, looking like something out of a fairy tale. Lainie would have loved seeing it, he thought.

Stop it.

Instead he turned to look at the course, the red and blue flags of the gates marching their way down the slope. It had taken him a while to learn to win on this mountain. It had taken him a while to learn to win at downhill. He'd eaten snow more times than he'd have liked. He'd placed in the lower echelons for longer than was prudent for his career.

But he'd never been the kind of guy to take no for an answer. When he wanted something, he went back at it again and again, for as long as it took to make it happen. Some called it stubbornness; he liked to think of it as determination.

J.J. shook his head. It was like Manny told him, you aimed at a goal, you visualized what you wanted, and you made it happen.

He blinked.

You made it happen. So why hadn't he and Lainie made

it happen? Why was he standing on the side of this mountain, missing her just as much as he ever had, more than five weeks after he'd last seen her? No other woman had ever gotten in his head like that before. No other woman had refused to fade away. No other woman had made him a better person. So why the hell was it that the one time he found a keeper, she was the woman who couldn't believe in him? Sure, he could tell himself he was giving up and he should try again, but there was a point where if you didn't accept that enough was enough, you were an idiot.

J.J. turned to the start house. "Hurry the hell up, Hermann," he said in German. "I want to get on the course."

Lainie hurried over the grounds of the resort to the crowd of people who swirled around the apron of the course. She could hear the cheering and the cowbells as a racer flashed over the finish line. She'd ditched the little rental Peugeot in what might have been a parking spot or might have been a ditch, it was hard to be sure. It didn't matter.

What mattered was finding J.J.

Of course, what happened after that, she hadn't a clue. All her thought, all her effort had been bent on just getting here. Now that she was, she hadn't any idea what came next.

She hurried toward the sound of cheering. A loudspeaker crackled and spit out a burst of French. Ahead she could see the final slope of the downhill course and the apron at the bottom, ringed by a crowd of people ten or twelve deep. She didn't know where J.J. was staying or how to find the athletes. Unless she found J.J. or Kurt Madsen, it wasn't likely anyone on the ski team would be able to help; somehow, she had a pretty good idea that every race a couple of women showed up claiming to be J. J. Cooper's girlfriend.

Ex-girlfriend, she reminded herself.

She wasn't going to think about that, though. She was going to find J.J. The leader board didn't show a time for him; hopefully, that meant he hadn't gone yet. Her best move was to catch him at the bottom, after his run. If she could catch his attention, hopefully they could talk long enough to agree to meet for coffee or something. And what came after, she'd trust to faith.

Out of the mix of French in the announcement, she suddenly heard J.J.'s name. And she began to work her way through the crowd to the front.

Hell, was J.J.'s first thought as he exploded out of the starting gate onto the course. Only three hours had passed, but it had changed everything. New snow blanketed the slope, gripping his skis to slow them down, obscuring the ice-covered underlayer.

Those first instants out of the gate were crucial, the chance to use the power in his legs and arms to add as much speed as possible before he settled into the tuck he'd do his best to maintain the rest of the way down the mountain. A minute and a half to ski the course. A minute and a half to justify his existence.

The speed of his passage sent the snow crystals biting into his cheeks. Automatically, he set his body for a turn, legs tensing to offset the g-forces. And skidded for a heart-stopping instant on a patch of ice that lay beneath the new powder, invisible.

That was downhill, taking it all out on the edge and bringing it back. It wasn't about beating Hermann or any of the other racers—it was about beating the course. It was about pulling the best possible performance out of himself, eking every bit of speed from every second. Like Franz Klammer in the 1976 Olympics, taking every chance, riding on the edge of disaster all the way, because that was when you skied the ultimate run. That was when you found the ultimate performance, when you skied without fear.

A man could do that when he didn't have anything to lose.

Lainie worked her way to the front of the crowd, her heart hammering. The jumbo screen showed J.J. flying down the mountain, flinging himself over the edge of a knoll, never breaking his tuck. And then she saw him appear at the top of the slope, a speeding figure in blue, flying down to the finish, flying down to her.

J.J. flashed over the finish line to the sound of frenzied cheering. He looked to the leader board for his time, even as he straightened and dropped his hands. Pushing up his goggles and pulling off his helmet, he brought himself around in a careless curve that he wasn't even conscious of.

1:20:04. Enough to nudge him to the top, just barely. He scanned the crowd, waving to Suzanne Madsen. And then he froze, his gaze caught by a flash of glossy hair and dark eyes. In disbelief, he looked again. It was Lainie, standing there at the rail, cheering for him.

Lainie.

He stared at her incredulously. And in that instant he knew beyond a shadow of a doubt.

He was in love with her.

He brought himself around to a stop in front of her, unable to believe that she was really there.

"Surprise," she said, with a smile that looked a little tense around the edges. "Congratulations. Looks like you're in the lead."

"For now," he said unable to stop himself from reaching out

to catch her hands. She was real, he thought as he touched her. "Talk about sights for sore eyes. What are you doing here?"

"I thought I'd come see things for myself," she said. "Isn't that what you've been telling me to do?"

"It's worth seeing."

"I believe you," she said, staring into his eyes, and he knew the words meant far more than just the race.

He pulled her toward him and she flowed into his arms.

"I missed you so much," she said, pressing her face to his neck.

There was a smattering of applause from the crowd. Only the thin plastic of the snow fence lay between them, but she was warm and delicious and *there,* he thought in amazement.

Lainie sighed. "You were right, J.J., in everything you said. I blew it."

"So did I."

"I didn't believe in you, but I do now." She raised her head to look at him. "I want to try again. I want to make this work. I want to do it better."

He caught her face and fused his mouth to hers. "God, I love you," he murmured, stupidly grateful to be getting another chance. "I'm sorry I screwed up. I want to do it better, too."

"I know we can," she breathed against his lips.

Time slid away in the warmth of the kiss, the feeling of homecoming and awakening desire. Someone nearby laughed and J.J. stirred. "So, you want to do it better, huh? How about if we go to my hotel room and get started on that right now?"

She laughed and pressed a kiss on him. "Later. First, you have to see whether you've won."

"Don't have to, sweet girl." He tightened his arms. "I already have."

Epilogue

Mother's Day, Eastmont, VT

"Five bucks says he faints."

The scent of burning charcoal and grilling meat drifted up into the warm late spring air as Gabe, Nick and J.J. stood around the barbeque behind the Trask family farmhouse.

Gabe shook his head at his brother's comment, beer in one hand, spatula in the other. "I say he won't even make it into the room." The edge of one of the patties began to smoke and Gabe reached for the spray bottle.

J.J. splashed it with beer.

Gabe glowered at him. "You just poured Sam Adams on my burger."

"Consider it a marinade," J.J. said. "Anyway, you're both wrong. I've got a twenty that says the minute things get going, he'll kick all the doctors out and do it himself."

Gabe and Nick stared at each other for a heartbeat. "How'd we miss that one?" Nick asked, turning to look across the grass to where Jacob hovered over Celie.

A very pregnant Celie.

"No fair," Gabe complained, flipping the burgers onto a platter next to the grilled buns. "You're already set to make money on the twins bet."

"Is it my fault that I'm a genius?" Ignoring Nick's snort, J.J. picked up the tray and walked toward the picnic tables that sat under the spreading cover of a maple tree. Red-and-white checked tablecloths fluttered in the breeze. The Trask women circled around him, laying out food or finishing up table settings. J.J. walked up to Lainie and glanced down at the bowl she held. "Potato salad?" he asked with a sniff.

"Burnt offerings?" She nodded at the tray he held.

"It's a sign of my devotion to you." He pressed a kiss on her, thinking you had to love a woman when she was not only gorgeous and yours, but had food in her hands. "Just think, you marry me, you can look forward to a lifetime of it."

"I thought I was marrying into a lifetime of glamour."

"Shows what you know."

She set aside the food and wrapped her arms around his neck. "I'll show you what I know." The kiss was short but full of promise, full of the complexity and meaning that seemed to deepen by the day.

"Make way for the mothers," Nick said behind them.

"Oh, you," Molly Trask said, but her cheeks pinkened.

"Can you call a pregnant woman a mother?" Gabe asked.

"I think you call her whatever Jacob wants you to," J.J. observed, watching Jacob hover protectively over Celie as she walked over. J.J. moved to pull out a chair for her and Jacob helped her settle. "How's the baby baking going?"

"The buzzer's about ready to go off," Celie said ruefully

and rubbed her stomach. "I don't know if we've got twins in there or an entire hockey team."

"When's the big day?"

"A month," she said.

"Hadley will help out," Gabe offered magnanimously as they sat down. "She's got experience with delivering babies."

Hadley threw him an amused look. "I seem to remember you telling me you were the catcher in high school."

Celie laughed. "Thanks for the offer, but I'll have all the help I need." She laid a hand over Jacob's and looked at him fondly. "Jacob's going to be there with me the whole time."

Gabe, Nick and J.J. looked at each other and burst out laughing.

* * * * *

Don't miss Her Christmas Surprise,
the fabulous new book from Kristin Hardy,
available from Mills & Boon® Special Edition
in December 2008.

*Mills & Boon® Special Edition brings you
a sneak preview of Cathy Gillen Thacker's*
The Rancher's Christmas Baby...

*As teenagers, Amy Carrigan and Teddy McCabe
made a solemn vow to each other: if they didn't
find their soul mates by thirty, they'd start a
family...together. Now, with everyone around her
having babies, Amy is afraid motherhood will pass
her by. That's when the sexy rancher pops
the question. If best friends can't help each
other out, who can?*

Don't miss this heart-warming new story in
THE CARRIGANS *mini-series, also featuring
a special centenary free story, available next
month in Mills & Boon® Special Edition.*

The Rancher's Christmas Baby

by

Cathy Gillen Thacker

"I had no idea it was this bad." Amy Carrigan reached over and took the hand of her best friend, Teddy McCabe, the day after Thanksgiving.

He squeezed her hand reassuringly. "Same here." Being careful to keep to the other side of the yellow tape surrounding the century-old community chapel in downtown Laramie, Texas, Teddy let go of her hand and walked around, surveying what remained of the previously beautiful church.

The once towering live oak tree that had been struck by lightning at the advent of the previous night's thunderstorm had a jagged black streak down what remained of the trunk. The rest of the tree had taken out the bell tower and fallen through the center of the church roof.

By the time the fire department had arrived, the white stone chapel was engulfed in flames. Nearly half the wooden pews had been destroyed. And though the exquisite stained-glass windows were amazingly still intact, the walls were covered with black soot, the velvet carpeting at the altar beyond repair.

Fortunately, no one had been hurt, and plans were already being made to restore the town-owned landmark.

"Do you think they're really going to be able to get this restored in three weeks' time?" Amy asked.

"Given the number of volunteers that have already signed up to help with the cleanup, yes," Teddy replied.

"Trevor and Rebecca were supposed to have the twins' christening here on the twenty-third."

"We'll get it done," Teddy promised.

Amy hoped so. Although there were numerous other churches in the area, the community chapel was where everyone got married and had their children christened. It was small and intimate and imbued with tradition and hope.

Amy had dreamed of being married here.

Teddy studied her. "Everything okay?"

"What do you mean?"

"You've seemed blue. You hardly cracked a smile during the Thanksgiving festivities yesterday."

Amy had been hoping no one would notice.

She walked around to survey the damaged landscaping around the chapel. "I had a headache."

Teddy ambled along behind her. He had a good nine inches on her. And though they *both* owned ranches and worked outdoors—she growing plants, Teddy breeding horses—one might have a hard time discerning how physically fit she was because she was so delicately boned and slender.

However, it came as no surprise to anyone that Teddy had ranching in his blood. After all, he had the broad shoulders and strong, rugged build of the McCabe men. Being around him like this always made her feel impossibly feminine…and protected.

"Headache or heartache?" Teddy probed.

Amy returned wryly, "Thank you, Dr. Phil. But I really don't need your psychoanalysis."

"That, my friend, is debatable." Teddy placed both hands on her shoulders and turned her so she had no choice but to look at him. "Come on, Amy." His grip tightened ever so slightly, the warmth of his palms transmitting through the fleece vest she wore. "Tell me what's going on."

Her skin tingling from the unexpected contact, Amy knelt to examine a fire-singed Buford holly bush. "It's nothing."

Teddy gazed at her compassionately. "Is it the birthday you have coming up in January?"

Amy glared at Teddy and stepped away. "Way to cheer me up, cowboy."

He exhaled. "Thirty-two is not old." He could say that because he was almost thirty-five.

Amy headed toward the parking lot located behind the chapel, where her pickup truck was parked. "It's not young, either."

"You have a lot to feel good about. A family who loves you and a lot of friends. Not to mention the best plant-and-tree nursery in the area."

Amy did feel proud. Over the last ten years, she had grown her business from a rented greenhouse to a prosperous concern.

"True, you don't have a house yet…." Teddy conceded with a frown.

Not like the one he had on his Silverado Ranch, anyway. "Now you're dissing where I live?"

The lines on either side of Teddy's mouth deepened. With the familiarity of someone who had been her friend since elementary school, he said, "You don't have to live in a tiny little trailer."

Amy shrugged off his concern. "It suits me just fine right

now. Besides, I want to pour all my money into expanding."

Laurel Valley Ranch currently comprised fifty acres and ten greenhouses. She grew everything from Christmas trees to perennials and starter plants, and even had a husband-and-wife team working for her full-time now.

"Then if it's not that…is it the time of year that's getting you down? The holidays…"

Not surprised that Teddy had seen through her defenses, Amy blurted out, "Can you really blame me?" Tears blurred her eyes. "Everywhere I look, everywhere I go, I'm reminded that Christmas is for kids—and I don't have any! And at the rate I'm going I might never have any!"

To her surprise, Teddy looked as if he were feeling the same. "Then, maybe," he said slowly, "it's time you and I both revisited the promise we made to each other."

Amy backed up until her spine touched the back of her pickup. "I was twelve and you were fifteen!"

Teddy propped a shoulder against the door, blocking her way into the driver side. "It doesn't mean it wasn't a good idea."

Amy stared at him, wishing she could say she was shocked by what he was proposing. The same crazy, irrational thought had been in the back of her mind for months now. She'd just been too romantic at heart to bring it up.

She took a deep breath and repeated the vow they had made. "You want us to marry and have babies together— as friends? Not two people who are wildly in love with each other."

Teddy exuded McCabe determination. "We said then if we didn't find anyone else to start a family with by the time we were thirty, that's what we would do. And let's face it," he continued ruefully, "we passed that mark a while ago."

Amy's heartbeat kicked up a notch and she put her hands on the metal door panel on either side of her, steadying herself.

"It's not like we haven't been looking for a mate or been engaged," Teddy argued. "We have. It didn't work out for either of us."

Teddy's march to the altar had been abruptly cut short two years ago. Amy hadn't fared any better herself; her engagement had ended in a firestorm of embarrassment and humiliation, five years prior.

Teddy took both her hands in his and looked down at her with a gentle expression. "I'm tired of waiting, Amy. Tired of wishing for that special someone to show up and change my life. Especially now that Rebecca and Trevor have had twins. And Susie and Tyler are expecting their first child."

Amy tightened her fingers in his. "It seems everyone we know is getting married, settling down." Her two older sisters, his two triplet-brothers…their friends and former schoolmates…

He held her gaze deliberately, his hazel eyes reflecting the disappointment he felt about the turn life had taken. "Except us."

Silence fell between them as a church bell began to ring in the distance.

The Christmas spirit that had been absent in her soul took root again.

"So what do you say?" Teddy took Amy's chin in his hand and a coaxing smile tugged at the corners of his lips. "How about we make this a Christmas we will always remember?"

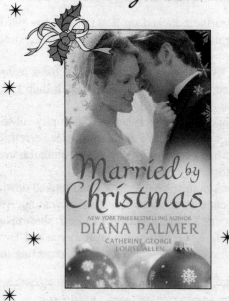

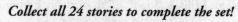
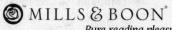

Celebrate 100 years of pure reading pleasure with Mills & Boon®

To mark our centenary, each month we're publishing a special 100th Birthday Edition. These celebratory editions are packed with extra features and include a FREE bonus story.

Plus, you have the chance to enter a fabulous monthly prize draw. See 100th Birthday Edition books for details.

Now that's worth celebrating!

September 2008

Crazy about her Spanish Boss by Rebecca Winters
Includes FREE bonus story
Rafael's Convenient Proposal

November 2008

**The Rancher's Christmas Baby
by Cathy Gillen Thacker**
Includes FREE bonus story *Baby's First Christmas*

December 2008

One Magical Christmas by Carol Marinelli
Includes FREE bonus story *Emergency at Bayside*

Look for Mills & Boon® 100th Birthday Editions at your favourite bookseller or visit
www.millsandboon.co.uk

4 FREE

BOOKS AND A SURPRISE GIFT!

We would like to take this opportunity to thank you for reading this Mills & Boon® book by offering you the chance to take FOUR more specially selected titles from the Special Edition series absolutely FREE! We're also making this offer to introduce you to the benefits of the Mills & Boon® Book Club—

- ★ FREE home delivery
- ★ FREE gifts and competitions
- ★ FREE monthly Newsletter
- ★ Exclusive Mills & Boon® Book Club offers
- ★ Books available before they're in the shops

Accepting these FREE books and gift places you under no obligation to buy, you may cancel at any time, even after receiving your free shipment. Simply complete your details below and return the entire page to the address below. You don't even need a stamp!

YES! Please send me 4 free Special Edition books and a surprise gift. I understand that unless you hear from me, I will receive 6 superb new titles every month for just £3.15 each, postage and packing free. I am under no obligation to purchase any books and may cancel my subscription at any time. The free books and gift will be mine to keep in any case.

E8ZED

Ms/Mrs/Miss/Mr ....Initials ....

BLOCK CAPITALS PLEASE

Surname ....

Address ....

....

....Postcode...............................

Send this whole page to:
UK: FREEPOST CN81, Croydon, CR9 3WZ